The Wild Warriners

*Four brothers living on the edge of society...
scandalising the* ton *at every turn!*

Tucked away at their remote estate
in Nottinghamshire are the *ton*'s
most notorious brothers.

The exploits of Jack, Jamie, Joe
and Jacob Warriner's parents—their father's
gambling and cheating, their mother's tragic
end—are legendary. But now, for the first
time, the brothers find themselves the talk of
the *ton* for an entirely different reason…

Because four women are about to
change their lives—and put them firmly
in society's spotlight!

Find out what happens in:

Jack's story
A Warriner to Protect Her

Jamie's story
A Warriner to Rescue Her

And watch for Joe and Jacob's stories—
coming soon!

Author Note

I have a thing for old Hollywood musicals. The glorious Technicolor, breathtaking Cinemascope and stereophonic sound captivated me as a child. Back in the days of VHS, when you had to tape things off the TV, I had a great collection of them which I would watch over and over again. *Singin' in the Rain*, *Calamity Jane* and *Meet Me in St Louis* are three of the greatest films ever made, if you want my opinion, but the best of all is *Seven Brides for Seven Brothers*.

I *love* that film. I adore the premise. Seven down-on-their-luck brothers, living in a shack in the middle of nowhere and eking out a living from the land. Looked down upon by the rest of the community because they're a little bit wild, they're all desperately in need of a wife and yet never meet any women at all—let alone court one.

In homage to that wonderful film I've created my Wild Warriners. Four brothers tainted by the dreadful reputation of their hideous ancestors, practically broke and forced to toil on their estate because they can't afford to pay anyone else to do it. And all desperately in need of that special someone. Their perfect match.

This story is the first in the series and follows Jack Warriner, the eldest brother and head of the family. He's proud, stubborn and used to being in charge. What he needs is a feisty woman to stand up to him...

A WARRINER
TO PROTECT HER

Virginia Heath

MILLS
BOON

First published in Great Britain 2017
By Mills & Boon, an imprint of HarperCollins*Publishers*
1 London Bridge Street, London, SE1 9GF

Large Print edition 2017

© 2017 Susan Merritt

ISBN: 978-0-263-06784-2

Printed and bound in Great Britain
by CPI Antony Rowe, Chippenham, Wiltshire

When **Virginia Heath** was a little girl it took her ages to fall asleep, so she made up stories in her head to help pass the time while she was staring at the ceiling. As she got older the stories became more complicated—sometimes taking weeks to get to their happy ending. One day she decided to embrace her insomnia and start writing them down. Virginia lives in Essex with her wonderful husband and two teenagers. It still takes her for ever to fall asleep...

Books by Virginia Heath

Mills & Boon Historical Romance

The Wild Warriners

A Warriner to Protect Her

Stand-Alone Novels

That Despicable Rogue
Her Enemy at the Altar
The Discerning Gentleman's Guide
Miss Bradshaw's Bought Betrothal

Visit the Author Profile page
at millsandboon.co.uk.

For Tracy Croft.
Mentor, friend and feisty heroine.

Chapter One

1st December 1813. One month, three days and approximately eighteen hours remaining...

The thin cord dug into her wrists painfully. Letty ignored it to focus on the practicalities. She barely opened one eye and peeked through her lashes. The Earl of Bainbridge's crinkly, grey head was lolling sideways, swaying slightly with the motion of the carriage—eyes closed, mouth slack— and she experienced a moment of relief to know he had finally nodded off. She risked opening her eyes properly for the first time in the better part of an hour, raising her head carefully from the seat to look out of the small strip of window still visible between the dark curtains which hid her from the world.

It was black as pitch outside.

A good sign.

It meant they were deep in the countryside, miles from any life, and the fact she could not even see the stars suggested this part of the Great North Road was edged with sheltering trees. Bainbridge's tatty coach was also flying along at speed, another indicator that they were a long way from the next inn or village. So far, each time the driver had approached one, the wheels had slowed and he had rapped loudly on the roof. Then the Earl had violently restrained her, his gnarled hand clamping tightly over Letty's already gagged mouth, the point of his boot knife pressed ominously against her throat as they had either passed through or the horses were quickly changed.

As he dozed, that very knife was still resting on his knee, his fingers loosely clasping it. Just in case. There seemed little point in trying to wrestle it from him when her main priority was escape. The last time she had showed any signs of struggle, Bainbridge had swept the back of his hand maliciously across her cheek with such force, his signet ring had sliced through the soft skin on her lip, leaving it now swollen and painful around the gag. For protection, she had pretended the blow had rendered her unconscious and had not moved a muscle since. If it had achieved nothing else, it had given Letty time to think.

As stealthily as she could, she rose to sit up and silently edged her bottom incrementally towards the door. If she could reach the handle, she could throw herself on to the road. After that, if she survived, she really had no idea what she was going to do. It was not really much of a plan, but as she had no desire to go to Gretna Green and she would much rather be dead than married to Bainbridge, it was better than nothing.

The Earl began to snore. But it was erratic on account of his upright position, the sort of snoring which woke a person up. There was no time to lose. Letty stretched out her bound hands and lunged at the handle desperately and, by some miraculous twist of fate, she managed to do this as the carriage veered slightly towards that side. She crashed into the door, wrestled with the handle and it flew open, taking her with it and tossing her sideways.

Instinct made her curl into a ball before she hit the ground, to protect her head and her limbs. Still the impact was sheer agony, pushing all of the air out of her lungs and blinding her with pain. Sharp stones embedded themselves in her skin as she rolled; muddy water shot up her nose and seeped through her closed eyelids, stinging them mercilessly. Almost as a blur in the distance, Letty heard a shout go up from the carriage, now further ahead, then the squeal from wheels when the brake was suddenly applied.

She rose to her knees, forced her bruised and battered body to move, practically dragging herself into the dark and silent trees. Then she ran. There was no thought as to direction. Just as long as it was away from the road, it didn't matter where she was going. She ignored the way the tangled branches seemed to reach out and grab at her clothing, nor did it matter that the deeper she plunged into these woods, the darker and more terrifying they appeared. Nothing could be as terrifying as being caught again by that dreadful man.

In the distance, she could still hear their angry voices, yet with every yard, those voices became fainter and fainter, spurring her to put even more distance between them as she ploughed recklessly forward. Until her lungs burned and her muscles screamed and she could run no further.

What Jack *should* have done was go straight home. But hindsight, in his experience, was overrated. It only served to bring about regrets, and frankly, Jack Warriner had quite enough of those already. So what if he was now drenched to the skin and frozen to the bone? The inn had been warm, the ale good and the company, for once, friendly. He had meant to stay for just the one drink. Just to clear the dust of the road from his throat and to enjoy a few minutes of respite from all of the responsibilities which stifled him before he wound his way down the last three miles to home. But one drink had soon turned into three. And three became six. Then the innkeeper had brought out the whisky and someone else had produced a fiddle, and before he realised it, he had been singing loudly with the rest of the patrons, stamping his feet, clapping his hands and behaving like a young man without the entire oppressive weight of the world on his shoulders.

Now he was paying for his rare moment of weakness. The rain was impressive, even by December's standards, and would have been coming down in heavy, vertical lines had it not been for the wind. But to compound Jack's current misery, as he fought the inevitable after-effects of far too much alcohol in too short a period of time, the relentless north-easterly was forcing the fat rain drops almost horizontal. Right into his face.

Thank goodness there was only a half a mile or so left. Soon he would be home. Safe in the house which ate money for breakfast, luncheon and dinner. His grand stately pile, the opulent legacy of his lofty title, a leaking, creaking, millstone around his neck. The place where all hopes and dreams were mercilessly crushed under the hobnail boot of responsibility, while Jack sunk deeper and deeper into debt with every passing year. Just thinking about it made him lethargic.

And slightly nauseous.

Or perhaps that was merely the whisky and the ale. Jack wiped his dripping face with the back of his sleeve and almost lost his seat when his horse suddenly reared noisily. He struggled with the reins to bring the beast under control and that was when he saw her. Almost like a ghost, the woman appeared out of the trees. Her skin eerily pale in the flimsy moonlight, hair and thin dress plastered to her body, eyes as wide as saucers as she stared back at him. Then she fled, wet skirts and a pronounced limp hampering her progress.

It took several seconds for his alcohol-impaired

mind to register what else he had seen. A vicious gag. Bound hands. Sheer terror.

She was stumbling ahead of him along the narrow, rutted lane which led to his house as if her very life depended on it. Judging by the state of her, it probably was. Jack's wits finally overpowered his inebriation and he swiftly directed his horse after her.

'Miss! Wait! I mean you no harm.' The wind carried away his words.

As he came alongside her, Jack bent low in the saddle and grabbed her arm. She spun around and tried to extricate herself from his grip, fighting like a cornered fox to escape him.

'I mean you no harm!'

He could tell by the way she struggled that she was exhausted. Shouting at her was not going to calm her.

'Let me help you.' He said this quietly and he saw her blink as she heard him. To prove it, he released the grip he had on her upper arm and held up his gloved hands as if in surrender. Automatically, she went to bolt and he forced himself not to try to stop her. It was the right thing to do. She hesitated. Turned back. Her wide eyes locked on to his and she simply gazed at him, as if she were searching the depths of them to the man he was inside, to see if he could be trusted. Then, almost as if all her strength and determination was gone, she began to slip to the ground.

Jack managed to grab her arm again before she crumpled into a heap and used all of his formidable strength to pull her now deadweight body on to his saddle. He cradled her in his lap; her damp flesh was like ice and it made him wonder how long she had been out here, exposed to the winter elements. She felt so very delicate in his arms. Precious.

He tried to work the gag free. It refused to move. Rainwater had sealed the knot tight and whoever had tied it had done it so harshly, he could not move it. This close, he could just about make out the bruising on her face. Her lip was badly cut and swollen, suggesting she had been beaten as well as bound. And the very fact he had discovered her stumbling blindly along a deserted lane, past midnight and wearing what appeared to be only a bedraggled, sleeveless silk gown meant she had probably managed to escape. Only then did it suddenly dawn on him that her captors might be searching for her. Whoever had bound and beaten this delicate woman was not going to be the sort of person to listen to reason. If she had escaped, it went without saying they would stop at nothing to get her back. Whoever she was, she needed his help.

Without thinking, Jack kicked the horse into a gallop, holding the reins tightly with one hand while the other held his unconscious passenger close to his body to keep her safe. He ignored the sting of the wind and rain on his face. Nothing else mattered but getting her home and to safety. Markham Manor might well be in dire need of a new roof, but at least his troublesome ancestors had had the good sense to surround it with a twenty-foot wall and an archaic pair of similarly proportioned gates which weighed a ton. He had a feeling tonight, for the first time in over two hundred years, the Warriners might actually need them.

Chapter Two

One month, three days and approximately sixteen hours remaining...

Jack carried her limp body into the hallway and shouted for his brothers at the top of his voice. Used to jumping to attention at his tone, they arrived one by one on the landing. First came Joe, the second youngest and only four years his junior, and by far the one he was keenest to see first. He took one look at the woman and the physician in him burst to the fore.

'I'll get my things.' And he was gone again.

Then came Jacob, the youngest, who crossed his brother on the landing, dark hair on end and rubbing the sleep from his eyes. Close behind him limped Jamie, the closest in age to Jack. Both men instantly sprang into action the moment they spotted the burden in Jack's arms.

'What the hell?'

Jacob just stood and gaped as he reached the bottom step, trailing after Jack as he hauled the woman into the high-ceilinged great hall which now served as the drawing room. He had already lowered the woman on to a sofa by the time Jamie managed to get there. Like the brilliant soldier he had been before his injuries, it did not take his brother long to assess the situation.

'Where did you find her?'

'She just appeared in the middle of the road. She was conscious then.' That she had failed to regain consciousness in the last twenty minutes was a worry. In the dim lamplight, her skin now had a grey pallor beneath the caked mud which did not bode well.

'Any signs of whoever did this to her?' Jamie asked.

Jack shook his head. 'But the storm is still raging outside. Even if there had been an army right behind me, I doubt I would have heard them. Make the place secure!'

Jamie responded immediately to Jack's command, turning to Jacob. 'Get my sword and pistols from my bedchamber, and grab something for yourself. We're going to close the gates.'

The two brothers were gone by the time Joe returned with his medical kit. Despite the fact there had been no money to send him to university again this year, Joe had still relentlessly studied medicine in the vain hope he would one day qualify as a doctor. He had done since he was a young boy. What he did not know about the workings of the human body was not worth knowing. He watched Jack carefully cut through the gag and the cord at her wrists, then remove them, before kneeling to examine her.

'She's like ice, Jack! We need to warm her up.' Joe fished in his bag for some scissors and began to cut the woman's clothing open from the hem up.

'What do you think you are doing?' Jack exclaimed, because somehow stripping the poor girl seemed a bit extreme.

'I have to get her out of these wet things, Jack, and dry her off or it will be impossible to warm her. Hypothermia can kill. Fetch some blankets.'

For once, Jack did exactly as he was asked. His younger brother might well bow down to him on all other matters, but in this situation, he trusted Joe more than anyone else to help the stranger. Secondly, Jack had precious little medical knowledge, had no idea exactly what hypo-whatever-it-was meant and it felt morally wrong to stand by gawping while she was relieved of her clothing. Wasting no time, Joe was in the midst of his examination when Jack came back, his patient's torso thoughtfully now covered in a coat.

'I do not think she has suffered any broken bones, though until she is awake, it is difficult to know for sure. There are cuts and bruises all over her—see?'

Jack passed the pile of blankets towards his brother and glanced down at the poor girl's visible bare arms and calves. His brother was not wrong. Filthy wounds and grazes marred the pale skin. 'Look at the bruising here.' Joe pointed to the left arm. 'If I had to take a guess, I would say she had a bad fall from something and landed on her side. Judging from the size and colour of the bruise, it's a miracle her arm or collarbone did not shatter from the impact. Some of these punctures are quite deep. The cut on her lip is nasty too. And her wrists have been rubbed raw by the cord around them—those wounds are angry and prone to become infected. She had to have been tied up for hours. I need to clean them all thoroughly.'

Relegated to the role of nursemaid, Jack busied himself by boiling kettle after kettle of water and traipsing the heavy buckets backwards and forward from the kitchen to the hall, leaving his brother to do what was necessary and feeling impotent in the process. As each layer of grime and embedded grit was removed, Joe commented on how miraculous it was that the woman was not more injured, yet she did not regain consciousness nor did she lose her deathly colour. Despite the now roaring fire in the enormous stone fireplace and the heap of blankets that swaddled her, her core temperature did not increase. Her swollen lips were blue tinged, her hands and feet like icicles.

'She must have been out in the cold for hours, Jack. I am worried she actually *has* hypothermia. She's barely breathing now and her pulse is definitely slowing.'

'What can I do?' Because there had to be something. The idea of her dying in their house tonight was horrifying. Not after he had done his best to save her, seen the stark terror in her eyes.

'You gather her up, Jack—share your body heat with her while I finish with all of the other injuries.'

'Share my body heat?' It sounded far-fetched, but Joe had proved to be right before. 'How exactly do I do that?'

'Hold her in your lap like a child.' Joe lifted her carefully at the base of the shoulders, exposing her bare back. They swaddled the blankets around her like a baby's shawl and Jack sat so the pair of them could manoeuvre her into his lap.

It was all well and good Joe telling him to hold her like a child—but it was blatantly obvious she was no child. There was too much of her, so his brother tucked her legs up beneath the covers to warm her extremities, while Jack smoothed his palms briskly along the sides of her arms in an attempt to create some heat from the friction. Her back and bottom were so cold he could feel the chill through the layers of woollen blanket and his clothing, and if she had not been breathing he would have thought he was holding a long-dead corpse. He gathered her close protectively and wrapped his arms about her, hoping she would absorb whatever warmth she needed from his body, crooning to her as his brother towel-dried her sodden, matted long hair before wrapping a blanket around her head too.

'If she was awake, I could make her drink something. Warm milk or tea might help to speed up the process.' Joe ran his hands through his thick dark hair in agitation. 'I suppose I could try and spoon some into her?'

All Jack could do was shrug. He had no clue as to what should be done and from his position beneath the girl, he was hardly in a state to assist his brother further. Being powerless was not something he excelled at. He hated feeling so useless when he was usually the one in control. All he could do was continue to hold her cradled in his arms, searching her wan face for signs of life. As he waited for Joe to return from the kitchen, his other two brothers returned. Both looked as if they had just walked through a hurricane.

'Only an idiot would be out in that!' said Jamie, shaking off the rain. 'But the gates are bolted and we saw nothing in the lane. If somebody turns up, we'll all deny any knowledge of your mystery damsel until we know what the hell this is all about. How is she?' He limped painfully towards the sofa and stared down at the still bundle in Jack's arms.

'Joe's patched her up as best as he can for the time being. Now we're trying to get her warm.'

Jamie did not instil a great deal of confidence

with his next words. 'I've seen many a man killed from exposure to the elements. It's when they stop shivering you have to really worry. Is she shivering?'

She was not. Jack did not want to think about what that meant. 'She won't die!' Not if he had anything to do with it. 'Joe is fetching some warm milk.' As if milk was some magic medicine nobody had known about which would miraculously cure a poor girl who was almost frozen to death. Jack stared down at her. She was so still, and so frighteningly pale, she could almost have been carved out of alabaster. He remembered the fear he had seen in her wide eyes when she collided with him and hoped those awful few minutes would not be the last she was doomed to remember. 'I don't even know her name.'

Jacob, so far silent, went to the pile of wet clothes discarded on the floor and began to rifle through them.

'She was not in the army, fool,' Jamie said dismissively, 'I doubt she will have her rank, surname and number written on her petticoats.'

'You'd be amazed what ladies keep in their petticoats.' Jacob did not look up from his task. 'Although to know that, you would have to know how to charm the ladies, Jamie, which you don't.' He sat back on his heels and triumphantly waved a small square of intricately embroidered linen. 'I, on the other hand, am very charming. Her name is Letty.' He balled up the damp cloth and threw it at Jamie's head. 'It says so on her handkerchief.'

Jack stroked his index finger gently over her cheek and willed her to wake up. 'Letty. Letty, sweetheart, can you hear me?'

Letty. Letty, sweetheart, can you hear me?
She did not recognise the voice, but it had a calming lilt to it even though it came from a strange man. It was not Bainbridge and it was not her uncle. That was all that mattered. Letty struggled to open her eyes, but they would not budge. She was so very tired. So tired she did not have the strength to be frightened. Something was pulling her upwards to a place she wanted to go, yet something, *someone*, held her firm, preventing her from floating away. She was cocooned rather than imprisoned. Safe.

She felt something warm trickle down her throat. She couldn't taste it. Strong arms around her. More of the warm liquid. *Letty. Try to swallow, sweetheart.* Sweetheart? That was nice. Nobody had ever called her sweetheart before. *We need to warm you up.* Now that she considered it, she was cold. Every part of her ached. Not surprising considering what had happened to her. Bainbridge. The carriage. The woods.

Panic came afresh. What if they had found her? She forced her eyes open. Intense blue eyes met hers. *You're safe, Letty.* They were beautiful eyes. Troubled eyes. Reassuring eyes. *I am going to look after you, sweetheart. I promise.* The deep lilting voice crooned against her ear. She sighed. It was all she had the strength to do and her eyes fluttered closed again. The painful gag was gone. And he was holding her.

There were worse ways to go.

Chapter Three

One month and one day remaining...

Letty experienced the sensation of falling and it woke her with a start. It took her a few moments to focus in the daylight, but when she did two pairs of identical blue eyes were staring down at her. Frightened, she had intended to scream; the strangled mewling noise she managed was really quite pathetic.

'Shh...' said one of the pairs of eyes kindly. 'Everything is all right. You are safe here.'

She could make out the blurry edges of the speaker's face. Dark hair. Smiling. Next to him stood another man who looked strikingly similar. They were definitely related. The same dark hair, the same deep blue eyes, but he was frowning. She knew those eyes.

'My brother rescued you from the road,' the

smiling man said, stroking one of her hands, 'You have had a bit of a fever and you are badly bruised, but miraculously you have made a very fast and splendid recovery. What you need to do now is rest. Give your body time to heal. In a few days, you will be as fit as a fiddle.'

Letty tried to speak, to ask where she was. However, her mouth felt so woolly, her tongue would not move. Her eyes flicked to the frowning man and he continued to frown, until the smiling man next to him gave him a sharp nudge in the ribs and he forced himself to smile. It did not touch his eyes. Letty could not quite make out whether the emotion swirling in those fathomless blue depths was concern or annoyance.

'Why were you tied up and wandering in the woods?' The smile slipped off his face as he stared down at her.

Again her stupid tongue would not move and she made some garbled sound.

'Leave her be, Jack. You can interrogate the poor girl once she is better.'

Interrogate? Were these men her enemies, too? She did not recognise either of them as her uncle's or the Earl of Bainbridge's men—yet that didn't mean they were not in their employ.

'Here, Letty, take this medicine. It will help you to sleep.'

She was powerless to stop the spoon being pressed against her lips and recognised the bitter taste of the liquid. Laudanum. The exact same drug her uncle had forced down her throat before he had handed her over to Bainbridge. Letty struggled as best she could. To her surprise, it was the frowning man who came to her aid. The one with the familiar deep blue eyes.

'Stop it, Joe. If she doesn't want it, you shouldn't force it on her,' he commanded.

The young man instantly withdrew, concern etched on his handsome face. 'I don't want her to be in pain, Jack. She needs to sleep.'

Apparently, enough drops of the liquid had already entered her system because her eyes were suddenly very heavy. She felt another hand touch her face softly. She knew immediately whose hand it was and also knew she liked this man's touch.

'That's a good girl. Close your eyes, sweetheart. Everything will be all right...'

It was still dark when she woke properly, but not so dark she could not see. Opening both eyelids, however, proved to be problematic. The left one would not open at all. The room was strange. The bed was warm and comfortable, and every bone in her body hurt like the devil.

The only illumination in the room came from a solitary candle on the nightstand and the moonlight streaming through the uncovered window panes. Letty tested her arms and found that she could, in fact, now move them. The tight cord her uncle had bound her with was gone then. Those bonds had left their mark on her wrists though; they were both sore and painful. She reached her other hand over to touch the opposite arm and felt her left wrist bound with bandages. More bandage bound her upper arm. She attempted to sit up, but gave up when her head began to spin and pound once again.

Bringing her hand to her face, Letty felt her swollen lip. It was sore still, although the cut caused by Bainbridge's signet rig was healed over. She must have been here asleep for hours for that to happen. Or days? Further probing led to the discovery of a huge lump on her temple. It was hot and tender, the bruising spread over the front of her forehead and just above her left eye. The lid felt swollen and explained why it was so difficult to open. She probably looked a fright. Her hair felt gritty and matted with a substance she did not recognise, but suspected was mud. She was also beyond thirsty.

For a few minutes she simply lay there, wondering what to do and trying to take in the unfamiliar surroundings. The bedchamber was large and simply decorated. There was a plain, mahogany dressing table against one wall and a matching, and equally enormous, wardrobe on the opposite one. The small nightstand next to her and the bedstead were the only other pieces of furniture. The heavy curtains at the leaded windows hung open, giving her a good view of the night sky beyond. The steady patter of raindrops on the glass suggested that the dreadful weather had not improved at all. The window was closed, but not barred or locked. That was a good sign surely—unless she was so high up escaping from the window was an impossibility. There were lots of castles in Scotland, after all, and the walls and ceiling did have an air of the ancient about them, although the ceilings were too low to belong to a fortress.

Letty scanned the rest of the room for clues. There was one large rug on the wooden floor. It looked to be good quality despite its obviously advanced age. The lack of artwork on the walls or little knick-knacks strewn about gave the room a distinctly impersonal feel. She had no idea whether she was in an inn or a private house and, as she was completely alone in the room, there was nobody to ask. There was also nobody to help her. However, the bedchamber door was open, which made her feel better. If she was a prisoner, then her captors would hardly leave her unattended with the door open—not after what had happened in the carriage. Perhaps she was safe at last?

Slowly, Letty shuffled her body to a more upright position, pausing to let each new wave of dizziness pass. Her shoulder throbbed, the wrist on her left hand was still immensely painful and her left ankle was also a bit tender, but other than that she had escaped the carriage remarkably in one piece. Stretching out her good arm, she could just about touch the rim of the cup on the nightstand. She used the soles of her feet to push forward a little more until she could grab the top of the cup with her finger and thumb. Judging by its weight, she thought the vessel must be filled with liquid. However, the flimsy grip she had on it was not strong enough. The cup slid out of her fingers and crashed to the wooden floor below, taking the precious fluid with it.

The noise created a flurry of activity, accompanied by manly-sounding grunts, on the floor on the other side of the bed. A bewildered dark head appeared first, blinking eyes heavy with sleep, taking in the surroundings as he dragged one hand over his face and through his unruly hair. 'You're awake!' he slurred, peering at her through semi-closed eyes.

'Sorry,' she croaked, 'I dropped the water.' Letty did not recognise him as one of her abductors, but there was something oddly familiar about him. Bizarrely, she had the distinct impression she could trust him and that she was safe with this complete stranger. Then she remembered him as the man who had prevented his accomplice from forcing more laudanum on her. If either of them had meant her harm, she was certain he would have held her down so the drug could be properly administered.

'It's all right.' Stiffly, he raised himself to his feet and stretched his back and neck before shuffling around the bed to the nightstand. He was tall, and from what she could make out, broad to go with it. Older than her, but not by more than a few years. She felt a pang of guilt for inconveniencing him, whoever he was. It could not be very comfortable, or warm, sleeping on the floor. With his back to her he poured a fresh cup of water, then sat on the mattress next to her and guided it carefully into her good hand, wrapping his warm palm around her chilled fingers until he was sure that she could manage it alone. Letty greedily drank every drop so he refilled the cup without her having to ask. 'It's the laudanum,' he explained gruffly. 'My brother says it makes you thirsty.'

How his brother knew this, she had no idea, but he was right. Letty could not remember ever needing to drink quite as much as she did at this moment. She sipped the second cup more slowly, feeling self-conscious as he watched her. Even befuddled and crumpled from sleeping on the floor the man in front of her was very pleasant to look at. He was nothing like the men she had known in the *ton*. His hands were obviously used to hard work and had felt calloused when they'd rested briefly over hers.

'My name is Jack Warriner, in case you were wondering.'

Jack Warriner was also a man who spent a great

deal of his life outside. Even in the poor light of the bedchamber she could see evidence of a tan— tiny white crinkles fanned out from the corners of his eyes suggesting that he often squinted in the sun. Yet his accent was not coarse and his diction unmistakably pointed to that of a gentleman. The untucked, and undone, linen shirt he still wore emphasised his wide shoulders and strong arms. The thick column of his throat would look stran- gled in the high collars favoured by the men in so- ciety. And what gentleman of means would sleep on the floor next to an injured stranger? Such an onerous task would be delegated to a servant while the master slept. Unless he was her guard and was merely lulling her into a false sense of security? He was the sort of large, imposing man who would be suited to the job.

Letty watched him carefully as she finished the last drops of her water before passing the cup back to him.

'More?' he asked, lifting the stoneware jug for emphasis and she shook her head gingerly. 'You gave us quite a scare, Letty, I don't mind telling you.' How did he know her name? 'I found you in the road. You passed out, no doubt from all of the trauma and the cold, and you've been out like a light since. My brother Joe is training to be a physician. He patched you up, so you probably have him to thank for saving your life.' His tone, his delivery was matter of fact. 'Do you remember how you came to be bound and gagged and wandering alone in the forest?'

Before she answered his questions, she had a few of her own before she trusted him with the truth. Her uncle was no fool. He would offer an impressive reward to anyone who found her. His own future depended on her marrying the odious Bainbridge. And if the Earl was looking for her and retrieved her…well, she already knew how cruel he could be. She pretended to think and then shook her head. The motion caused a fresh wave of dizziness which he spotted.

'Lie still. Try not to move your head too much.'

'Thank you, sir. You are being very kind.' Letty attempted a smile in the hope he would not realise she was already suspicious.

'Call me Jack,' he said with a wave of his hand, 'everybody else does.' The corners of his own lips curved upwards slightly, giving some respite from the perpetual frown he had worn since he had awoken, but it was still not a smile. He stared at her awkwardly for a few seconds before speaking again. 'Would you like some more medicine?'

She shook her head. The black void that came with the laudanum would rob her of any control. Besides, if she needed to escape quickly from here then she needed to be lucid. She also needed to plan an escape route.

'Can you tell me where I am… Jack?'

He sat back down on the mattress again, disregarding any of the rules of propriety, and sighed, as if answering questions was a great chore to him. 'You are in my home. Markham Manor. In deepest, darkest, dankest Nottinghamshire. Retford is the nearest village, almost three miles away, but if it's a proper town you need, then Lincoln is probably the closest.' That put her in the north of England. Just. A long way from Gretna Green at least. 'I found you near the woods a good mile away. Soaking wet and frozen stiff. I reckon you had been out in the storm for a couple of hours before I came along. I have no idea where you sprang from either and since nobody has come to claim you, I think we can assume whoever tied you up was not able to follow your tracks. My brother Jamie has battened down the hatches in your honour, in case they come visiting, and is taking turns with my youngest brother Jacob to keep watch, so you are safe.'

For some inexplicable reason, Letty believed him. She had actually done it! She had escaped Bainbridge and now she was hidden in a house. Her relief must have been obvious because he shot her a dubious look which suggested he did not believe her pathetic claim to have no memory of the event.

'What day is it?' The passing of time was her only hope now, yet she had no idea how long she had been here.

'It is past midnight so it must be Friday.'

Letty risked another tenuous shake of the head. She could not work out how much longer she needed just from that information. 'The date?'

Intelligent eyes sought hers and she had the uncomfortable feeling that he could see into her very mind and knew she was lying. 'As I said, it's past midnight, so I suppose that would make it the fourth.'

'I see.'

'Yet you have not enquired as to the month, so I must assume you remember some things. Are you sure you have no memory of what happened?'

Letty looked down towards her hands. This man

had been nothing but kind to her so lying to him made her uncomfortable—but there was no guarantee he wouldn't be tempted by a ransom, so with no other choice she did it anyway.

'I do not recall the accident at all.' She would never, ever forget it. Her heart began to knock against her ribs at the falsehood and her palms felt sweaty. What she was claiming did not sound plausible to her own ears.

'Do you remember any details about your family, Letty, so that I might be able to inform them of your predicament?'

Letty would rather die than admit the truth. If her uncle knew where she was then her life might as well be over. Correction—it likely would be over and pretty sharpish, too, if he and the Earl of Bainbridge's hideous plan came to fruition in the next few weeks. No matter what, she needed to stay hidden until then. She stared down at her hands again and shook her head. 'I am afraid I do not… My head feels so dizzy.'

Whilst this was true, she only mentioned it to stop him probing further. Lying was not something that had ever come naturally to her. Her mother and father had always caught her out when she had tried to do it, joking that her guilt was plainly written all over her face. Just in case he could read it in her eyes, Letty hastily closed them with a sigh, but not before she saw scepticism in his own intelligent blue gaze. 'Perhaps I will feel better with a little more sleep,' she mumbled, trying her level best to sound exhausted rather than terrified of imminent exposure, and felt him rise from the mattress next to her.

'Perhaps I should fetch my brother so he can check on you. You have been very ill.'

'There is no need to wake him at such a late hour. I have already inconvenienced you and your family enough. I shall sleep for another few hours, I think.'

She heard, rather than saw, him hesitate for a few moments as he decided whether or not to grant her request. 'I will be right here next to you should you need anything,' he said gruffly, perhaps a touch begrudgingly. Then she heard the rustle of blankets and the sound of him easing his big body back down on to the hard, uncomfortable floor.

Letty was peculiarly grateful that he did not intend to leave her alone in her current state. She felt too vulnerable and his solid presence was strangely reassuring. 'I am so sorry for being so burdensome,' she added lamely, hoping to convey to him her appreciation for all that he was doing for her despite the fact she was lying through her teeth. He grunted in response, but offered no soothing words to contradict her nor did he make any attempt to prolong any conversation between them. She heard him punch the pillow into shape and hoist the covers over himself as he settled into a suitably comfortable position to sleep in.

Whilst Jack Warriner lacked the gentlemanly politeness she was accustomed to, Letty could not help but admire his honesty. He did not want her here, she was a huge burden, but he would not turn her away just yet either. She would be safe here, temporarily. It was a small weight off her mind. A day or two of respite in this remote oasis was a blessing to be sure, although she would have preferred not to have been flung from a speeding carriage in order to have achieved it.

On the other hand, neither her uncle nor the odious Earl was likely to take her escape lying down. Now she was out of their clutches, if she managed to make it intact for her twenty-first birthday, both men were now in very precarious positions indeed. She was not entirely sure what the penalty for abduction, forced marriage and then bridal murder was—but she would be extremely surprised if either of them was allowed to live if they were ever sentenced for the crimes. They would move heaven and earth to find her, and to silence her, and they would endeavour to do so well before the fourth of January.

Letty could not afford to rest on her laurels while she recovered. She needed a plan. A proper plan this time, which would keep her safely out of harm's way until it was too late and she would have full control over her inheritance. She also needed to think of something to tell her clever, reluctant host. Bumbling excuses were not going to work indefinitely on him. But could she really risk telling him the truth? Until she knew more about the situation and the man himself, it would surely be prudent to keep quiet. In the last few days, Letty's blind trust in mankind had been smashed to smithereens with a pickaxe. Trusting anyone after what she had been through was not going to be particularly easy.

To her side, she heard the steady deep breathing of a man already lost in slumber. Letty had never shared a bedroom with a man before. A few short weeks ago such a scandalous act would have brought ruin to her name. Then she had cared a great deal about her reputation—as if it was all that mattered. Of course, she had not realised her

life and liberty were in danger and she had believed she would be free to select the husband
of her own choosing from the ranks of willing
gentleman who swarmed around her at every so-
cial function. Her enormous fortune gave her the
pick of the bunch, so there had been no need to
be hasty. Years ago, when she was young and
foolish, she had even written a list of attributes
the lucky candidate must possess. He had to be
handsome, witty, titled, an excellent horseman,
a connoisseur of the theatre, a patron of the arts,
the absolute envy of all her friends and, of course,
and most importantly, he *had* to be *hopelessly* in
love with her.

Whilst she had managed to find suitable gentlemen with nearly all of those qualities, the last one
was always the sticking point. After several Sea-
sons her youthful hopes had become quite jaded.
So far, she had not found one man who she was
wholly convinced loved her, Letty the woman,
rather than Violet the Tea Heiress. Her huge fortune, instead of giving her a reassuring sense of
comfort, had become a massive weight on her
shoulders. Did anyone of her acquaintance actually like her for herself? Or was it merely the
piles of pound notes and all the luxury that came

with her legendary generosity that drew people to her? She could never tell.

There was one promising candidate who was already close to proposing marriage—the Duke of Wentworth. However, Letty could not quite fathom him out either. Until she did, there was no way she was going to commit to something as permanent as marriage. She was still young; what was the rush? Besides, for a while now she had been distracted with other thoughts. Ideas of actually doing something with her fortune, something that mattered, something which gave her shallow, empty life some purpose. Perhaps create a home for foundlings? Other orphans who were all alone in the world, just as she was, but who did not have the benefit of a fortune to keep them safe, fed and warm. Unfortunately, while she had been lamenting the huge burden of her fortune and what to do with it, and putting off journeying on the path to find her one true love, she had neglected to consider her uncle's personal ambitions for *her* money or the fact that she was bound by law to do his bidding until she reached the age of majority.

Which was only one month away now, give or take a few hours.

Chapter Four

Exactly one month left...

Jack eagerly swapped his nursemaid duties with Joe well before dawn. The hard floor had not been conducive to sleeping on for any longer, not that he ever had time to sleep in, but still, even by his standards the hour was early. The mystery woman had been in his care for a few days now. However, last night had been the first time she had been in any state to speak for herself and her cagey responses to the questions he had asked her did not quite ring true. In fairness, the poor girl had been bound and gagged and horrifically abused beforehand, so it was hardly surprising she was reluctant to trust him, but as she was now his responsibility, he reasoned he did have the right to know what sort of trouble he had brought to his own door.

And she was going to be trouble.

He knew that with the same certainty he knew the sun would rise every morning. Trouble had been Jack's constant companion for a decade; he knew the scent of it too well to ignore.

He wasn't surprised when he found Jamie already up and dressed in the kitchen. Since his brother's return from the Peninsula, he apparently did not sleep. And he smiled even less than Jack did. Both states worried him, yet he had no idea how to fix them. Jamie had always been a closed book. Any loose pages he once had were now glued together firmly and no amount of cajoling would pry them free again.

'I thought I would head to the village and see what I can find out about our guest.' After cradling the woman in his arms for hours and sleeping alongside her for two nights, much as he did not want to, he already felt responsible for the chit. And strangely protective. Clearly he was going soft in his old age.

Jamie handed him a steaming mug of tea and an assessing stare. 'Good idea. I've been thinking much the same myself. It is fairly safe to assume the girl is in danger, but if you go there asking questions, you could stir up a hornets' nest.'

'I am not a fool.'

'I never said you were; however, you are not known for your subtlety. I'll come with you and show you how it's done.'

Without thinking, Jack allowed his gaze to wander to his brother's wounded leg and regretted it instantly when he saw his face cloud with fury. 'I am not a blasted cripple, Jack! I can still ride a horse.'

He was in no mood to try to reason with him today. Jack had barely slept properly in three nights so his temper was closer to the surface than usual and he would likely say something which couldn't be undone. Since Jamie had come home, he was still so angry at the world and convinced he was good for nothing. Any attempts at brotherly concern about him over-extending himself and putting back his recovery would only aggravate him further.

'I shall saddle the horses then.'

It was market day in Retford and by the time they arrived the square was already bustling with activity. At his brother's suggestion, they went directly to the inn in search of breakfast and information. It made sense. If strangers were in the area, they would be staying at the inn. Jack would not have thought of that first, so perhaps having Jamie in tow would prove to be beneficial.

'Just eat your food and listen. The trick to good recognisance is to appear disinterested. If we hear anything vaguely interesting, leave it to me to do the probing.'

Jack grunted in response, a little put out by his brother's lack of faith in his abilities. Jamie selected a table in the centre of the dining room and they ordered food, then his brother disappeared to do some quiet digging and left him to his own devices. For want of something useful to do, he scanned the patrons to see if he could see anything suspicious and conceded that perhaps his brother was right. He knew nothing about gathering information subtly. In fact, his relationship with subtlety of any sort could best be described as tenuous. Jack was a doer and acknowledged his usually straightforward methods of getting to the truth might not be what was needed today. Because it was market day, almost every face was new to him—and therefore, by default, instantly suspicious to his untrained eyes. His first instinct was to go and thoroughly question them all, which was exactly what his military-trained brother had feared he would do. 'You cannot help yourself, Big Brother,' he had said as they had ridden over, 'you are too used to being in charge.' Acknowledging his own character flaws always made Jack wince; having them pointed out correctly by a sibling was galling.

At the bar, Jamie had sidled up to the innkeeper. Being a recently returned war hero from the infamous family who lived near the forest made him of significant interest to the innkeeper. The locals did love to gossip and the Warriners had given them plenty to feast on over the years. Jack watched the man ask his brother question after question with barely contained curiosity and, as usual, Jamie dealt with them with his customary surliness, staring into his drink and never meeting his interrogator's eyes. To all intents and purposes he appeared exactly like a man who wanted nothing more than to be left alone rather than one on a quest for information. Jack had to admire that talent, even if he was still slightly sulking and did so begrudgingly.

A few minutes later, Jamie limped back to the table and spoke in a voice so low, Jack had to strain his ears to hear it.

'There are a group of men from London staying here. A pushy lot, by all accounts, who the innkeeper would be glad to see the back of. They have been here since the morning after you found your damsel in distress. Came in soaked to the skin, despite the two fancy carriages they arrived with. The carriages and half the men left the next day, leaving three of them behind. The rooms were all booked under the name Smith. The innkeeper says they've been asking questions about a girl. An heiress, by all accounts.' Jack raised his eyebrows at this news. 'They are claiming she has been kidnapped and they are searching for her. They haven't surfaced yet this morning, but he expects them presently on account of it being market day and filled with new people to talk to. So far, each morning they have done the same thing. They ask questions, eat and disappear for the day. He has no idea where they go to—but they come back very frustrated. As if they are in a great hurry to get the job done.'

Jamie shot him a warning glance as their breakfasts were brought over. How he noticed the impending arrival of the food was also impressive, Jack mused, seeing as Jamie was not facing the kitchen and would have needed eyes in the back of his head to have seen anyone behind him. The innkeeper's wife plonked them down unceremoniously in front of them, her hostility towards not one, but two Warriners so early in the morning written all over her face.

'Have you paid for these?'

Their father's legacy still blighted them. The bastard had been dead seven years and still the locals believed a Warriner equalled nothing but bad debt and aggravation. Jamie shot the woman an evil look and was about to put her in her place when Jack intervened. 'I paid up front, Nelly. As I always do.' He was trying to build the broken bridges, had been trying for years to mend them, and as much as the slights still wounded he understood them. For centuries the Warriner family had always been a bad lot and it would take a darn sight longer than seven years for the brothers to repair the damage their ancestors had wrought. It was only in the last eighteen months that Jack had been able to lure a few rag-tag tenants back to his land and even they were not originally from around these parts. Nelly sniffed and stalked off.

'Perhaps they are Letty's family searching for her? Maybe she *was* kidnapped.' Conjuring the image of her terrified and running away from him

made Jack feel a strange combination of protectiveness and fury all over again.

Jamie shrugged. 'Or that is exactly what they
want us to think. They could hardly tell people they are the kidnappers and they would like
their hostage back now, can they?' That argument
made a lot of sense too. 'Besides, if they are above
board, why the name Smith? It's too convenient,
Jack. My gut tells me it's not right.'

As Jamie's guts had saved his soldiering bacon
on more than one occasion, Jack decided to go
along with them. They ate in virtual silence in
order to overhear the tangled conversations around
them. In the main, they were all tradesmen here
to make some coin. One or two piqued their interest, but nobody mentioned a bound and gagged
girl in the woods.

Their food was long finished and they were
about to leave when three burly men walked in
and scanned the room like hawks seeking prey.
Jamie picked up his empty mug and pretended to
drink. 'Here we go. This is them, I reckon.'

The three men instantly split up and began approaching the other patrons jovially, moving from
group to group after friendly handshakes were
exchanged and ever closer to their table.

'Remember. Act bored. And keep your mouth shut.'

Jack gave his brother a sarcastic look. 'I appreciate your confidence in me, Jamie.'

'Hello, gentlemen—might I trouble you for a few moments?' The man who pulled up a chair next to them was all politeness. Jamie flicked him a detached look and shrugged. Jack copied.

'Do you live locally?'

'What's it to you?' Jamie replied suspiciously.

'Merely a friendly enquiry, sir.' The man's diction was crisp, but his appearance belied it. Underneath the fine clothes and the oily smile, he was not from the gentry, Jack was certain of that. He might lack Jamie's skills as a spy but he knew a wrong 'un when he saw one. This man had fists like hams, for a start, and a nose which had been often broken. The bridge had collapsed beneath his forehead before jutting out at an odd angle, making him appear more like a bare-knuckle fighter from a travelling carnival than a discerning gentleman of taste passing along the Great North Road. A fine, white jagged scar bisected one cheek. Its presence spoke volumes. This man was a close acquaintance of violence.

'My friends and I are looking for someone. A

young lady.' The man gave them a knowing smile. 'There's a reward.'

Jamie stared down into his empty mug as though he was only interested in how soon he could fill it up again. 'A reward, you say?' It was quite a masterly performance. Casual disinterest which gave the interloper just enough hope the lure of money *might* tempt him.

'Indeed. A handsome one. A hundred pounds to anyone who aids in her safe return.'

Jamie let out a slow, impressed whistle. 'A hundred pounds—that's a lot of money. Why so much?' He glanced casually at Jack, his lips curved in a disbelieving half-smile before he turned back to their visitor. 'Is she wanted by the Crown?'

'No. Nothing like that… She has gone missing.'

'We are on the road to Gretna Green. Hundreds of young girls go *missing* along this road every single year. If yours doesn't want to be found…' Jamie shrugged again, allowing the implication to ferment.

'Unfortunately, we believe the young lady in question was kidnapped rather than eloped. Her family are extremely keen to have her back. They fear for her safety.'

'If she's been kidnapped, why not wait for the ransom demand and simply pay it?' Jamie was back to being bored again. His amused eyes met Jack's. 'We are not the sort of men to take on a gang of kidnappers. Not even for a hundred pounds. We value our own lives too much.'

The man smiled and nodded. 'I understand, gentlemen—but the lady in question is rather... resourceful. *If*...she managed to escape their clutches, it might explain why no ransom demands have been made yet.' It all sounded so reasonable—yet alarm bells were ringing in Jack's mind. 'All I would ask is that you keep a watchful eye out for her. She is gently bred, unfamiliar with the area and there are so many places she could get lost here. If you did come across any information as to her whereabouts, her family would be very grateful... And it might prove to be very lucrative for you gentlemen also. Everyone wins, as it were.'

Jack had had enough of playing the mute sidekick. 'If we did see her, what does she look like?' He ignored his brother's warning glare.

'Very pretty. Blonde hair. Green eyes. Only twenty. She's quite a striking little thing. A bit prone to fancy though, as so many young women are, and after such an ordeal there's no telling what sort of state her poor mind will be in...' The man shook his head as if he were genuinely concerned and it raised the hackles on Jack's neck further. 'Her family are hoping to get her back quietly. You understand. The poor girl would be ruined if the world knew what had happened to her. If you see or hear anything, you can find me here at the inn.'

'And your name is?'

'Smith. Mr John Smith.'

'And the girl's? Is she a *Smith* too?'

'No, sir. I merely work for the family. Her name is Violet.'

'No surname?'

The man smiled again, but it lacked any sincerity. 'That's right, sir. The family would prefer not to create a scandal...the young lady would be quite ruined if news of her abduction leaked. Therefore, I am certain you can see now why the family are keen to get her safely returned into their loving arms as swiftly as possible.'

Jamie pierced the stranger with his steely glare. 'If the reward is one hundred pounds, then I am assuming the family is important. That is a large amount of money for a lady of little consequence.

Therefore, it stands to reason they can spare more than a paltry hundred pounds for her safe return, don't you think?'

The other man stood, his face a frozen mask. 'May I enquire as to your names, sirs?' There was suspicion in his cold eyes now as they flicked between them.

Jack stared back, all smug arrogance. 'Warriner. I am Jack and this is my younger brother Jamie.'

For a second he saw Jamie silently querying the logic behind giving this fellow their real names, then realising it was sensible. If they aroused this man's suspicions he would likely check on their story and a great many of their neighbours would happily sell the 'Wild' Warriners down the river.

'Well, Mr Warriner, I am sure the *family* would be open to negotiations. Should you have anything of…interest to them.'

Jack laughed and slapped his brother heartily on the back. 'I think me and you should go heiress hunting, Jamie. What do you say? What could we do with at least a hundred pounds, aye?' Never a truer word was spoken although it was a drop in the ocean compared to what he actually needed to stop the rot in their ailing fortunes.

Jack smiled enthusiastically back at the still-loi-

tering man, ignoring the bad taste in his mouth
which came from coveting the reward and for
hoping the scarred, creepy fellow was, indeed,
telling the truth, despite his gut feeling that he
wasn't. The Warriners could do with one hundred
pounds. It might be enough to send Joe to medical school for a while and ease his guilt at failing
to get his brother there sooner.

Then again, wanting that money already felt
disloyal to Letty, although he had no idea where
his overriding loyalty to her had come from. Unless it was just the crushing burden of yet more
responsibility he did not need. Jack apparently
had a soft spot for damsels in distress. 'Where
did you last see her, Mr Smith?'

The man's expression instantly changed to one
of friendliness again, believing he had won them
over. 'We suspect she might have been taken along
this section of the Great North Road.'

'You *suspect*?' Jack shook his head at his
brother and laughed derisively. 'So we would not
be chasing a fact—merely a suspicion? Only about
ten villages and a hundred square miles of Sher-
wood Forest to search then!' He stared back at the
man with pity. 'I think my brother and I can find
better things to do with our time than searching

for a needle in a haystack—but I wish you well with your search. If, by some miracle, we do hear something, rest assured, Mr Smith, you will be the first to know.' For good measure, he toasted him with his own empty mug.

Chapter Five

Still just one month to go...

Her attentive physician tied the last of her clean bandages, then sat back on the mattress to smile at her. 'It is indeed a miracle you are this hale and hearty. I was convinced you would die when Jack brought you home, yet now there are just a few sprains and cuts left to heal. You obviously have a strong constitution indeed. A day or two of rest and I dare say you will be as good as new.'

Letty certainly felt better. And cleaner. The youngest Warriner, Jacob, had brought her a bucket of hot water, some soap and towels at her request, so she had managed to rinse the mud and grit from her hair. She was sat up in bed, her belly pleasantly filled with food and dressed in a freshly laundered gentleman's shirt. She bestowed her healer with one of Violet's best smiles—the one which had been fêted in society as the most stunning of the Season—and hoped her swollen lip would not spoil its impact. 'Thank you, Doctor. I am grateful for all you have done.'

'I am no doctor yet,' he said a little wistfully, 'but perhaps one day.'

This surprised her. 'I was certain you were a proper physician. Your medical knowledge is excellent. Without your help, I do not doubt I would have died. Why do you not get a proper licence to practise medicine?'

He stood and busied himself with tidying away the soiled bandages. 'I study and read extensively, and I am sure that one day I will qualify. However, it is not just my efforts that saved your life. The majority of your thanks should be directed at my brother Jack. He was the one who brought you home and he has scarcely left your side since your arrival. He was the one who spent the nights tending to your fever and making sure you were kept warm.'

Letty recalled the eldest Warriner had slept on the floor beside her last night. Clearly, he had spent a few nights on that hard floor on her behalf—odd when he had appeared so suspicious and put upon, although, for reasons she could not fathom, his diligence did not surprise her. 'Then I shall extend my gratitude to him also, *Dr* Joe, as soon as I see him next.'

He had not been there when she had awoken this morning, which at the time Letty had been relieved about. Jack Warriner saw too much. Whether or not he really was a good man, as both of his younger brothers had suggested, she would have to see. However, neither Jacob nor Joe Warriner had been guarded in their answers this morning when she had bombarded them with a stream of questions. Thanks to them, Letty now knew for certain she was not a prisoner in this house. Jack Warriner had found her on the road and brought her home, and by doing so, had saved her life.

Home was a four-hundred-year-old manor house surrounded by thirty acres of park and farmland. Mostly farmland. The Warriners grew wheat and raised sheep, and hardly moved in the sort of circles Bainbridge and her duplicitous uncle did. Apparently, only the second eldest, Jamie, had been to London and then only once on a fleeting visit, so they would have no idea who she was either.

They all worked on the land, with the exception of Jamie who had only recently arrived back from the war, and was still recovering from the damage Napoleon's army had done to his body. The three younger brothers also had enormous respect for Jack. It shone out of their eyes whenever he was mentioned in a conversation and they clearly deferred to his leadership on all matters of importance.

The Warriners were fiercely loyal and hugely protective of one another, the sort of tight family bond Letty had never experienced, yet always yearned for. They loved one another. It was plainly obvious and she could not help envying them for that. It must be nice to know there was always somebody there for you, ready to support you or simply to commiserate with when times were tough. To always have someone to turn to. Letty had not had such support since the untimely death of her parents at seventeen. She had ostensibly been all alone in the world—yet nobody had really pitied her because she was the Tea Heiress after all, as if her money could somehow fix her broken heart, or banish her loneliness and make everything bright in the world again.

If something happened to one of the brothers, the others would move heaven and earth to rectify things or would support each other in their grief. She had been missing from Mayfair for days—

and sincerely doubted anybody had missed her at all. Not really. Her swathes of friends might comment on her absence at a ball or afternoon tea, but Letty was not convinced any of them genuinely cared enough to investigate the true cause of her absence. She did not possess one true friend, the sort a girl could confide in or depend upon. Nobody had ever assumed she might want one and she had no idea how to go about getting one. And that was a humbling thought, as well as a depressing one. She had more money than she could ever spend in one lifetime, yet she envied the Warriners.

She got the impression life was tough for the family—although such disloyalty had not been vocalised explicitly—and she suspected the main obstacle between Joe qualifying as a doctor, and not, was decidedly financial. That might work in her favour. In her experience, those in need of money were easily bribed and her father had often commented on the benefits of 'greasing a few palms'. In a few weeks, she could easily fill the palms of all four Warriners with gold and still not make a dent in her reserves.

And then again it might not. If they desperately needed money quickly, they could well sell

her back to Bainbridge if the opportunity presented itself. At least Bainbridge could pay them
instantly—Letty would have to wait weeks to get
her hands on her own money. The appointment
was already made with the solicitor on the day
of her birthday to sign the papers which would
give her her longed-for independence. It was also
the day she would consign a generous portion of
it to the charitable trust she intended to set up in
her name and begin carving out a new life filled
with noble purpose rather than pampered inertia.
Once that was done, she intended to begin searching for premises right away and nobody would be
able to stop her.

Her uncle had always been most dismissive of
her desire to put her money to work and had refused to allow her to spend it on anything apart
from gowns and fripperies she did not need and
had long ago ceased to want. But on that glorious day, in one month's time, she could do with
it whatever she pleased. The Warriners might not
want to wait.

The fact that she had not been attended to by
the family servants niggled. It was almost as if
the brothers were intent on keeping her presence
here a great secret. Why would they do that un-

less it was for sinister purposes? Was it for her protection or was it for theirs? The most pressing problem was that Letty really did not know if this family was to be trusted.

Until she did, it was probably sensible to have an escape route. As soon as Joe left her on a quest to fetch her some tea, Letty eased her legs over the side of the bed. After carefully testing her weight on her bad ankle, she hobbled across the room to the faceted, leadlight window and peered out.

Markham Manor was indeed in deepest, darkest, dankest Nottinghamshire. One side of the estate was fringed with dense woodland. The outer edge of the estate ran directly alongside the River Idle, so unless they came by boat or battled their way through the trees, the only way Bainbridge could enter the grounds was to the east, and via the narrow, rutted dirt lane her rescuer had found her on. A lane whose only destination was here.

In the distance, Letty could just about make out the high wall which she now knew enclosed the Warriners' land. She also knew the huge gates were now locked because Jacob had moaned about the effort it had taken to do so and the splinters he had received in the process. A little further along, and purposely hidden behind tangled vines, was a smaller gate, a secret escape route which sounded positively medieval and very romantic. The Warriners of old must have needed such a device, as well as a great deal of fortified protection, if they had built such defences, yet those same defences now gave Letty a great deal of peace of mind. She had been here three days and nobody had come a calling. The more time passed, she hoped, the less likely it was they would do so.

Directly below her window was a cobbled courtyard which housed a large iron pump handle and a small mountain of buckets balanced haphazardly on top of each other. Other than that, the courtyard was bare. Her bedchamber must face over the kitchens then, in the rear of the house and well away from prying eyes in the lane. The drop from her window to the courtyard was significant enough to cause injury, she estimated, yet not quite high enough to result in death. There was trellis alongside her window, covered in the gnarled old branches of a wisteria left quite barren by the winter. If she had to, she could lower herself from it carefully and make a dash for the woods.

Satisfied the outside was safe, Letty turned and began to hobble towards her bedchamber door to investigate the layout of the house when the door opened and Jack Warriner strode in.

Then stopped dead.

She was wearing his shirt. That should not have come as a surprise because his brother had dressed her in his shirt when they had transferred her unconscious body to Jack's bedchamber because the only other one in any habitable state had mould creeping over the damp, cracked walls. Except the sight of her standing there in it was simply staggering. She had legs. Lovely, shapely female legs which were bare to mid-thigh where the tail of the shirt hung. And the most wonderful golden hair Jack had ever seen. A tumble of corkscrew ringlets fell past her shoulders, the short curls around her face framing it like a halo. His words dried in his throat and his eyebrows shot up as he stared at the beautiful creature right in front of him.

Emerald-green eyes stared back at him in surprise before she crouched and her arms covered her thighs. 'Would you mind turning around, please!' she squeaked and his wits returned.

'Yes, of course! Sorry!' Jack spun on his heels and faced the door, grateful for the opportunity to catch his breath and simply breathe.

There was a woman in his bedchamber.

Because after seeing her legs there was no way he could continue to think of her as a patient. There had not been an actual woman in Markham Manor since his mother had died a decade ago and he could barely remember the last time he had seen a woman's bare legs. May? Last spring, in Lincoln? Although at the time he had not really taken much notice of the tavern maid's legs because he had had to travel home before dark and he was more concerned with other parts of the woman. Perhaps he should have, because surely one pair of legs was much like the next? What was it about these particular legs he suddenly found so alluring?

He heard her scramble back towards the bed and the rustle of the covers as she made herself decent. 'You can turn around now Mr... Jack.'

Somehow, seeing her sitting up in his bed, all tousled and proper, made it worse and he felt the falls of his breeches tighten uncomfortably. She looked as tempting as a baker's window and, by God, he was desperate to taste her. But he had no time to spare to consider such unexpected yearnings, definitely not for a woman in his care and definitely not when he sensed impending danger.

'We need to talk... Violet.'

Her lovely eyes widened further in alarm at the use of her proper name and Jack finally knew for certain she had been economical with the truth. However, it was difficult to be annoyed at her for the omission. In her shoes, he'd have probably done much the same.

'There are men in the village looking for you.' A look of terror washed across her delicate features which he experienced an enormous desire to soothe. 'We did not alert them to your presence here. I thought it prudent to talk to you first before I entrusted them with any information.'

She visibly sagged with relief, the motion causing the open neck of the capacious linen shirt to fall to one side, exposing the smooth, pale skin of her delicate, feminine shoulder. Jack's groin tightened again and to cover it, he sat down heavily on the mattress in front of her. 'I think it is time you told me the truth. Don't you?'

Her golden head bobbed in assent, causing the blonde curls nearest her face to bounce. He suppressed the urge to reach up and touch one. Run his fingers along the length of it to see if it actually did feel like spun silk. She worried her bottom lip nervously with her teeth, drawing his hungry eyes there too. Her mouth was pink and plump and ripe for kissing. For some inexplicable reason, Jack was sorely tempted to kiss her. Not that he would, of course. The poor girl was frightened enough already, the last thing she needed was his case of rampant, wholly inappropriate lust.

'How many men?'

'Three. The others and their coaches have gone elsewhere to search for you, although I doubt they are too far away either. There are not many villages in this part of the county. They claimed to be working for your family.'

Her expression hardened. 'In a manner of speaking, they are.'

'They also claimed you were abducted, although I gather you would rather not be returned to them?'

He watched a flurry of emotions play on her face. Fear, confusion, mistrust, then finally acceptance. She stared back at him levelly. 'Those men—was one of them an older man? Grey hair tied back in an old-fashioned *queue*?'

Jack shook his head. 'No. The man I spoke to called himself Mr Smith. He had a scar across his cheek here.' He swiped his finger in a jagged line down his own cheek to the jaw in demonstration.

'Layton. His name is Layton. He works for the Earl of Bainbridge.' She sat back on the pillows, tucking her knees to her chest and hugging them. It was an unconscious gesture which suggested she needed to protect herself from whatever it was these men had come to achieve. It sparked something visceral inside him. Something primal and male and territorial. It made him want to slay dragons for her—a ridiculous notion which suddenly came out of nowhere and blindsided him. She could be lying through her pretty teeth, yet that made no difference to his urgent need to be her knight in shining armour. What was wrong with him? It wasn't like him to be so fanciful. Jack did not usually have those sorts of feelings for women. He liked them well enough...but always in a pragmatic and sensible way. He had never been a *romantic* man—although a part of him was certainly feeling that way if he was thinking of himself as her knight and conjuring imaginary dragons in his obviously addled mind.

It was probably because of the golden hair, he reasoned, he had always had a penchant for blondes. The legs were a bonus, of course, and then there was the fact that she was lying in his bed. Staring a little warily at him with her beautiful green eyes. She regarded him thoughtfully for several moments, then sighed.

'Letty *is* my name. It is the name I prefer to be called, at any rate, because my mother used to call me it as a child. However, my full name is Violet Dunston.' She paused briefly as if he should recognise the name, and when he didn't she seemed a little surprised, but continued. 'My parents died in a carriage accident a few years ago and since then I have been under the guardianship of my father's brother. Whilst I have never been particularly close to my uncle, I had no reason to suspect he wished me ill. He moved into my family house to fulfil his guardianship duties, although apart from that we really had little to do with one another.'

'A few weeks ago, he introduced me to the Earl of Bainbridge, a man old enough to be my grandfather who apparently had expressed a desire to marry me. Unsurprisingly, I was not thrilled with the proposal and turned him down. He is a completely odious man, who has already outlived two wives and has the reputation for being a dreadful gambler. I was surprised he would even condone such a proposal. However, since then, my uncle has been relentless in his insistence that I marry the vile man—because they were friends, or so I was led to believe. We argued about it a great deal and eventually my uncle ceased pressing the suit. I assumed I had convinced him that Bainbridge was the very last man on earth who I would consider marrying. Unfortunately, I could not have been more wrong.'

Just thinking about her uncle's treachery made her angry. All this time she had been duped into believing he had only wanted the very best for her...but he had designs on her fortune just like every other man who came knocking on her door. 'On the night in question, I had only just dressed for a ball and was waiting for the carriage to be brought around when my uncle asked to speak with me. He offered me a glass of wine, which stupidly I drank. It was laced with laudanum. I was barely conscious by the time Bainbridge arrived, but I overheard the gist of their conversation nevertheless. Bainbridge had agreed to give him half of my fortune in return for my hand in marriage—payable as soon as Bainbridge could obtain legal access to my money. It is held in a trust, you see, until I reach the age of majority. They tied me up and I was taken to a carriage bound for Gretna Green.

'By the time I came to, we were speeding along the road. I told Bainbridge that no court in the land would condone a forced marriage. I threatened to have the pair of them arrested and tried for their crime and that I would move heaven and earth to have the sham of a marriage annulled if he succeeded.' Her voice wavered then, because Letty still could not quite believe it herself. 'He laughed, claiming he had no great desire to be shackled to me for any longer than was necessary to get his hands lawfully on my magnificent stack of money and said...' her voice faltered '...he said that if I failed to comply and made his life difficult, then I would force his hand. He said I would find it difficult to get a marriage annulled from the grave.'

Jack Warriner's dark eyebrows came together fiercely as he absorbed her words. Other than that, she really had no idea what he was thinking. His very handsome face was quite inscrutable.

'So you were kidnapped, then?'

Letty nodded. 'Yes—but effectively by a member of my own family. If they find me, Bainbridge will drag me to Gretna Green. As soon as we are married, English law grants him my entire fortune.'

'And then your uncle would receive his half?'

'My father left him nothing in his will, aside from naming him as my guardian and giving him some control as trustee of the estate. As soon as I turn twenty-one, control of my entire inheritance reverts to me. The blood money earned by selling his niece to Bainbridge was obviously more palatable to him than living out the rest of his days with nothing.'

He stood and pinned her with his stormy blue gaze, giving nothing about his ultimate intentions away.

'I need to talk to my brothers.'

Then he stormed to the door.

Chapter Six

Thirty days and twelve hours left...

'Violet Dunston?' Jacob exclaimed and then appeared frustrated when all of his three brothers stared back perplexed. 'Seriously? Do you three never read the newspapers?'

'I don't have time to read the newspapers.' By the time Jack finished his never-ending round of daily chores, he could barely stand, let alone read.

'Scarcely a week goes by without a mention of society's darling Miss Dunston. She is the *Tea Heiress*.'

Jack was losing patience. 'Spare us the dramatics, Jacob. Surely it is quite apparent none of us knows what you are blathering on about. Kindly put us out of our misery, Little Brother.'

Jacob leaned forward on the scarred kitchen table as if imparting some great wisdom. 'The

Dunston family were *serious* tea importers and by serious I mean they made oodles of money from it. Or they did, before old man Dunston sold the business for a king's ransom. I believe he died a few years ago. Violet Dunston is an only child; heiress to it all. Lock, stock and barrel. She is a renowned beauty and now that I've seen her I have to concur.' Watching the twin smiles of male satisfaction appear on Jacob and Joe's faces caused Jack to experience an unfamiliar pang of jealousy, but he held his tongue. His siblings all had eyes, after all, except the thought of his brothers sharing the magnificent spectacle of Letty's legs particularly bothered him. He needed to find her more suitable clothing as soon as possible. Something shapeless, large and concealing. Something that would put a stop to his brothers' wayward gazes. Begrudgingly, he turned his attention back to his youngest brother.

'The gossip columns are filled with speculation about whom she will choose to marry. It is all anyone can talk about. The gentlemen of London are falling all over themselves to court her.'

Jamie, always the least impressed by anything, was scathing. 'Hardly a surprise when the girl is obscenely rich. I should imagine, just like her uncle and the Earl of Bainbridge, they would be delighted to get their hands on all of that lovely money. She could have a face like a horse's behind and they would probably still want to marry her.'

'True,' agreed Jacob, 'but it is not only fortune hunters who are courting her. There are a few wealthy peers too. I read something about the illustrious Duke of Wentworth throwing his hat into the ring, and he is as rich as Croesus and has his pick of the ladies. She's famously charming— in fact, Miss Dunston is viewed as a diamond of the first water. An *incomparable*.'

An incomparable! If ever Jack needed proof that his misplaced lust was barking up the wrong tree, there it was. Letty had queues of eager, *solvent* suitors and would never look twice at a humble Warriner for anything more than necessary protection. She was so far out of his league he would need a stepladder to reach her. Perhaps twenty stepladders. Not that he had hoped for more, of course. Lust was a natural, human response to such a beautiful woman. Even bruised and dishevelled, Letty *was* a beautiful woman, so his instantaneous and physical reaction was also, therefore, quite understandable. Besides, Jack was too pragmatic, too wise to be disappointed in the ways of the world and too burdened already to even consider something beyond the carnal. These overwhelming feelings of protectiveness towards her obviously stemmed from the unyielding and irritating sense of responsibility he had been cursed with since birth. She was a damsel in distress. Ever since his mother, he had a soft spot for them. He had found Letty stumbling in on the road to his house, therefore, until he could take her safely home to Mayfair, it stood to reason she was also his responsibility, just as his mother had been. Another one. To add to the thousands he already had and didn't need.

Lucky him.

'We will need to get her back to her people in London as quickly as possible if her life is in danger. There must be another relative there who can keep her out of harm's way while this uncle and Bainbridge are brought to justice.' And out of his sight.

'It's too soon to make her travel yet.' Joe immediately leapt to her defence. 'Yesterday she was still burning with fever. She needs a few days to properly recuperate.'

'Nobody is planning on moving her yet. With that Layton and his cronies still at large in the village, a trip now might arouse suspicions. I will not put either her life or any of yours in danger by acting rashly. Once the dust has settled and I deem it to be safe, I will return her.' Although how Jack was going to pay for an unforeseen trip to London without their finances suffering too much, he had yet to work out. All of the spare money left over from last year's harvest had already disappeared in new lead for the decrepit roof on the east wing. Every other penny had been accounted for. He supposed they could overnight in one inn on the way there and on the way back he could find a quiet barn somewhere…

'You will not be making the trip alone. It's too dangerous. I will be coming with you,' Jamie announced. Nobody dared point out that Jamie was lame and in no state to endure such a long and demanding ride south. However, he had apparently already considered it himself. 'I might be useless on my feet, but I can still sit on a horse and shoot straight, should the need arise.' And nobody commented on the peculiar arsenal their brother now housed in his bedchamber either. Not after Jacob had found out the hard way that the former soldier slept with a knife under his pillow. 'Do any of you know how to cover your tracks or live off the land?' He scanned their faces and shrugged smugly. 'I thought not.'

As always, Jamie made a valid point. Despite his physical limitations, he would be useful to have around. Especially if the Earl of Bainbridge's men decided to follow them. 'All right then. It's settled.' He pointed at Joe and Jacob. 'You two can stay here and convince those scoundrels all the Warriners are where they should be, in case they come calling. Layton has nothing to link us to the girl as yet—I would prefer to keep it that way. Jamie and I will escort her back to London.'

'You most certainly will not!'

Letty had become increasingly anxious waiting for Jack Warriner to return to her room and appraise her of her fate, so she had wrapped herself in a blanket, hobbled down the creaky wooden staircase and followed the sound of male voices. Now, it seemed, she had timed her arrival to perfection. 'I cannot go to London until the fourth of January!'

Jack stood and glared at her. 'Your family will know how best to keep you safe.'

'To the best of my knowledge, my entire family only consists of one treacherous uncle. To return me to him is tantamount to signing my death warrant! I am too well known and there are too many people who would sell me down the river for a reward.'

'Surely there must be someone else you can go to?' He was looking at her as if she was clearly stupid and his patronising tone rankled.

'I believe, sir, I would remember if I possessed any other living relations. Do you think I have mislaid them somewhere?' Her head had started to spin, but she ignored it. 'For the time being, I would prefer to hide, just for a few days while I decide what to do next. Perhaps I could remain hidden here?' Without thinking she cast her eyes around the shabby room and smiled kindly. 'I can pay you, if it's money you require.'

The three younger Warriners all exchanged a telling look. Joe winced. Jamie shook his head and Jacob simply closed his eyes.

'I don't need your damn money, woman!' Jack stalked towards her in outrage. 'We are not paupers, *Miss Dunston*, and I resent the implication. Whilst you are here, you will remain as our guest and that is that. Taking you safely home as soon as possible is the *right* thing to do. I find it hard to believe there is nobody in London who is worried as to your whereabouts and would be a more suitable guardian for you than myself. There must be somebody—a cousin, a close friend, perhaps?'

She had to make him understand. 'The Earl of Bainbridge and my uncle will find a way to silence me if they have any inkling I am alive. I know of their nefarious plan, remember? They will be in fear for their own lives now. Don't you see? Desperate men like that will resort to desperate measures. Travelling anywhere, even in the dead of night, will put my life in danger.' The toll of the last few days had made her body weak. Her knees threatened to buckle so Letty locked them to stand proudly in front of this domineering man who thought he knew best. 'You have witnessed already the lengths they are prepared to go to. Not only will my life be in danger, yours will be too.'

'Then that settles it. You will remain here for the entire month,' Jack decreed.

An entire month! Here? 'Once I am fully recovered I will seek sanctuary with the local authorities of my own accord. I will not be held responsible for putting you and your brothers at risk.'

'I do not hold the authorities in Nottingham in particularly high esteem. Once they know you have been here, with the Warriner family, I doubt they will act with the necessary diligence your circumstances demand. I believe I am quite capable of protecting you and my brothers against any threat for a month, Miss Dunston.' Letty went to interrupt and he stayed her with his hand. 'It is settled. My decision has been made. Until I can return you to London and alert the proper authorities there as to what danger you are in, you are now my responsibility and will abide by my rules.'

'But you are four men, Mr Warriner! Four men and I am a woman alone.' Letty had intended to sound reasonable, but the words came out in a screech. She had only thought to stay here for a few days, not several weeks. If she were ever to be discovered here her good reputation would be in tatters.

'Yet you are safer here than you would be out there!'

A very valid point. She remembered the huge gates and walls. The isolation. Nobody knew she was there. The idea had merit, but she had to be in control. 'Only on the condition that I recompense you for your services.' Surely her money would give her the upper hand against this domineering man she hardly knew?

Jack's thunderous expression said it all. 'Out of the question.'

Letty shook her head stubbornly, a movement which brought about a wave of dizziness so intense she had to grab the doorframe for support. 'I will not be in your debt, sir. You have already done so much and I can well afford it.'

The three seated Warriners all stared at their feet in silence. Clearly she had said the wrong thing again, because Jack was looming over her now.

'I do not require money for doing a good deed, madam. As the master of this house, it is my responsibility to keep you safe, and after what you have told me, I honestly believe the best way to do that is to hide you here. You will not return back to London until I deem it safe to do so. It is decided.'

It took a great deal of pride not to burst into frustrated tears at his dictatorial tone. 'Decided? Am I to have no say in my own future?' Such a concept was beyond ridiculous. Letty always got what she wanted. He stared back, his steely blue glare unmoved. 'I am not a child or a chattel, Mr Warriner. I am perfectly capable of looking after myself. *You* have no authority over me!'

As parting shots went, she was quite proud of it. His intense blue eyes narrowed as he digested her words and Letty decided now would be the opportune moment to make a well-timed exit. The walls of the room had begun to sway and tilt quite ferociously as she turned smartly to storm back upstairs. Letty took two steps forward, then the floor began to list too. Her grand gesture of defiant independence collapsed the moment her knees did and she found herself crumpling woozily to the floor. Most irritatingly, it was Jack's strong, capable arms that caught her. He lifted her into them as if she weighed practically nothing, with a distinctly paternalistic, put-upon expression on his face.

'Joe?'

'She's still weak from her ordeal—she shouldn't be out of bed. No wonder she swooned.'

Jack did not even bother responding to his brother, he merely turned with Letty still in his arms and began to walk briskly towards the staircase. It was disconcerting being held so close by him—yet bizarrely not in a bad way. She felt safe, protected and stupidly impressed by his strength and undeniably manly physique. And he smelled positively sinful. Some sort of spicy, fresh, male smell which Letty wanted to inhale deeply while she burrowed her face into his neck. His overbearing, single-minded, irritating neck. 'You can put me down. I can manage.' There would be absolutely no burrowing. Not while he was being so... domineering and non-compliant.

His irritatingly beautiful, blue eyes flicked to hers for a second. 'We can't have you *swooning* now, Letty. Can we?' The very idea of it seemed to amuse him, which of course, seriously rankled.

'I am not a woman known for swooning, Mr Warriner. Anybody who knows me will tell you that.' Not that there was anyone left alive who truly knew her. Her parents had. Everybody else saw what they wanted to see and Letty found it easier to hide behind that convenient façade than allow anyone to see she was lonely and unhappy. 'Had I not been forced to wander in a freezing forest for hours in the rain, after being bound, gagged and abducted, it would not have happened today.'

He stared ahead, apparently bored. The dark stubble on his chin tempted her fingers to touch it, so she clasped them ineffectually across her middle as he started up the stairs.

'Are you too proud to let me pay for your services?'

Silence.

Clearly it was time to become the confident Violet Dunston. Whenever she met a brick wall, and Jack Warriner was definitely a big, thick, brick wall, Violet's charm had never failed to quietly knock it down. Men, especially, were particularly responsive in her experience. She could not spend a month being dictated to by this stubborn man. She would run mad.

Letty unclasped her hands and rested one palm gently over his heart, moistened her lips to give them some gloss and peeked up at him through her lashes in the manner which she knew all men found utterly delightful. 'Perhaps I could fund your brother's medical studies, Jack?' For good measure she blinked a little erratically so he could see just how long and lovely those lashes were and how very upset she was by his insistence on being in charge. 'Surely you would allow me the pleasure of doing that one, small thing out of gratitude.' Something which would keep this infuriatingly dictatorial male in check.

He glanced down at her face and she was certain she felt his heartbeat speed up beneath her fingers, but when his jaw hardened and those dark eyebrows came together in a forbidding line, she realised she might have seriously misjudged the situation.

'You might have my brothers falling all over themselves to do your bidding, Letty, and I am sure you are quite used to getting your own way in practically everything with your *fêted* beauty and *piles* of money, but your pouting and flirting will not sway me. You can stay here for as long as I am prepared to be your keeper—and once I decide it is safe to take you back to London, then you will go. In the interim, you will do as you are told, Miss Dunston, because I am master of this house and you would do well to remember it. No amount of pretty eyelash fluttering is going to change my mind.'

Chapter Seven

Twenty-eight days remaining, give or take a few hours...

Letty stared at the trunk full of outdated ladies' dresses with a sinking heart. The heavy brocades and stiff skirts would take hours and hours to turn into anything vaguely presentable, even with her talent with a needle. She had dispatched Jacob up to the attic to find her something to wear, other than Jack's shirts, and this was the best he could come up with. With amazing forethought for a man unused to having women in his house, the youngest Warriner had also brought his mother's old sewing basket down too. Now that she was more herself again, altering these clothes would give her something to do while Joe had confined her to yet another day of bed rest, which frankly she did not need.

'Thank you, Jacob. I am sure I can make use of these. I have not been allocated a maid yet. Now that I am feeling better, could one be arranged?'

'A maid? Of your own?'

'Yes—somebody who is handy with a needle and good with arranging hair. And could you ask your cook to vary the menu a little bit? Whilst the roast meat is always very nice, I find the lack of sauces and the boiled vegetables a little bland.'

Jacob's face began to split into a wide grin. 'I have no authority regarding the distribution of *staff*, Letty, or the menu choices. You should probably ask Jack. He organises all of those things.' His eyes were twinkling mischievously. 'However, perhaps he might be more open to such requests if they came from you. You are our *guest*, after all.' He looked like he was about to burst out laughing. 'Aside from that, is there anything else you require?'

'Some tea would be nice, Jacob. In about half an hour? And I don't suppose you could bring some cake with it?'

He playfully tugged his forelock. 'I shall see what I can do, Letty.'

Left alone, the silence of her lonely room began to feel oppressive. Letty was already way beyond bored with staying in bed, certain that it was Jack who was insisting she rest rather than have her under his feet. For the sake of peace, she would comply today, but wild elephants would not keep her in this bedchamber tomorrow.

Her only company came in the shape of either Joe or Jacob Warriner and usually only briefly when they could be spared from other chores. They brought her tea or books or whatever else she requested—but those visits were still few and far between. Thus far, she had not had any dealings with the gruff Jamie and she had only seen fleeting glimpses of the domineering master of the house since he had unceremoniously deposited her back on his bed two days ago, after her failed attempt at getting him to bend to her will.

The fact he had seen straight through the reasons for her flirting was embarrassing. Usually men scurried around Letty to please her, even without her resorting to using her feminine wiles. When she did bestow one coy look or a faint flutter of her eyelashes, even the most hard-nosed gentleman was won over and keen to earn her good favour. She was the *Tea Heiress*, after all. Judgemental Jack had managed to make her feel like a fool, and what was worse was the fact that she had been the one trying to make him feel off-kilter. Instead, it had been her pulse which had ratcheted up several notches; her kilter that was off.

Being held in that man's arms had been overwhelming enough. She had felt protected, delicate and, despite his grim demeanour, quite special. Galling when she was so determined to be independent. It almost felt like she'd taken a step back towards the old Letty, the one who wanted to marry a man to feel worthwhile. But touching Jack's hard, warm chest had been, frankly, beyond heady. Letty had never experienced a reaction to a man quite like that one. She had wanted to curl her arms around his neck instantly and experience how splendid she imagined it would be to be draped fully against him, properly wrapped in those magnificent, ungentlemanly muscled arms. Shamelessly staring up into his fathomless, beautiful blue eyes...

Oh, stop it, Letty! She had a tendency to be prone to flights of fancy and silly daydreams—but to be having such thoughts about a man who saw her as a great inconvenience and was completely immune to her womanly charms was ridiculous. Jack Warriner was not the sort of gentleman she usually favoured. Yes, he was handsome and, yes, he was deliciously burly and easy on the eye—but he was also a stubborn, dominant and unbendable male! Just like her uncle. A man who refused to listen to her—and, although she sincerely doubted Jack shared any of her insidious uncle's other, reprehensible character traits, Letty was all done with domineering males. Her fanciful mind had no place constantly wandering back to *him*. She knew exactly the sort of man she wanted and that man was nothing like Jack Warriner.

He was someone more like the Duke of Wentworth, for example. A polite, solicitous and gentlemanly man. Letty doubted he was that interested in her fortune, because he had a vast one of his own, although one could never tell. She supposed the title could be considered a bonus, except she had little interest in such things any more. The trouble with Wentworth was that he was a collector of all things beautiful and he always had to have the best of everything. The opulent new house he was having built in Mayfair was a great source of society speculation and he had reportedly sent out emissaries to the furthest reaches of the globe to bring back rare treasures to fill it with. Despite his charming manner and seemingly besotted demeanour, Letty had a horrible suspicion his interest in her stemmed from the ridiculous label she had been given of an *incomparable*. The *diamond* of the Season. And being desired simply as another adornment to a man's house, rather than for the woman she truly was, was somehow worse than being merely a source of income. At least money had a use. Ornaments got dusty when their appeal faded and the owner forgot about them. Until Wentworth proved otherwise, Letty was not particularly tempted to become his duchess either. Whoever her future husband turned out to be, he had to be hopelessly in love with *her*.

Not a handsome, domineering farmer to whom she was an unwelcome burden. She wanted a man who would put her on a pedestal, didn't she, not one who put her in her place... Although, in typically contrary fashion, she immediately decided it was quite refreshing that he had not fawned all over her. She quite respected his strength of character even though she disliked his heavy-handed approach. That intrigued her. He was the first man she had encountered who appeared totally oblivious to the fact she was an heiress—in fact, any mention of her money seemed to get his dander up. And he was very, very handsome. Those eyes of his were positively swoon-worthy and his muscles were so...so...

Clearly, she had to get out of this dull room or she was in danger of running completely mad if she was actually debating the merits of Jack Warriner as a potential suitor! He had three equally handsome brothers, two of whom were closer to her own age and both thoroughly charming. If she was going to have peculiar fancies for a Warriner brother, she would do better to direct them towards the capable, kind physician Joe, or the roguish, flirtatious Jacob. Any Warriner, in fact, who was not Jack.

With a sigh, she padded across the bedchamber to the large wardrobe and rooted through it for something which would render her decent enough to eventually leave this room. All she could find were more shirts, plain waistcoats and breeches. After comparing a few pairs for size, she pulled on a soft pair of buckskin breeches which were far too big around the waist but fit her well enough everywhere else. A quick rifle in the sewing basket produced a reel of scarlet ribbon. She cut off two lengths. One was tied tightly around her waist to hold up the sagging breeches, the second she used to tie back her unruly hair. With no hairpins apparently anywhere in Markham Manor, and no maid as yet, it was the best she could do with such limited resources. Her request, made via Joe yesterday, for some feminine items to be purchased on her behalf in the village came back, also via Joe, with a terse '*Are you mad, woman?*' from He Who Must Be Obeyed.

Now she considered it fully, she was prepared to concede that the oldest, most irritating Warriner had made a valid point. The purchasing of anything feminine for a house filled with men was a tad suspicious and, if she wanted to remain out of Bainbridge's gnarly clutches, she should probably make do with her ribbon. Although making do was not something she was used to. If she was being completely honest, it was not something she had ever experienced—which made her feel like some spoiled, selfish brat and the sort of woman she loved to loathe.

But she wasn't incapable of making do, was she? And she certainly wasn't useless. Hadn't she already proved herself to be resourceful by escaping her captors? If she could do that, then she could fashion herself a perfectly serviceable wardrobe without inconveniencing her vexing host further or tipping off Bainbridge's lackeys as to her whereabouts. Besides, she could hardly roam around the house in men's breeches, even if they were surprisingly comfortable. Imbued with a self-righteous sense of purpose, she had soon ripped open the sleeves of one of the dated gowns and had spread the fabric pieces on the floor to cut.

Jack tossed his wet greatcoat in the hallway and took the stairs two at a time. His trip to the village this morning had bothered him. The reward money was no longer a generous one hundred pounds. It had been raised to a princely five hundred and the whole village was buzzing with the excitement. Folks in this particular corner of Nottinghamshire rarely, if ever, saw such a vast sum of money in one go and the anticipation of securing those riches had inspired several packs of locals to form teams scouring the forest and neighbouring areas. It was only a matter of time before some of them made their way up the lane towards his house—and if they found the gates bolted to them, they would become suspicious. Hardly anybody trusted a Warriner at the best of times. A wary, non-compliant Warriner would likely result in a siege when five hundred pounds was at stake.

Much as he railed against the prospect of keeping her here for the entire month, moving her now was completely out of the question. And much as he wanted to avoid the prospect of spending any more time in that minx's company, he needed to tell her of the heightened danger. While he was about it, he was also going to set some well-needed boundaries. Letty Dunston was running his two younger brothers ragged with her demands.

No, that was not strictly true. Neither was run ragged—it was more that they were eagerly hopping up and down to do her bidding, which was taking them away from their usual chores and forcing Jack to pick up the slack. Only yesterday, when Jacob was supposed to be chopping wood for the fires, he had learned his brother had, instead, taken himself off to the village because Princess Violet had asked for some biscuits.

Biscuits indeed! Biscuits were not going to keep the house warm or the sheep fed. And the woman apparently needed a near-constant supply of tea brought to her bedchamber, yet barely drank more than a single cup at a time. Last night, when Joe had helpfully wrapped the pot in some towels to keep the heat in it longer, she had complained that her tea was now too stewed to enjoy properly and sent his foolish brother to bring her a fresh pot. Had Jack not been avoiding the temptress, he would have stormed up there and given her a piece of his mind right away. Tea was an expensive commodity. So were biscuits, when the only place you could get them from was the local bakery because not one of the Warriners knew how to bake the damn things.

But he was avoiding the temptress—and temptress was the only word for her. Every time he laid eyes on her he was tempted. His mouth dried, his blood heated and his eager groin hardened. When he had carried her up the stairs he had been only too aware of the way her trim waist had curved out to a fine pair of rounded hips. He had also remembered, with far more clarity than he was comfortable with, the soft press of her unrestrained bosom resting against his body as he held her. Carrying Letty to his bedchamber held a great deal of appeal—although his rampant mind and body would have preferred the circumstances to be very, very different.

However, the woman was quite certain of her appeal towards the male sex, and was not averse to using it to her own advantage. The brazen way she had walked her fingers up his chest when he had carried her back upstairs had been one of the most calculated displays of feminine manipulation he had ever seen. The fact she had tried to use her wiles on him in an attempt to control him, and the fact that his body had betrayed him and reacted instantly to her touch, was beyond the pale. Worse still, now random images of her kept creeping into his dreams and disturbing his sleep. And his work had suffered too. Jack had thought about nothing but blasted Letty all morning and only a small fraction of those thoughts had been concerns for her safety. That hair. Those seductive green eyes and, God help him, those legs! Even avoiding her, she was driving him to distraction.

He eyed the open bedchamber door cautiously. There was no avoiding her now. They needed to talk about her precarious safety and he needed to stop having errant thoughts about her and remember she was another unwelcome responsibility he did not need. She was a spoiled heiress and an armful of trouble. Mentally fortified, Jack strode purposefully in and stopped dead in his tracks.

The damn woman was going to kill him!

First there had been delicate bared shoulders,

then the loose hair and long legs and now her fantastic bottom was displayed to him in all of its round, feminine glory as she was, for some inexplicable reason, bent on her knees on the floor rather than recuperating in his bed. At this rate, his imagination would be able to piece her intriguing parts together bit by bit—and it only made him wonder more about the parts he had not seen. And if he wasn't mistaken, her tempting bottom was currently encased in *his* breeches. How exactly was he ever supposed to wear them again knowing they had touched that magnificent backside?

'Ahem.'

Her golden head whipped around at his cough and she smiled at him around a mouth full of pins. A slight blush touched the apples of her cheeks in a most becoming fashion and he wondered, rather uncharitably, if it was genuine or another beguiling feminine tool she could summon at her will.

'I need to talk to you.' Jack stood stiffly at the doorway, unsure of whether or not he should enter. It was his room, after all, but while she had laid siege to it, it felt wrong to just barge in. There was already the air of the feminine about it. She had made the bed differently. The pillows were plumped and stood on their sides; the bedcovers draped in an aesthetically pleasing fashion.

He watched her carefully pop the pins back into his mother's old pincushion and then sit up on her heels. 'Talk away. I am all ears.' She wasn't. She was all hair and legs and curvy bits, but that was not what he needed to discuss. The bed suddenly loomed larger in the room.

'I am afraid your Mr Layton has upped the reward for your safe return.' Jack saw a flash of panic cross her face and realised with dismay that she had immediately assumed he had surrendered her for the larger amount of money. As if he were a low, immoral creature who would do such a thing! 'I do not need Mr Layton's five hundred pounds, Letty.' The numerous, urgent things he could do with five hundred pounds did not bear thinking about. 'I prefer to earn my money through honest labours. Thank you for your lowly opinion of me, though.' He ignored the fact that his father would have pocketed the money without a moment's hesitation. As would all of his other dead ancestors. A Warriner with morals was a new, and decidedly outrageous, anomaly which the world was clearly still not ready for, despite almost a decade of him trying to change the past, yet still he was mortally insulted.

'I did not think you would hand me over to him, if that is what you are insinuating, I was just thinking how much more attractive a prospect finding me has suddenly become to all and sundry. I think it is *you* who has a lowly opinion of *me*, Jack, if you believe I would think such a thing about you after all you have done for me, although I am not sure quite what I have done to deserve it.'

He could see now that he had really upset her. Her green eyes became greener when she was troubled, her golden eyebrows were drawn together and she frowned. Now it was Jack's turn to feel bad for his uncharitable assumptions. Letty had no idea of their wild Warriner reputation and he could hardly admit to a rampant case of lust as the cause of his disgruntlement. 'I'm sorry, Letty. The implication was uncalled for. We Warriners are considered the scourge of the earth, thanks entirely to my forebears. Unfortunately mud sticks and we are doomed to be tarnished by it for ever. It makes me defensive—although in this case unfairly.'

She dazzled him with a smile then. A proper

smile that made her fine eyes sparkle and transformed her face from a thing of beauty into some sort of transcendental manifestation of total perfection which rendered him momentarily stunned. 'Then I shall forgive you, Jack. Perhaps we should start this conversation again?'

Or perhaps he should just give in to temptation and run over there and kiss her. When he found his voice it came out a little strained. 'In view of the increased incentive, I believe it would be prudent to expect visitors to come here searching for you. I have told my brothers to re-open the gates, Letty, but do not panic, during the night they will be secured again. Those ridiculous fortifications will only serve to arouse suspicion during daylight hours if they are closed. If anybody arrives, I shall have to appear willing to co-operate. I will invite them in and listen to whatever they have to say—and, however long that takes, you will have to remain hidden up here.' The lovely smile had slipped.

'I have to stay in this room.' Whilst she was grateful for his protection, Letty would go quite mad confined in this one place for hours on end with nobody to talk to.

'No, of course not. Only if and when we have

visitors. The four of us will take it in turns to work near the top of the lane. That road is the only way in and out of Markham Manor. If we spot anyone, the man on watch can alert the rest of us to an impending visit and you can slip up here.' He stared at her seriously. 'Just in case anyone should force their way up these stairs, I need to show you something.'

He motioned for her to follow him and, intrigued, she did. He led her down the landing a little way to a painting on the wall. The portrait was undoubtedly a Warriner. Almost jet-black hair, handsome features and striking blue eyes stared back at her. 'This is Sir Hugo Warriner. A troublesome fellow by all accounts—but then most of my ancestors were. He had the enormous wall built around the house when he decided to help Mary Queen of Scots plot against Queen Elizabeth. Fortunately, his involvement in high treason was never discovered, or else I would not be here. Old Hugo was a cautious fellow—he also installed this.'

Letty watched fascinated as he opened a secret door in the oak panelling and then peered inside. 'A priest hole?'

'More of a Hugo hole really.' Jack grinned rak-

ishly like his troublesome ancestor, showing a
row of perfectly white straight teeth, and somehow being roguish suited him. For a moment she
caught a glimpse of the young man who lurked
beneath the serious exterior, the one he hid from
her and perhaps the rest of the world, too.

Of course, it helped that when Jack Warriner
smiled he became even more handsome, if such
a thing was indeed possible, and the way his deep
blue eyes sparkled make her feel all fizzy inside,
like champagne. 'I doubt he would have been
charitable enough to consider hiding a worthy
fugitive. I believe this little room has hidden a
great many Warriners in its time. My ancestors
have always had a canny knack of being on the
wrong side of everything. They fought with King
Charles during the Civil War, supported the Jaco-
bite uprising—there is even a suggestion that one
of them was a member of the gang who tried to
blow up Parliament with Guy Fawkes—but again,
he was never caught. In fact, history is peppered
with infamous, and decidedly slippery, Warriners.
I am yet to find any evidence of a good one…but
I live in hope.'

Letty laughed then, as she was sure she was
meant to. 'Well, you and your brothers are good

men, so I can only assume the family has changed its errant ways. Your father would be proud to know that he did such a good job with you all.'

His face clouded briefly. 'I doubt it…however, I digress. Should you feel threatened in any way, Letty, or hear someone coming whom you do not recognise, I want you to come here. It locks from the inside. Do not open it unless either myself or one of my brothers comes to tell you the coast is clear.' He promptly closed the panelling again and stood stiffly beside her as he stared at Sir Hugo's picture rather than at her. 'I will keep you safe, Letty.'

'Thank you, Jack.' After everything he had already done for her, plain old words were a poor expression of her gratitude. All at once, she felt emotional at his continued kindness. It was on the tip of her tongue to say I am in your debt and will repay you as soon as I am able, but stopped herself. The last time she had offered him a reward he had reacted badly and, as they had declared a truce, of sorts, bringing up the subject of money would probably bring stern Jack back. Letty rather liked the slightly shy Jack. Without thinking, she laid her hand on his forearm and watched his blue eyes fall on the place where it rested. 'I shall sleep easier now.'

Their oddly intimate moment came to an abrupt end when he simply nodded and stalked off in the direction of the stairs.

Chapter Eight

Twenty-five days remaining...

When Letty woke she decided she was all done being treated like an invalid. Today, she would breakfast with the family, whether they liked it or not, and explore the house. Aside from her one trip downstairs when her head was still spinning and her eyes practically crossed, she had no idea what the rest of Markham Manor was like. As nobody had yet come to attend to her because it was still dark outside, she washed in the ice-cold water on the nightstand, before pulling on the breeches and a fresh shirt and tying back her unruly hair in the scarlet ribbon. Barefoot, because she had no idea what had become of her evening slippers, she padded out of the bedchamber and headed down the creaking, wooden staircase.

The sun had not risen properly, yet the servants

had lit no candles to illuminate the dim hallway. However, it was plain to see that the standard of cleanliness was not quite what it should be. It wasn't filthy, nor was it overly messy, but there was an air of neglect which Letty supposed came with a house full of men who did not have the exacting household standards a woman did. The mistress of a house would ensure the corners and nooks would be properly dusted and the house properly maintained.

As she wandered slowly along the hallway, her critical gaze saw plenty of evidence of the servants' slackness. The wooden panelling looked to be in dire need of a good coat of fresh beeswax to bring out its lustre, the rugs needed beating, the floors polishing properly and the beautiful leadlight windows would positively gleam with a treatment of vinegar. So far this morning, she had not encountered one of the lazy staff, which was a shocking disgrace. At her house in Mayfair, she ran a tight ship. Her servants were busy from six o'clock, ensuring everything was properly done so the correct standards were maintained. The servants here were practically fleecing the Warriners!

If she could do nothing else in the short term

to repay the brothers for their benevolence, she could take the servants in hand and make this house shine. It might make them like her. And when her fortune was hers to control she would buy new furniture to replace the old and purchase each of the brothers a special gift...

She paused and sighed. There it was again, her pathetic need to get people to see her worth. Her true worth rather than the value of her fortune, yet she was using her fortune to try to buy their favour. She really needed to stop doing that. If she truly wanted to be liked for herself, then perhaps it was time she stopped feeling the urge to buy their affections. For the next few weeks, Letty was basically a pauper who was doomed to accept the Warriners' charity. What better opportunity to find out if she possessed the characteristics of a woman who was liked purely for herself?

Joe and Jacob already liked her, or at least she thought they did. She had no idea what Jamie thought of her and was not entirely sure she particularly cared—but she wanted Jack to like her. She really wanted Jack to like her...at least then she would not feel quite so awkward about liking him as much as she did, even though she got precious little back except for commands or put-upon stares. Although, as he had been her own personal knight in shining armour, she supposed it was only natural that she would like him far more than his equally handsome brothers. Most of the time, she got the distinct impression she irritated him. If she could do something useful to repay him for saving her, Letty would definitely feel better about the whole thing. Especially as he vehemently refused to take her money.

Markham Manor was actually quite a charming old building which certainly did not deserve to look quite so dingy and neglected. The ceilings downstairs were high and vaulted, while the aged oak panelling gave the whole manor an air of gravitas Letty found pleasing. With a good clean, about a hundred candles, some fresh flowers and a few homely, feminine touches, it would be a delight.

Letty pushed open one of the many closed doors off the long passageway and was surprised to find the room beyond draped in dust covers. Behind the next two doors it was exactly the same, which was odd. Why would so much of the house be closed up when the four brothers were in residence? The fourth door led to a formal dining room dominated by a long banqueting table, but no sign of breakfast. The dull layer of dust on the mahogany suggested this room has not seen a family meal in some considerable time. Yet another mark against the staff. Meals should always be served in the proper setting. It was uncivilised to do otherwise. In her mind's eye she had already pictured a large formal dining room in her foundling home; cheerful, happy conversation over a plate of good food. If such things were good enough for foundlings, Jack and his brothers should insist on such things as their due. Shaking her head, she closed the door and continued onwards. Finally, she found herself at a pair of large, arched doors which opened on to the impressive great hall she had glimpsed on her one trip downstairs. A roaring fire burned in the biggest stone fireplace Letty had ever seen, casting the room in a warm, cosy glow. She could have easily stood in the grate with all four Warriner brothers and there still would be space for another person.

This room looked to be in full use despite the fact it was currently vacant and the welcome heat drew her in. Evidence of the four men who lived here was everywhere and made it easy to determine exactly who sat where. Next to the big, comfortable chair closest to her was a neat pile of books topped with a folded pair of wire-rimmed spectacles. A weighty tome lay face down on the chair: *On the Fabric of the Human Body* by Andreas Vesalius. That meant this was Joe's seat. Across from that she recognised several London newspapers strewn about the floor in front of a brocade sofa. As she already knew Jacob had a penchant for society gossip, he had to sit there.

Closer to the fire sat another chair twinned with an enormous footstool. On the side table were some medicinal bottles, clearly pain relief for the dour Jamie, although the easel and paints nearby surprised her. She wandered over and was taken aback at his current work in progress. For a withdrawn man with a military past, she did not expect to see a beautiful watercolour picture of a garden filled with fat, blooming roses. Obviously, Jamie hid a poetic heart to choose such a romantic tableau. Intriguing.

Finally, opposite Jamie's chair was the sturdiest but shabbiest-looking chair of the lot. Jack's seat. The ancient upholstery bore the indents where his big body rested to such an extent she could instantly picture him there, sat leaning slightly to one side if the over-worn left arm was any indicator, although Letty doubted he spent much time relaxing. Piled next to the chair were ledgers, books on animal husbandry, arable crops and a dull-looking pamphlet entitled *The Manner and Proper Drainage of Clay Soils*. The sight of so much work occupying what should have been his leisure time troubled her. The proverb 'all work and no play makes Jack a dull boy' immediately sprang to mind. It probably explained a great deal about his character and the burdens he carried. Despite his patriarchal bearing, Letty estimated Jack to be well shy of thirty. This manor, an estate and the responsibility of his brothers was a considerable load for such a young man to take on his shoulders. Yet he carried it effortlessly, just as he had carried her effortlessly up the stairs in his strong, comforting arms.

She allowed her fingers to trail lightly over the back of his chair and spotted another book tucked down between the arm and the seat. Curious, she plucked it from its hiding place. She instantly recognised it. *The Soldier's Daughter* was one of her favourite plays, although it had not been on the London stage for a few years now, but she had fond memories of seeing it as it was the first production she had been taken to see by her parents upon her come-out. It had been responsible for her life-long passion for the theatre. Jack had good taste in plays, as well as a sense of humour about his ancestors. Two things she liked about him. Three, if you included his arms.

Letty's stomach rumble reminded her she had come down here in search of breakfast first, so she carefully slipped the slim book back into its hiding place, feeling a new affinity with Jack Warriner. They had something in common, albeit a very small thing in the grand scheme of things. Why such a thing mattered, she could not say, aside from the possibility that the pair of them could converse on topics which did not always have to be about her current predicament. It would be nice to get to know him better—the real man she had glimpsed a few days ago rather than the overbearing master of the house—the man who grinned rakishly and yet took his responsibilities seriously. Letty was rather drawn to that version of Jack.

Back in the hallway she heard the distinctive sound of hearty male laughter and followed it to the kitchen. All four of them were there, sitting around a big oak table, sharing the noisy, boisterous sort of family camaraderie Letty had never known, even when her quiet parents had been alive. While the brothers were blissfully unaware of her presence, she simply stood and listened, enjoying the way they parried insults and quips to and fro. It did not take long to get the gist of the conversation—Jacob had made yet another conquest. A farmer's daughter. The brothers were joking about the possibility of her father coming after him with his pitchfork if word ever got out. The youngest Warriner apparently took all of the ribbing in his stride and looked inordinately proud of his achievements with the farmer's wayward daughter.

It was Jack who spied her first and instantly brought his brothers to heel. 'There is a lady present!'

Four sets of deep blue eyes swivelled to her spot by the doorway and both Jack and Joe stood politely.

'I am not sure you should be out of bed, Letty,' said Joe with his usual air of concern, 'Do you feel dizzy or light-headed?'

'I am feeling perfectly well, Dr Joe, although I am positively *dying* of boredom stuck in that room.' Letty boldly walked towards the table in case anyone wanted to argue and pulled out the only spare chair. Instantly, Jack sprang to attention and solicitously pushed it back in when she sat. He had gentlemanly manners, too. Another thing to like. 'I thought I might have breakfast with you all. That is if you do not mind my company?' She smiled at the men hopefully. One of her real smiles rather than one of Violet's. A test for herself.

'It will be delightful to see a pretty face at the table rather than this ugly lot.' Jacob grinned back at her. 'Would you like some tea, Letty?' She nodded happily to be included and was surprised when it was Jacob who poured, in the absence of a servant, while Joe wandered to the hearth and retrieved a covered plate and placed it in front of her. He whipped off the silver cloche and her face fell at the sight of yet more bacon and shrivelled-looking fried eggs.

'Is everything all right?' He stared back at her, concerned.

'Would you ask your cook if I might have something different this morning? Only I have had bacon every day so far and I am not overly fond of it. Some sausages, perhaps, or some scrambled eggs?'

There was a moment of strained silence at her

request, then Jamie scowled and pierced Jack with his stare. 'I am not cooking her anything different.'

Jacob grinned at his brother. 'That's because you can't cook anything different, Jamie. I, on the other hand, have a particular way with eggs.' He went to stand, but Jack stayed him with his hand.

'We eat what we are served in this house, Letty, and we are grateful for it.'

The four men focused intently on their plates as if the discussion was now over. Letty considered letting sleeping dogs lie, then decided she could not. These four men obviously worked tremendously hard, so it was a travesty that their lazy staff should hold so much power. The youngest Warriners clearly found it easier to step into the breach rather than bring the help to heel. As she had suspected, this was an area in which she could make a contribution.

'Please do not be embarrassed. I would hardly expect four men to know the best way to deal with unruly servants. Fortunately, it is an area in which I have a great deal of expertise.' Letty had been running her Mayfair house since the age of seventeen as her uncle was not used to dealing with such a large household, or, indeed, even interested in learning. If anybody could get the best out of the Markham Manor servants, it was her. 'Why don't I oversee the indoor staff while I am here? It would be no trouble. If nothing else, I can improve the quality of our meals.'

For effect she picked up the abandoned silver cloche and popped it back over her plate. 'It is a sorry state of affairs when the servants are too lax to serve breakfast. We are *grateful* for what we get indeed! Where is the choice? Why, there is not even any jam on the table! How can one be expected to have a civilised breakfast without preserves? I fear that your good natures are being taken gross advantage of by all of your servants. I intend to speak to your cook personally and explain the proper way for a good kitchen to be run.' For emphasis, Letty stood and picked up the offending plate. 'Where might I find your belligerent chef?' Because things were going to improve at Markham Manor starting right now. It would be her gift to this generous family. One which would cost her nothing but her own efforts. 'And whilst I am about it, I should like to speak to your housekeeper as well. It is criminal the way the housework has been neglected. The maids need to be told to dust all of the nooks and crannies and their work needs to be thoroughly checked to see it is up to standard.'

Letty would start with the kitchen and then move on to the rest of the staff. By tonight, this house would run like clockwork. She smiled reassuringly at the stunned-looking gentlemen in front of her, except their reactions to her sudden decisiveness made her nervous. Joe and Jacob exchanged a telling look before staring mournfully at their empty plates, while Jack's jaw hardened. Jamie Warriner rose slowly to his feet and folded his arms angrily across his chest.

'I am the belligerent cook. And the current lazy housekeeper.'

Letty had not been expecting that. 'Surely not?' Her eyes scanned the other faces around the table for confirmation. Only Jack met her gaze, although she could not accurately discern what stormy emotion was currently swirling in those cobalt eyes. Annoyance? Shame? Pride? Perhaps all three? She stared at him beseechingly. 'Are you having difficulties hiring servants?'

That was clearly another wrong thing to say, judging by the snigger which emitted from the vicinity of Jacob and cut through the brittle silence like a knife. Letty turned to him in question and even he began to look guilty. The wretch had encouraged her to talk to Jack about the staff when she had enquired about a personal maid and now she had a sneaking suspicion he had led her on a merry dance for his own amusement. He had set her up for a fall and she had indeed fallen for it like a silly, spoiled fool. Whilst she enjoyed a good joke as much as the next person and had always had an enormous appetite for mischief, Letty had the distinct feeling she had just horrifically insulted Jack Warriner. Inexcusably insulted him, if what she was coming to suspect was the case, and that was too awful a prospect to have to contemplate after all he had already done for her.

Jacob's guilty smile slipped off his face under her scrutiny and he coloured up in embarrassment. 'It's not so much we have difficulty hiring servants, Letty, it's more we have difficulty paying for them…oomph!' He sagged when Joe's elbow collided sharply with his ribs and knocked the air out of him.

Realisation began to dawn. Her outburst had not only been crass; it had been cruel. Unforgivably cruel. 'There are no servants at Markham Manor, are there?'

Jack stood, clearly furious, and his voice was more clipped and frigid than she had ever heard it.

'I am sure back in London you have an army of obedient servants to cater for your every whim, *Princess* Violet. Here, we have to work for our supper. Seeing as you are now up and about, and we are apparently stuck with you, it's time you stopped leeching off our hospitality and earned your keep. Fortunately, you have helpfully pointed out how criminally the housework has been neglected. It is difficult to find the time or energy to dust every *nook* and *cranny* when you have to work in the fields from sun up to sun down. Therefore, those *neglected* nooks and crannies are now yours, Miss Dunston. I look forward to checking your work later. I would hate for the standards to not be properly maintained.'

The walls of the kitchen shook with the force he put into slamming the door on his way out.

Chapter Nine

Twenty-four days and fourteen hours...

Complete humiliation had never brought out the best in him, but for some reason, complete humiliation in front of Violet Dunston was worse than any Jack had ever experienced before. And he had a wealth of embarrassing experience to draw upon. When she had declared her intention to take his cook and housekeeper to task for their ineptitude, he had wanted to curl up into a ball and die from the shame. It was one thing to know your home was turning into a crumbling hovel before your very eyes, but it was a very different kettle of fish to have it pointed out by the most beautiful woman you had ever seen. A very different, totally unappetising kettle of fish indeed when he had spent the night lusting after her. Again. Clearly he was a glutton for punishment.

Doubtless her good opinion of him was now in question, especially at his surly reaction, and that bothered him a great deal too. For once, he wanted to be judged on his deeds rather than his family's past, and as Letty's views had not been tainted by the locals he had been hopeful she would regard them as decent, civilised people. However, his pride would never allow Jack to show her how much her thoughtless words had hurt him, so he had barked at her in retaliation instead, because attack had always been his default form of defence.

Even now, after a full day of hard work in the constant pouring rain, he was still smarting. He knew she had meant well and suspected Jacob had a hand in her belief that they had staff, but neither of those things were any consolation. The lofty lord of the manor *should* be able to afford servants. That was the way of things. He could hardly blame her for her blatant disbelief at his failure to provide something so fundamental when he owned a house with fifteen bedchambers, even if only four of the damn things were safe to sleep in. How was Letty to know the last of their servants had left a year before his father had drunk himself to death? Understandably, they were unforgiving of the Earl of Markham's habit of prioritising his brandy ration over their wages. The fact the man had put his brandy above everything else, the welfare and futures of his four motherless sons included, was even more unfortunate. If he had not felt an overwhelming responsibility towards his younger siblings, Jack would have cheerfully joined the fleeing servants and never looked back. Except, after their mother had chosen death rather than seeing them all grow up, Jack could not be cruel enough to desert them, too.

When the selfish old bastard had finally turned up his toes when Jack was just twenty, there had been nothing left for the boys except weed-choked fields, huge debts lodged with every merchant from here to Nottingham and the reputation of being the lowest of the low and little better than vermin. It was widely held that the family would cheat you in business, despoil your women and sell their own grandmother on a whim for their own benefit. Those that remembered his father in London, where he had been all of those things and had then scandalously compromised an heiress into marriage to round it off, probably thought much the same still, too. Nobody trusted a Warriner.

They had even less respect for the Earl of

Markham, a title his father had bandied about to justify his selfish vileness to such an extent it was now infamous, so Jack had never bothered using the tarnished title he had inherited with the crushing debt and crumbling house, in the hope the unpalatable legacy would blur with the sands of time. Seven arduous years on, they were still tarred with the same old brush and Jack sincerely doubted anyone would work for him even assuming he could, somehow, miraculously pay their wages. Those old wounds ran too deep, no matter how hard he tried to improve the family's reputation.

Of course, it did not help that all four of them were the spitting image of their feckless father. Everyone assumed the similarities went much further than skin deep and that it was only a matter of time before history repeated itself. The villagers were so wary of the Warriners that no shopkeeper would even allow them to open an account. Everything had to be paid for in cash there and then. No leeway, no benefit of the doubt, no better than any common vagabond who happened to be travelling through Nottinghamshire. Servants? That would be a funny joke if it wasn't entirely on him.

With a grunt he hauled down a fresh bale of hay

and heaved it on to his shoulders to carry to the few cows in the other barn. Not that it wouldn't be nice to have the extra hands. Especially as the health of the farm slowly recovered and required more and more of his time. Two years ago, his working day was ten hours long. Now it was nearer fourteen and that was pretty much nonstop, even in winter and with his brothers pulling as much weight as he did on a daily basis.

The cows, horses and chickens needed feeding twice a day in this weather. The sheep on the grazing land fed themselves, but thanks to the heavy clay soil, needed constant supervision. The stupid animals were forever getting stuck in the mud, or stranded in the flooded areas nearest the river, and the least said about the constant risk of foxes the better. But the lamb he raised was good quality and he received a reasonable return for it now that he was building up a good relationship with a butcher in Lincoln. He was paid a little lower than market price for it, in view of the risk involved in doing business with a Warriner, but it was a start. It was a shame nobody would do any business with him closer to home. The long treks to the cathedral town and back wiped out a whole day he could ill afford to lose—but beggars could not

be choosers. At least somebody bought his pro-
duce. Even the wool made some money, although
not nearly as much as he needed or as much as it
should.

Despite all of the work and the paltry financial
rewards, Jack was secretly proud of his achievements. In seven years he had turned the majority
of this estate from barren wasteland into farmland and with no outside help at all. He had single-handedly rebuilt two of the dilapidated tenant
cottages, cleared the tangled brambles from the
plots around them and rented them out. Granted,
for a pittance and the few pounds' return a year
was not much of an income, but it was consider-
ably more income than this land had raised in his
lifetime, not to mention the joy that came from
gradually clawing his way out of his father's debt.
If only the price of corn would improve, then he
might be able to turn an actual profit. In another
few years, if the roof of the house held up and he
could find the time to fix up the remaining tenant
cottages, and after he had paid for Joe to finally
go to medical school and then perhaps send Jacob
to university, he might be able to employ one or
two people to help ease his burdens. It all seemed
very far away and he dared not hope.

And now he had a blasted tea heiress criticising him. Perhaps he should have taken her up on her offer to pay him to hide her, except being paid to do a good turn for another did not sit well with him. It was something his father would have done unthinkingly—which, categorically, also made it the wrong thing for Jack to do as a matter of principal. Whilst there was no doubt he could use the woman's money, his pride would never allow him to accept her charity—because that was what it would be. Charity. If he had a decent home, rather than a ramshackle manor, and if he'd had proper servants as earls were expected to have, she never would have offered such a preposterous thing after her horrific ordeal. But the bewitching Letty Dunston saw things exactly how they were and had offered him money because she meant well. In the same, humiliating way she had meant well when she had commented on the disappointing food and the dire state of his dusty nooks and crannies.

Jack had never asked for hand-outs and he never would. He toiled and suffered and paid his own debts and stood proudly in front of those who judged him. If it killed him, which he suspected it all probably would in the end, he would turn this family's fortunes around—and perhaps their reputations, too—and the tart opinions of well-meaning heiresses would not change that. He doubted she'd done a day's work in all of her charmed life, so what right did she have to judge him anyway?

And why should he care one way or another what the girl thought of him? He hardly knew her despite his odd feelings for her and, at best, their acquaintance was only temporary. As soon as it was safe for her leave, she would merrily skip back to her perfect life and become the darling of society again. He sincerely doubted she would ever give him a passing thought he was so far beneath her.

Perhaps it had escaped her notice, but *he* was the one doing *her* a huge favour. If his humble home was not good enough for the princess to live in, then she could go elsewhere as he had originally wanted, to people who were more her sort or who would happily take her money to keep her safe. But as soon as he thought it he discarded it. He knew that he didn't trust anyone else except himself and his brothers to keep her safe, so she *would* remain in his house until the blasted fourth of January, when he could finally stop thinking about the minx every minute of the blasted day and feeling so ashamed of who he was in her presence.

* * *

Letty was exhausted. Up until this moment, it had been a word she had blithely thrown about when she had been shopping for hours in Bond Street or had danced every dance at a ball. Now she fully understood what being truly exhausted meant, she promised herself she would never say it in vain again. She also had new respect for her maids, although there were at least ten of them in her Mayfair house working downstairs alone and she was only one. Nevertheless, Letty experienced an enormous sense of accomplishment when she cast her eyes critically around the great hall. The vaulted room looked positively homely thanks to her labours and she was looking forward to showing it off.

Unfortunately, there was nobody to show it off to. She had spent almost the entire day completely on her own after insulting the master of the house so spectacularly at his breakfast table. Afterwards, Joe had dismissed Jack's order that she pull her weight as merely his temper talking and had insisted she continue to rest in her bedchamber. Jacob had apologised profusely for his mischief and told her to do the same.

'Jack has a temper,' he'd said with a shrug. 'But it disappears quickly.'

Then the two youngest Warriners had donned heavy coats and plunged out the back door into the elements to begin their own work, leaving her alone with Jamie. The most taciturn Warriner did not offer her platitudes or reassurances. Instead, he wandered to a cupboard, pulled out buckets, mops and brooms, then silently put on his own coat and disappeared after the others. But she had seen the fierce loyalty towards his brother and the latent hostility in his eyes.

She supposed they all thought she was not up to the task and that she would admit defeat before she had even started because she was a silly, spoiled heiress who was completely out of touch with the harsh realities of life. And perhaps she had been a few weeks ago. Not one of the brothers thought her capable of anything resembling work and, despite her own significant reservations, her pride refused to allow her to live up to their low expectations and surrender. There was more to her than everybody realised. She had determination and drive. She was capable of more than lighting up a ballroom or shopping for ribbons. She always excelled in everything she put her mind to.

Letty had escaped kidnap and survived a night in a frozen forest. If she could manage that, she could certainly clean this house.

And she had cleaned. Slowly at first, but once she got the hang of it there had been no stopping her. Years of supervising her own servants had taught her that polishing and dusting required vigour and it took her a while to learn the proper application of polish or how to avoid unsightly smears. Using all of her pent-up rage at her traitorous uncle and Bainbridge she had scrubbed and swept and buffed until her arms screamed and her back ached. Now, not a speck of dust dared linger in any of the corners. The old Persian rug had been beaten to within an inch of its life, largely because she had pictured the Earl of Bainbridge's wrinkled face in the centre of it and had found thwacking it therapeutic. The windows glistened and the chandelier shimmered in the soft candlelight. It had made her smile to see the transformation and went a little way toward easing the guilt she felt at her horrendous faux pas.

Once the room was clean, Letty had then set about rearranging it to make it look pleasing. After hunting under the dust covers in the adjacent rooms, she had found more furniture which suited the main room. Now, the worn chairs favoured by the brothers were covered in soft throws and cushions she had salvaged and she had added another chair for herself, as well as a low footstool and some well-positioned extra candlesticks. If she said so herself, it was a vast improvement on what it had been before. The only thing missing was a cheerful bunch of flowers—and she sincerely doubted she could summon one of those at will. A house which could not afford servants would hardly have its own hothouse. But perhaps some branches of holly and some cheerful winter berries would not go amiss?

A quick dash upstairs to rummage in the trunk of old clothes and she procured a pair of lady's walking boots. They were a bit big—Mrs Warriner was clearly built in a sturdier fashion than Letty—but she padded them out with an extra pair of thick woollen stockings, then headed to the back door through the kitchen, clasping a pair of lethal-looking shears she had found.

Leaves and flowers were homely and Markham Manor could do with a lift. Letty pulled on a heavy greatcoat which was hanging on a peg by the door and clomped out. The crisp fresh air was a welcome change from being stuck inside. Even the rain was refreshing. For several seconds she simply stood and enjoyed it all before she went hunting for foliage to complete her masterpiece.

Finding holly in the early evening darkness proved to be more of a challenge than she had first anticipated, meaning she had to trudge further from the house than she'd intended. Eventually, she found some and began snipping away with the shears until movement in the distance caught her eye.

Initially, Letty was scared and darted behind the bush in case it was somebody sinister looking for her, but the more she watched the lone figure, the more convinced she was that it was Jack. There was something about the way he held himself, the long, sure strides, the broad shoulders, the strange attraction which pulled her to only him rather than any of his three brothers.

Letty owed him an apology and the chance to do it in private, rather than in front of an audience of his brothers, was too appealing an opportunity to miss.

Jack kicked open the barn door and set about breaking up the bale of hay and distributing it amongst the horses. He never heard her behind him until it was too late.

'Hello, Jack.'

At the soft sound of her voice he instantly stiffened, but did not turn around. Looking at Letty made him want her and he was still embarrassed at her obvious reaction to his failings. 'You shouldn't be outside.'

'It's getting dark and nobody can see me. I wanted to apologise for what I said earlier.'

'There is no need.' He didn't need her well-meaning pity either. He would rather pretend it hadn't happened. 'It was a misunderstanding.' Jack busied himself by refilling the water troughs from the big barrel in the corner and hoped she would go away and stop dredging the sorry episode up. Unfortunately, he heard her move to stand next to him.

'It *was* a misunderstanding—but that does not excuse my thoughtlessness. Without meaning to, I insulted you. I feel dreadful, if it's any consolation.' It wasn't. 'You must think me very spoiled.' He did. 'After everything you have done for me, I am heartily ashamed of myself.'

Jack really did not want to look at her, but his eyes strayed towards her anyway. She certainly looked like the dictionary definition of remorse. Her face was downcast, her delicate shoulders slumped and her lovely eyes were troubled. Even as he fought it, she plucked at his heartstrings. 'It really doesn't matter, Letty. I am over it.' And now he was lying to make her feel better.

'Still, I should like to make it up to you.'

His teeth ground together unconsciously in protest. 'For the last time, I do not want your money, Letty...'

'I know that. I also would not insult you by offering it again. But I can help in other ways. I have already started on the nooks and crannies.' The corners of her plump mouth curved up into a nervous smile. 'Although I have only done one room so far.'

Jack experienced a rush of guilt. 'I never really intended for you to do the cleaning.' She shouldn't have to debase herself like that, especially after everything she had gone through. It was not as if she was responsible for the mess. He was.

'I quite enjoyed it, actually. I had a sense of purpose which has been missing this last week. You have no idea how mind-numbingly boring staying in bed is.'

Her open smile made him feel a little better.

She was trying to smooth things over, therefore, he should meet her halfway. 'I should like to try it one day. A whole day of doing absolutely nothing appeals to me.' Why was he ruining a perfectly nice moment by complaining about his lot?

'Spoken like a man who would rather do everything himself instead of delegating. I get the impression you do far more than your fair share, Jack.' She gazed around the barn and noticed the hay bale he had brought. 'Why don't I help you now? You will be finished more quickly if both of us do it.'

Her assessment of his character followed by her offer to assist surprised him. Instantly he refused it. 'There is no need. I can manage.' Letty simply grinned and ignored him. She had discarded her lamp and branches and was pulling huge clumps of hay from the bale before he had finished his sentence, positively throwing herself into the task. Clearly she did not realise how dirty one could get in the company of horses. 'Try to avoid the end without a head on. Horses can be…unpredictable at times.'

Her laughter was not the tinkling sort he imagined normally issued from gently bred ladies. It was a throaty giggle accompanied by the occasional snort. It sounded positively naughty. God help him.

'What a gentlemanly way of putting it, Jack. But I am used to the *unpredictability* of animals. My horse has no manners at all. He is ruthlessly *unpredictable* at every available opportunity.' Methodically she distributed the hay as if she fed animals all of the time.

'You ride?'

'Like a hellion, I am told. I particularly like fast and fearsome horses like this fine chap.' She reached up to stroke the muzzle of Jamie's temperamental black stallion.

'Satan doesn't like to be stroked,' Jack said quickly.

Letty smiled and ignored the warning, and for once the troublesome horse appeared to welcome the attention, pushing his big head against her open palm like the biggest of flirts. 'You poor thing,' she crooned, 'What did you do to deserve such a horrible name? You're a sweetie, Satan, aren't you?'

In Jack's experience, the horse most definitely was nothing of the sort. 'Usually, the only human he allows near him is Jamie and even then he barely tolerates him. Jamie brought him home from the Peninsula with him. When I say brought him home, it would probably be more accurate to say that he stole him. The horse gave him so much trouble, he called it Satan, but despite all that Jamie still kept him.'

'I can't say I blame him. You are such a handsome boy, Satan, aren't you?' To Jack's amazement she then kissed the tip of the animal's nose before stepping away. It was a sorry state of affairs when a man found himself jealous of a horse. 'I bet he is very fast.'

'He is. Dangerously so. Jacob tried to ride him when Jamie first came home and Satan threw him in a ditch. We didn't see the horse for hours afterwards, not that Jamie was concerned. He simply shrugged and said Satan would come back when he was good and ready. And he did as well. Wandered back into the barn eventually as if nothing was amiss.'

'Do you think Jamie would let me ride him?'

'I don't think it's down to Jamie. Satan can be particular. He's a one-rider-only sort of chap. I doubt he would make exceptions, even for a hellion.'

'My mother used to tell me off for riding with reckless abandon and then she would tell my father off worse for encouraging me.' Her lovely face clouded at the memory.

'You were close to your parents then?' Now there was something he had no concept of. He had never understood his, let alone been close to them. Neither his mother nor his father had wanted much to do with their offspring.

'Indeed I was. It was always just the three of us. Until it wasn't. I miss them dreadfully.'

She had brought them up, so Jack decided she probably didn't mind talking about them. 'You said they died in an accident—how old were you when it happened?' He returned the water bucket to its proper place at the same moment she brushed the last of the hay from her hands.

'Seventeen,' she said without hesitation, 'Far too early to be without any parents—especially a mother. But I suppose you would understand how devastating that is. Jacob told me you were all still children when your mother passed away.'

'He was seven, I was fourteen.' Except he hadn't really had the opportunity to be devastated. His three younger brothers had needed a buffer between them and their father's belt strap, just as his mother had needed one from his father's drunken fists. Not that she had ever been grateful for his interference or tended to his bruises afterwards.

'You were even younger than I, then. How did she die?'

Years of being the wife of a Warriner, estranged from her family and all good society, the harsh realities of her isolation and the constant poverty had driven her to do the unthinkable. 'Suicide. She drowned herself in the river.' It had been swollen and raging after a week of storms, just as it was now, so she had jumped in on purpose without a backward glance because she mourned the life she had lost and could never regain.

Jack still hadn't fully forgiven her for leaving them, when they had loved her even though she could barely look upon them without seeing the face of her hated husband. The man who had compromised her into marriage to get her dowry and then had them chased out of London because of his mounting debts. Lord only knew what had happened to the dowry, but Jack doubted it went on anything sensible. Letty's face was filled with pity. 'And before you ask, my father followed her into the ground seven years later. He was fond of the bottle.' Why was he telling her that? Although it was hardly a secret. Being drunk was one of the few things his father had done well, to the detriment of everything else, and for some inextricable reason Jack had wanted to tell her because she appeared to care.

Letty stared at him for a long time, her golden head tilted to one side as she considered what he had unintentionally confessed. Where he thought he might see horror, or judgement, he saw only sympathy. 'Oh, Jack,' she said at last, with a sigh, 'now I understand why your brothers all look up to you so. You have had to be both a mother and a father to them all these years. And run this estate. What a lot to take on.' She smoothed her hand down his arm almost affectionately. He felt the touch everywhere. 'You should be proud. You have done an excellent job of it. Your three brothers are all good men.'

If he had been expecting a compliment, or an affectionate touch, he might have had a glib answer ready for her. Instead, he experienced a rush of gratitude so acute it caused a lump in his throat. Nobody had sympathy for a Warriner, not usually, which made Letty's reaction all the more special. He dipped his head to avoid her gaze and tried to change the subject.

'Why have you been picking holly? Surely it is a bit early to be making garlands for Christmas?'

She shook her head, the motion causing one damp corkscrew curl to bounce enticingly over one eye as she grinned. 'I thought I would make a pretty arrangement for the drawing room. A homely touch to cheer you all—perhaps it might even raise a smile from Jamie.'

The curl bounced again, tempting him. Unconsciously, Jack reached out and tucked it behind her ear, his fingers grazing the silky, soft skin of her cheek in the process and she smiled up at him. More words tumbled out unchecked.

'Sometimes it is difficult to know exactly what Jamie is thinking. Since his return home, his withdrawal worries me. I wish I knew what to do to fix it.' And there he went again, telling her things which he did not share with his family. Confiding in her. Letty Dunston was doing strange things to his heart.

'Perhaps you cannot simply fix it. I suspect Jamie needs time to come to terms with his experience of war himself before he can explain it to you. Give him time to heal mentally as well as physically. All grief heals eventually.'

'Maybe. It is hard to simply stand by and watch.'

'Why? Because you are used to being the one in control of everything?'

'I suppose.'

His fingers were still playing with the soft curls by her ear, lingering too long on her skin until he realised he was beaming back at her like a besotted idiot, something he was quite sure she was used to, but not something he ever did. Jack dropped his hand as though he'd been burnt and quickly turned back to finish his work. He really had no right to touch her like that, no matter how easy he found it to confess things to her, and quickly quashed the overwhelming urge to touch her again. The girl was trouble he did not need. Another unwelcome, unwanted responsibility. One who was only biding her time here until she could return to her splendid life and her fancy Duke, and one who certainly would not be impressed by his overwhelming attraction to her.

She stood waiting silently as he blew out the lamps in the barn, a task he instantly regretted the moment he turned around. The soft glow from the lantern in her hand cast her in an ethereal light which made her look just like an angel. Once again, she took his breath away and he could think of nothing to say to relieve the wave of desire which suddenly swamped him. Her beauty and his spellbound reaction to it almost made him physically flinch.

'Dinner will be ready soon,' he said abruptly. Standing alone with her, here in the dark, was foolhardy. If he was not careful, she would know he was attracted to her and he would spill out all of his troubles, and that would never do. Then she really would pity him, poor, unworthy pauper that he was, and he would look completely pathetic. It was far better she thought he saw her as a great inconvenience rather than the greatest of temptations. 'We should go.'

With brisker efficiency than he felt, Jack led the way out of the barn and secured the heavy door. They walked a few yards in painfully awkward silence while he racked his brains for something—anything—sensible to say which did not make him appear to be the lustful, uncivilised nobody he had a frequent tendency to feel around her.

'It's been raining for days.' Good grief! Was that really the best that he could do? Only the dullest of fellows talked about the weather. 'I am worried the river will flood.' And now he was burdening her with more of his problems, as if she would care about something so…mundane and beneath her.

'I suppose a flood would damage your crops, wouldn't it?' She was trying to make the best of his feeble attempts at scintillating conversation and he cringed inwardly at his lack of charm. Even Jacob had better luck with females than he did. This was a woman who was the darling of society. An incomparable. And he was a crass oaf who couldn't even afford one servant and became overwhelmed after receiving one, tiny compliment. But the die was cast, he had started the boring conversation, and he had to answer her polite question even if neither of them really cared about the answer.

'It is the wrong time of year for crops. However, if the river does burst its banks it can be dangerous for my animals.'

As if to prove a point, one of those animals cried out in panic. Letty's eyes widened. 'What was that?'

'A sheep.' And if Jack wasn't mistaken, it was a sheep in distress. Just what he needed in the pouring rain, despite the fact it got him out of being the dullest conversationalist Letty had ever had the misfortune to talk to and gave him an excuse to escape from her tempting presence. 'I will meet you back at the house, I need to go and see what is wrong.'

'Something, I suspect, you might find much easier with the lantern, don't you think?' She grinned and wiggled the lamp for emphasis and sealed his fate. 'I shall come with you.'

Chapter Ten

Twenty-four days and thirteen hours to go, give or take a few minutes...

Letty had never heard the sound of a panicked sheep before, but it was quite unsettling and almost child-like. The nearer they got to the pitiful sound, the more her too-big boots stuck in the sodden ground beneath her feet. More worrying, in view of Jack's sad tale about his mother's untimely death, was the unmistakable noise of the angry river as they trudged ever closer to it.

Jack had relieved her of her lantern and held it aloft following the noise deftly. He let out a frustrated groan when he spotted it. 'There it is.'

In the darkness, Letty could just about make out the shape of a sheep. Its head and flank were thrashing from side to side as it stood rooted to the spot. Jack simply stared at it in disgust. 'Their hooves become embedded in the mud. I live in hope the silly animals will eventually learn from their mistakes and avoid the river bank. But they are sheep and sheep are reliably stupid at all times.'

He put the lamp down on the ground and shrugged out of his heavy coat, passing it to Letty to hold, and then began to unbutton his waistcoat quickly. She watched transfixed as the second layer of clothing came off, unsure as to why he was stripping off, but when he gripped the hem of his shirt and began to pull that over his head too she began to panic.

'W-what are you doing?'

'Clearly you have never wrestled with a wet sheep, Letty, else you wouldn't ask.' The shirt joined the pile of clothes in her arms and he stood in front of her naked from the waist up and clearly irritated. 'They can be ridiculously absorbent.'

The glow from the lantern made his skin appear almost bronze and cast interesting shadows around the large muscles on his arms and shoulders. A dusting of dark hair fanned over his chest and narrowed before disappearing under the waistband of his breeches. Jack appeared blissfully ignorant of how vastly improper their current situation was and Letty was loath to appraise him of the fact in case he reassessed the situation and put his clothes back on. Did that make her a hussy?

Probably. But she didn't care right now.

'I will be soaked to the skin instantly the moment I touch it. At least this way, I will have something reasonably dry to put on afterwards.' He stood on one leg to tug off a boot. It was swiftly followed by the other one. She held her breath and scandalously hoped he would shimmy out of his tight breeches as well. Without the covering of his coat, the soft fabric clearly encased an impressive pair of thighs and a pleasingly firm, rounded bottom she had not noticed before. Had she ever noticed a gentleman's bottom before? If she had, it was no wonder she did not remember it. For several seconds she scanned her memories for the Duke of Wentworth's bottom and came up blank. Whatever his posterior resembled, all previous bottoms of her acquaintance paled into insignificance in comparison to her present company. To Letty's complete disappointment, the breeches remained resolutely on.

'This shouldn't take long.' With that, he strode purposely towards the sheep.

Further conversation proved impossible because Letty's body was behaving in the most peculiar way. For a start, she could not tear her eyes away from his powerful back as he grappled with the animal. How could she when those muscles moved intriguingly under his smooth skin? It took a tremendous amount of fortitude to force them elsewhere and even then they kept drifting back guiltily until she realised he could not see her eager staring with his back to her. After that, she allowed herself to ogle him shamelessly. His back, his broad shoulders, the muscles in his arms and his delightfully firm bottom were all studied far more than was really necessary because, it went without saying, they would be seared on her memory for ever. But as she did so, to her consternation her knees were definitely becoming increasingly wobbly and her heart was beating so loudly it drowned out the bleating of the panicked sheep. And she was hot. Very, very hot. All over.

Whilst such an unexpected display of his own nudity did not apparently bother Jack, Letty was definitely overwhelmed with the impact of his raw manliness. Her arms had involuntarily tightened about the warm pile of his clothing she held. Better that than to give in to the desire to march over there and touch him herself. But his garments were an unsatisfactory substitute.

How would he feel? She definitely should not allow her errant thoughts to wander there! Unfortunately, those thoughts were not done wandering and refused to listen to her.

Would his skin be soft like hers? She already knew his body would feel deliciously firm beneath her palms. Her fingers itched to be able to explore all of those indents and bulges properly. Just to be certain.

Letty had never experienced desire like this before. She had flirted with battalions of men, usually just for fun or because that was what everyone expected Violet to do, yet once or twice she had been curious about what it would be like to kiss a man. She had recently given a great deal of serious thought to kissing the Duke of Wentworth—just in case she did end up marrying the man. However, whilst she definitely wanted to kiss Jack, she also wanted to touch, lick and nibble him, too.

All over.

A new and blush-worthy development she had not considered before—even with her dashing Duke. She sincerely doubted she would ever be able to talk to Jack again without thinking about him *without* his clothes on. It was a good job it was dark. From the intense heat radiating from her skin, Letty knew she was flushed. Flushed rather than blushing all over, which was scandalous in itself. She should be horrified to witness such an improper display of naked male. Not be revelling in it. Fantasising about it. Wishing it would never end.

It did not take Jack long to dislodge the sheep's hooves from the mud and, rather ungratefully, the animal struggled in his arms as he carried it to the safety of firmer ground. 'You have done that before.' Letty's voice was undeniably hoarse as she attempted to sound nonchalant. For good measure she sucked in a few calming breaths in an attempt to bring her fluttering pulse under control. It didn't work.

'Too many times.'

He grabbed the shirt from her arms and to her total fascination, began to use it as a towel. First he rubbed it briskly over his head, unaware that in doing so the muscles in his arms bunched in a most appealing way and he gave her a glimpse of the two dark patches of hair beneath them which held her transfixed. Then he used the balled linen to roughly dry his exposed skin. It was on the tip of Letty's tongue to offer to do it for him and that shocked her so much she forced herself to stare at her feet rather than gaze longingly at his splendid body.

Too soon, he relieved her of his heavy coat and slipped it on, stuffed the sodden shirt into one of the pockets, then bent to pick up the lantern, leaving Letty still holding his waistcoat and her holly, painfully aware of the fact she could still see tantalising glimpses of his bare torso as they walked back towards the house and feeling very, very aroused by the sight.

When they entered the kitchen, Jamie Warriner took in the scene with his usual blank look, but his eyes lingered on Letty's flushed cheeks and wide eyes and she was certain she saw a flash of amusement in his inscrutable gaze.

'Dinner is in half an hour.' Then, as an afterthought, he smiled at her.

Oh, good heavens! He knew what she was thinking about his elder brother. A blush joined the flush and heated her face further. Letty probably resembled a beetroot. She tried to brazen it out. 'Excellent. That gives me time to freshen up then.' And to have a lie down, ostensibly, she reasoned, to think about how she was currently feeling. However, her legs were now so unsteady, Letty knew if she didn't lie down soon, she would probably fall down. Or swoon. Swooning was more likely. 'If you will excuse me, gentlemen.'

She was still clutching her bunch of holly as she scurried upstairs and didn't care. Jack had unsettled her. He kept doing that, she realised. His smile, his manner—rakish one minute, domineering the next—his kindness, fierce loyalty and, not least, his pride. He was absolutely right to be proud, she supposed. He had been so young when he had taken on the burden of responsibility for his brothers and the estate, something she found both admirable and touching. Then, of course, there were his gorgeous deep blue eyes and now his truly magnificent body was thrown into the heady mix. Letty gratefully sank down on the mattress and flopped back against the pillows to allow her mind to properly consider it now she was alone. One did not need a vast amount of experience with the male form to know when one had seen a singularly perfect specimen…

Jack stood next to Jamie and surveyed his drawing room. Letty had not exaggerated when she had claimed to have cleaned all of the nooks and crannies. He could not remember the last time anywhere in this dilapidated old house had ever felt so inviting or smelled so overwhelmingly of polish.

'She did this all by herself?'

'It was impressive to watch. The woman is a demon when she gets going. I genuinely feared for the windows when she started cleaning them.'

'And you didn't help her move the furniture?' Jack was still baffled as to how she had managed to drag in the heavy oak side table from the other room all alone. On the surface, Letty appeared to be such a delicate little thing.

'By the time I came home she had already moved it all. Neither Joe nor Jacob helped her either.'

Jack scratched his head and smiled. 'She's done a splendid job.' Who would have thought a spoiled heiress was capable of actual graft?

'Indeed she has. Your Letty is a feisty one.'

Jack was reluctant to take the bait, but knew from bitter experience it was better to tackle it head on rather than leave such an outrage unchecked. 'She's not *my* Letty, Jamie, so have your fun elsewhere.'

Jamie shrugged and feigned disinterest. 'Is she not? Perhaps I misread the obvious signals she was sending out.'

He couldn't ignore that. 'Signals?'

'You fluster her.'

'I do?'

'I'll say. Just now she was all pink and nervy. What did you do her?'

'Nothing. She apologised for this morning, we chatted and then I had to pull a sheep out of the mud.'

Jamie allowed his eyes to travel slowly down Jack's body and then pulled apart the front of his greatcoat. 'Like that? Where has your shirt gone?'

'You wouldn't wear your shirt if you were handling a wet sheep either.'

'That explains it, then. You gave her a show of your raw manliness—women like a bit of the untamed savage in their men. Displays of half-naked brute strength have a tendency to make females swoon. I don't suppose your Letty is any different.'

'Stop calling her *my* Letty. You know full well there is nothing untoward going on.' Much as he would like there to be. Jamie merely shrugged again, but it was a gesture loaded with meaning.

'I rather think she is *your* Letty, Big Brother. There are four devilishly handsome Warriners in this house, yet she has taken a fancy only to you. There is no accounting for taste.' Jamie turned and limped back to the kitchen, forcing Jack to follow him like a lapdog, desperately hopeful to hear more of his brother's tantalising theories, but Jamie did not elaborate. Instead, he poked the point of a knife into his boiling potatoes and pretended Jack did not exist. Asking anything now was tantamount to a confession of guilt and he did not need his astute brother knowing he was burning with lust and fraught with longing for the woman, so Jack poured himself some milk. He tried to choke it down nonchalantly when all he really wanted to do was shake his irritating brother by the shoulders and demand he explain himself. Immediately.

After an eternity, Jamie spoke again with far more measured casualness than even his acting skills extended to. 'I suppose it doesn't hurt that she is an uncommonly pretty little thing.'

Jack experienced a surge of possessive jealousy at his brother's comment. 'Is she? I can't say I've given it much thought.'

'Liar!' Jamie threw his head back and laughed

then, something he rarely did. Jack had never craved the satisfaction of punching his brother in the face more. 'Every time you look at her your tongue is hanging out and you practically drool.'

The best form of defence, even when your brother had your exact measure, was attack. 'I wonder if Napoleon's troops didn't injure your thick skull as well as your leg, Jamie. Clearly you have begun hallucinating.'

Jack stalked from the room to the boisterous sound of his brother's laughter, feeling a strange mix of emotions which unnerved him. Was Jamie right? Was it within the realms of possibility that a fêted society beauty might have taken a fancy to him? While the prospect warmed him, he would have to be an idiot to give the theory any credence. If she was flustered, it was probably due to his uncouth disrobing in the presence of a lady. At the time, he hadn't given it much thought. He always stripped to the waist when he rescued wet sheep. They all did. Now that he considered it, he supposed proper gentlemen would never do such a thing. His instruction in correct etiquette had been woefully neglected by both of his parents, so was it any wonder the poor girl had been shocked by his crass behaviour?

Letty's flush would have been pure embarrassment, not admiration for the *untamed savage* as his brother had suggested. Instead of being impressed at his display of brute strength, all Jack would have managed was to cement her opinion of him as a brute. The very last thing he should be doing was holding out a preposterous hope of anything else with her.

In Jack's experience, hope in any form was normally the kiss of death. Every single time he had experienced that fickle emotion, fate had had very different ideas. As if Violet Dunston, incomparable diamond from sophisticated London, would seriously lower herself to be with somebody like him. Even if he weren't a Warriner, he boasted little to tempt her. No money, poor manners, a crumbing house and the son of a man who had ruined another heiress once upon a time. Yes, indeed—plenty to turn her head there!

And besides, he had enough burdens in his life already, without yearning for the additional complication of a woman in it. Even if by some miracle she did find something attractive in his *brutish savageness*, wives and Warriners did not mix. The Warriner men were doomed to make women unhappy, and although he was not a violent man, like his father, or a drunk, again like his father, he was loaded with far too many responsibilities to take on another one and he could not bear the idea of reading the inevitable disappointment in any woman's face when she realised she had made a huge mistake in shackling herself to him.

Added to that, it certainly did not help matters that Jack's estate was in the direst of straits, he was tarred with the worst reputation possible, barely had twenty measly guineas to his name and was definitely not the sort of man an *incomparable* would ever consider as a potential mate in any lifetime, let alone this one. Not when she had wealthy dukes falling all over themselves to court her, who definitely did not need her money at all and could give her exactly the sort of life she had been born to live and doubtless yearned to get back to.

Chapter Eleven

Twenty-two days left...

'What are you doing?'

The barked question nearly caused Letty to lose her tenuous balance on the tiny occasional table she was teetering on. 'I would have thought it obvious, Jack. I am cleaning the chandelier.' The large, only remaining dusty thing in the vaulted hallway had been taunting her.

'You are going to break your neck, woman!' He strode towards her, looking simultaneously annoyed, windswept and enormous in his undone greatcoat. Unfortunately, this time there was both a shirt and waistcoat firmly in place beneath it. His big hands steadied the table and he stared up at her with barely disguised irritation. 'Get down this instant!'

Every time Letty heard his dictatorial tone it

grated and childishly she became more set on doing whatever it was he disapproved of, even though she knew he was right. Her position had been dangerously precarious and she should be grateful he had come to her aid. She should be, but she wasn't. 'No! Just look at all the dust and the cobwebs.' With a flash of ill-advised defiance, she wielded her feather duster on the dingy glass droplets again and the table wobbled ominously beneath her feet despite his hold on it.

Letty's arms waved as she tried to balance herself, only to find this completely unnecessary when his hands gripped her thighs in a most improper manner. 'Oh, for goodness sake, you stubborn wench!' Seconds later her feet left the table top as he hoisted her into the air until her shoulders came level with all of the cobwebs.

Suddenly, cleaning the silly thing as quickly as possible became her main priority, because his head was inches from her navel and those distractingly strong arms were wrapped very tightly just below her bottom. Never had a feather duster moved so fast, yet as rapid as her movements were, they did nothing to take her mind off their intimate position.

Letty could feel his breath on her skin. Warm,

slightly laboured, it floated through the soft linen of the shirt she was wearing. *His* shirt. The heat of his hands seared through the buckskin of her breeches, *his* breeches, until she was aware of the exact shape of his palms and the weight of each of his fingers pressed against her legs. And there was nothing else between the fabric and her skin. She had no underwear. The corset and chemise she had been wearing on the night of her abduction had been ruined along with her evening dress and slippers. Letty had never wished for a corset more than she did right at this moment, because it would have acted like armour. A boned and impenetrable layer of protection between this vexing man and her decidedly vexed body.

Almost desperately, she scrabbled for the last of the cobwebs. 'All done!' This was sung with far too much relief and in a voice a great deal more high-pitched than normal. 'You can put me down now!'

Misguidedly, she had assumed he would plop her back on the table and then help her down. He did no such thing; instead he carefully lowered her to the ground by sliding her down his body. Whilst this probably made sense in view of the feeble nature of the table she had chosen to use, the logistics of the task proved to be more disconcerting than merely being held aloft. It involved Jack's arms shifting position as he shuffled her downwards. They grazed over her bottom before circling her waist, his face now level with her breasts. That warm breath did peculiar things to those as it permeated the flimsy linen.

A moment later and her breasts were pushed flush against his chest, and Letty hoped he was not as aware of her suddenly pert nipples as she was, although she suspected they would be awkwardly apparent through the fine linen of his shirt now that only two layers of thin material separated them.

Her eyes locked with his as they came level. Up close, there were darker flecks of sapphire in the intense blue and his pupils were larger than she was used to seeing them. Unnerving. Her pulse leapt further when they briefly flicked to her lips. He blinked and for a moment Letty thought he might kiss her, so intense had the atmosphere between them suddenly become—but if he was as attracted to her as she was to him, he hid it well. Effortlessly, he lowered her until her feet came into contact with the floor; her neck tilted back to look up at him, reminding her of the huge difference in their heights. The peculiar exchange had probably taken no more than a few seconds in total, yet her fevered imagination had slowed it all down in order to savour the whole experience.

It was Jack who stepped back and broke the sensual spell she was under. 'Do not attempt to clean another chandelier without one of my brothers there to help you!' The gruff tone was a dash of cold water which brought Letty up short. 'And please try to keep yourself out of trouble for the rest of the day.'

He turned and strode towards the kitchen, that greatcoat billowing behind him as he disappeared around the corner. Letty heard the door slam as he left the building and realised her foolish idea that he might kiss her had been exactly that. Foolish. The man thought her the greatest of all inconveniences and clearly still did not like her despite her pathetic efforts to try to make him do so.

More than a little unsteady and now quite miserable, she considered admitting defeat. Jack Warriner would never warm to her and perhaps without the protective aura of her fortune to seduce people with, she wasn't particularly likeable. A sobering thought.

A defeatist's thought.

Letty had thwarted kidnappers, for pity's sake. If she could manage that then she could make Jack like her. Perhaps she simply needed to go about it in a different way...

As she had never cooked anything before in her life, the recipe before her might as well have been written in a foreign language, but now that the lower floor of Markham Manor was shining like a new pin, Letty was determined to serve a proper meal in the newly sparkling dining room. One with a sauce. And a dessert.

Letty had never as much as peeled a carrot before, so to make a meal entirely from scratch would gave her an inordinate sense of achievement. Her uncle had often accused her of being spoiled and having no understanding of the real world. She needed, her uncle explained in that patronising way that he had, a sensible man's guidance because she was incapable of being independent. Well, thanks to his treachery, she had learned a completely new set of skills recently which she had hitherto not needed. Escaping a moving carriage, for instance. Or dusting. Or doing laundry. Yet she had not only tackled each task with vigour, she had emerged triumphant, as she always did, and excelled at every one, with the exception of yesterday's unfortunate chandelier incident. Now she would teach herself to cook as well. What was that if it was not independence?

It had also been nice to be able to do something for this family who had taken her in. She had already developed a great affection for the three younger Warriners, even the taciturn Jamie, and there was no denying the physical attraction she had to their brooding big brother. Since their memorable meeting in the barn, closely followed by the peculiar incident in the hallway, he had been doing his level best to avoid her. That was plainly obvious to anyone with eyes and she clearly still irritated him, as even in the evenings when she sat in the drawing room with the whole family he remained aloof. She chatted and laughed with Joe and Jacob, occasionally Jamie added some pithy comment which made them all smile, while Jack occupied himself with his ledgers and barely grunted if she tried to include him in the conversation.

And there she had thought they were beginning to get along the other night. Only to spoil it by climbing on that silly table and making herself look inordinately silly in his eyes once again.

With Jack Warriner, every time she took a step forward, she seemingly took two steps backwards. She had never been more confused by a gentleman in her life. Men usually courted her good favour. Jack now totally ignored her.

If she said so herself, making dinner was a stroke of genius. For days now, Jack's unfriendly behaviour towards her had put Letty on edge. She was not used to being either invisible or disliked. People always adored her—well, on the surface they did anyway. Did they only see Violet, rather than Letty? The very fact that she continually thought of herself as two people, and only Letty was real, did little to ease her unease. Violet was rich, charming and enigmatic. The catch of the Season.

But Jack did not want her money, or appreciate Violet's charms, nor did he appear to like Letty very much. The real her. Once again Letty felt like an inconvenient burden to him and she was now so desperate for his approval she was prepared to try anything to get it. Something, she was prepared to concede, which was completely pathetic and said a great deal about her need to belong and, more to the point, her underlying lack of confidence.

Doing something productive for the family helped to alleviate some of the guilt she felt at straining their already limited resources and, if Jack would not accept her money, he was jolly well going to accept the fruit of her labours... and perhaps, if the way to a man's heart was truly through his stomach, he might stop treating her like a plague victim come to contaminate them and smile at her again. One of those unguarded, roguish smiles which made his eyes twinkle mischievously. The one which made her heart melt. She frowned. No wonder she needed to keep herself occupied. Every time Letty stopped moving, she found herself thinking dreamily of him. Usually without his shirt on.

When she had informed Jamie several hours ago of her intention to make dinner, his only reaction was to quirk one eyebrow, then disappear into the courtyard. When he returned a few minutes later, he handed her two dead chickens which were still warm, their broken necks swinging menacingly as she held them tenuously by their feet. 'There are vegetables in the pantry,' he had said and then had promptly disappeared outside again.

It was just as well. Cooking was proving to be much more troublesome than polishing and dusting, and the ancient cookbook she had found in the long-forgotten library was not a great deal of help. *The Art of Cookery Made Plain and Simple* was a misnomer. The recipe for 'Fowl à la Braise' was neither plain nor simple and took it for granted that the reader knew the fundamentals of the culinary arts before commencing. What, for example, did '*reduce*' mean? And how could one '*add enough flour to make a thick sauce*' if one had never made a sauce of any sort before? How much, exactly, was enough? In desperation she had added spoonful after spoonful to the pan, only to watch it congeal into lumps before her very eyes. Far from being in a sea of thick, delicious sauce, her fowl *à la Braise* was now floating in a stagnant pond in the middle of a heatwave. And with less than half an hour before dinner was due to be served, she was beginning to lose all hope of the final dish being edible.

Jack worked himself into a state of exhaustion. He had not needed to spend an hour in the barn chopping wood, the wood pile already being quite healthy, but he could not face going back to the house until it was absolutely necessary. Not while she was there, tempting him with her glorious riot of corkscrew curls and still wearing his breeches. Looking and not touching was killing him. Looking, while not appearing to look, was driving him insane. He had never been so frustrated in his life. Unfortunately, as it was almost dinner time it was absolutely necessary to go back inside so he could not put it off any longer.

With a sigh he piled up the last of the wood and shrugged on his coat. The last three days had been tortuous. He was wary of even glancing at Letty in case Jamie had been right and he did openly gape at her with his tongue out, drooling, and after he had shamelessly enjoyed the feel of her in his arms yesterday and had very nearly kissed her because he was so consumed with lust, the only course of action available to him now was to have as little to do with the temptress as possible.

In the mornings, Letty's company had been more bearable because he had a distinct purpose—eat breakfast and then leave as quickly as possible. But in the evenings…well, frankly they made him cringe. If sitting silently through dinner trying not to explode while conversation wafted around him wasn't painful enough, at the end of the evening he would then have to watch her perfect bottom sway up the stairs, in *his* breeches, on her way to bed. *His* bed. Both things drove him mad with unfulfilled desire. It was all he could do to mutter goodnight.

Things would be a lot easier if she was an ordinary-looking girl, but of course he was never that lucky. Instead she had those lovely, big green eyes and those plump, pink lips which appeared to have no difficulty talking. There was an animation about the way that she spoke which made even the most mundane topics sound interesting. But that was entirely the problem. Her life had been far from mundane. She knew everyone in London, had been invited to every ball, had danced with dukes and solvent earls, and even the Prince Regent himself.

Twice.

How exactly did a humble, financially embarrassed farmer from dankest Nottinghamshire even begin to compete with all of that? She positively reeked of effervescence. Jack probably stank of the sheep he wrestled like a savage. Half the time he felt unworthy, the other half merely miserable. Letty was perfect. There was no other word for her. And perfect, when you were a penniless Warriner with an incurable case of lust and no prospects, was intimidating. Jack used to be master of the house, but now he was reduced to being a slave to his urges, and a mute slave to boot.

Despite his inability to reciprocate conversationally like a civilised gentleman, or indulge his rampant desire, having Letty in the house made everything about the place seem a little brighter. Not to mention cleaner and more…homely. It was almost as if she belonged at Markham Manor—which was, of course, ridiculous. An *incomparable* did not belong here. With him.

He took a calming breath and then opened the door.

'Letty has been cooking!' announced Jacob with a grin.

Letty was stood at the table looking lovely, a leather-bound tome entitled *The Art of Cookery Made Plain and Simple* at her elbow and a huge smudge of flour on her cheek. It was quite an arresting sight. She looked like a beautiful depiction of the perfect farmer's wife. Jack managed a smile despite the sudden tightness in his chest. Farmer's wife? Where the hell had that come from?

'So I see.'

Joe was stirring a big pot on the range and appeared to be on the cusp of hysterical laughter. 'She has made Fowl à la Braise and potatoes—

which is apparently a fancy name for a chicken stew from what I can make out. For pudding we have baked apples with cream.'

'It sounds delicious,' he said carefully, although it did not actually smell particularly delicious. It smelled burnt—and ever so slightly fetid.

'Why don't you sit down, Jack?'

With a sinking feeling Jack realised he was trapped. He had to make conversation now after she had plainly gone to so much trouble. It was expected. 'Have you had a good day?' It was a reasonable start.

She smiled at him and gestured to the mess around them with a spoon. 'I have been learning to cook. I did not realise that it was so complicated—but it has proved to be very entertaining. I had originally intended to make an apple pie for pudding, but I am afraid that the pastry proved to be a little too challenging.'

'I see.' Dull. Dull. Dull. Jack racked his brain for another topic. 'The rain has stopped.' Good grief, could he be any more boring?

'It has?' This news appeared to cheer her. 'That will make your work easier.'

'I hope so, though it could take a day or two for the water to subside. Once it does, I should be spared from rescuing sheep for a few days. Three of them got stuck in the mud today. Sheep are such stupid creatures.' Much better. He had actually managed to string several sentences together quite effectively.

'They taste good, though, so that is some consolation.'

She gave him such a lovely smile and he found himself grinning back at her like an idiot before he checked himself. 'Indeed it is.' Jack took a grateful gulp of his tea.

'I think that the potatoes are done, Letty,' Jacob called from across the room. 'You had better get those plates ready, Jamie.' When Jack stood up, intending to help her, Letty turned to him and stayed him with her hand. It touched the back of his briefly and sent tingles up his arm.

'Sit down. The three of us can manage well enough. You work too hard, Jack.'

Letty insisted they all eat in the formal dining room so the brothers carried the steaming pots to the table, but when the lids were removed she stared at her creation with a sinking heart. They all did. It might well smell like food, but it looked terrible. The sauce around the chicken was thin, lumpy and grey in colour. The two chickens looked anaemic. The least said about the accompanying vegetables the better. Mush was a more fitting word for them now. Bland, pale, unappetising mush.

Jack politely served himself a chunk of the chicken. As he lifted the sorry-looking portion on to his plate Letty could see the tell-tale signs of feathers still on the greasy, gelatinous skin and winced. The spoonful of mush Joe served him landed on his plate with an ominous-sounding splosh.

'This looks lovely,' he said with the falsest smile she had ever seen and then he proceeded to help his brothers load their own plates with a completely straight face. Letty wanted to curl up and hide as she watched them all pick at the food dubiously. Poor Jack had no option but to fill a fork with the slop and choke it down.

'Mmm…' For good measure he nodded sagely, rolling his eyes at his siblings as if his mouth was filled with the nectar of the Gods and she realised he was actually being kind. To her. Letty wanted to die. But they all made a polite and valiant attempt at eating the meal despite the fact it was beyond awful. Jamie curled his lip in disgust and shovelled the food in fast, a technique he had probably learned in the army when the rations were terrible. Jacob and Joe appeared so disappointed upon swallowing their first mouthful, but they looked to their elder brother, who kept making encouraging sounds as he attacked his plate with gusto, and they did the same. At one point his eyes rested on hers. For once, it was not irritation she read in them, nor was it disappointment at the shameful ruination of good food at her clumsy hand. To her complete surprise he seemed to find the whole thing very funny.

'I am so sorry about dinner,' she blurted out and then instantly blushed from the roots of her hair down to the tips of her toes, 'It is a travesty.'

Those intense blue eyes lifted slowly from his plate and regarded her with obvious amusement. 'A travesty is a bit harsh.'

'How would you describe it, then?' Letty's cheeks were burning hot, but she forced herself to meet his gaze. 'I have even ruined the saucepans.'

For a moment he shrugged, then a devastating boyish grin transformed his face. 'There are some redeeming aspects. You make excellent tea—so the beginning part of the meal was very good.'

To her horror, both Joe and Jacob burst out

laughing. Even Jamie smiled. 'In the army I had to eat some pretty inedible things, Letty. But this? This is by far the worst meal ever to pass my lips.'

Letty buried her face in her hands and groaned. 'It all appeared to be so straightforward in the book.'

Jack's eyes were still laughing, but he spoke kindly. 'Perhaps you should have started with something simple first. I confess I have never heard of fowl *à la Braise* before today, but I think you should master something basic like roasting a chicken before you move on to something as advanced as trying to cook it *à la Braise*.'

'Would you consider boiled potatoes and carrots advanced? I ruined those, too.'

'You are being too hard on yourself.' The three other Warriners nodded enthusiastically, in a valiant attempt at making her feel better which failed completely. Feeling inordinately stupid and angry at herself, Letty stood and began to snatch up the still-full plates, stacking them in a pile in front of her.

'The baked apples might taste better!' Although she did not hold out much hope. The acrid smell of burning fruit was unmistakable.

To compound her misery, Jack started laughing.

'I thought the stewed chicken feathers were a particularly *nice* touch. I have never seen that before. Was it in the recipe or a little twist of your own?'

'I enjoyed those, too,' said Joe, fishing one from his mouth and waving it for emphasis. 'They gave the meal a little extra something...'

'Texture.' Jacob was holding his ribs, he was sniggering so much. 'If you ask me, there are not enough feathers in food. They are wasted in pillows.'

Letty pouted in consternation. 'I have never plucked a chicken before,' she admitted with the beginnings of a smile because it was funny. 'It was horrible. They were still warm. I gave up plucking when I thought one of the birds was still twitching. I foolishly thought the remaining feathers would burn off as they cooked. But at least I got one thing right. My fowl *à la Braise* was accurately named. It was truly foul.' The infectious sound of Jack's laughter was interrupted by the sound of a fist pummelling on the front door.

Chapter Twelve

Twenty days left and all is not well...

The five of them stared at each other, although Letty appeared truly terrified. She needn't have worried. Jack would slay dragons before he ever let anyone get near her.

'Go upstairs. Stay out of sight. We'll deal with this.' She didn't have to be asked twice and sprinted from the dining room with her lovely eyes wide.

The fist pummelled the door again and the four of them walked warily towards it. 'I'm coming!' Jack shouted with feigned irritation, conscious that his heart was threatening to beat its way out of his chest. This was his fault. No doubt the change in the weather had influenced this visit. For once, Jack was not pleased the incessant rain had stopped now that they had a fairweather search party at the door. He chastised himself for not realising this was bound to happen. Thanks to his own stupidity, he had inadvertently put Letty in danger. But he could flagellate himself later, when the threat was gone.

He turned to his brothers and whispered instructions. 'Whoever it is, we know nothing. We have seen nothing.' They nodded and headed into the great hall, led by Jamie. When Jack saw they were all sat in their usual places, pretending to be reading something, he slid open the latch and the heavy front door swung open. There were three men standing on the dark threshold, all with lanterns in their hands. Jack recognised only one of the men.

Layton. When this was all over, he promised himself he would enjoy making the weasel pay for his part in harming Letty. But not tonight. In the nick of time he remembered that calling him by his real name would tip the man off.

'Mr Smith? What brings you here at such a late hour?'

The scarred man leaned sideways to look suspiciously past him down the hallway before returning his gaze to Jack. 'Sorry for the unexpected disturbance, Mr Warriner, only we are still looking for the missing girl. After talking to some of the locals and after having been informed your estate was quite extensive, not to mention so remote, it occurred to me that Violet might have taken refuge here somewhere.'

The man's pale eyes searched Jack's expression for any sign of emotion which might give something away. He forced himself to appear amused. 'With your reward now at a princely five hundred pounds, you can be assured if either myself or my brothers had seen her, we would have delivered her safely back to you immediately.'

Layton smiled, although his eyes remained cold and inscrutable. 'I am sure you would, Mr Warriner. I am certain five hundred pounds would be extremely useful to a man in your position...' He would pay for that comment, too. 'However, the young lady in question is a resourceful thing. In her panic, she may well have ensconced herself in one of your outbuildings without your knowledge—'

Jack cut him off curtly. 'In her panic, Mr Smith? I thought the girl had been kidnapped.'

Layton never missed a beat. 'We now believe she may well have escaped her abductors, Mr Warriner. We have still received no ransom note and a few of the locals have mentioned seeing a young girl of her description on the night in question. They say she was all alone and obviously terrified.'

Jack had never seen a person lie so effortlessly. Nobody else had seen Letty, on the night of her escape or since. The only people who knew for certain she had been alone on the road hereabouts at that particular time were her abductors and him. The only truth in Layton's claim was the fact Letty had been terrified. That, Jack had seen first-hand. Now he knew exactly who her abductors were, the need to cause Layton harm was visceral. But Letty's continued safety depended on his performance right this minute.

'Perhaps you had better come in, Mr Smith. Seeing as the rain has stopped, we can all search the outbuildings together.' For effect he called to his brothers. 'Joe, Jacob—fetch some lanterns. We need to go outside.' Jamie would guard Letty in his absence.

The three interlopers stood in the hallway and Jack did not leave their side until Joe and Jacob came to relieve him. Both had donned coats and serious expressions. Jamie limped behind them, his limp more pronounced for dramatic effect. As he had hoped, his brother knew exactly what do without Jack needing to explain. For good measure, Jamie behaved exactly like a Warriner was expected to behave.

'If she's in our barn, then she's ours until you pay us for her,' he said with an unpleasant leer.

Layton eyed him with hostility. 'Perhaps…'

'There's no perhaps about it. If she's there, none of us will let her leave without our pockets being filled with that five hundred pounds.'

Jack stepped in. 'Now, now, Jamie… We can discuss terms *if* we find her. I won't let them sell us short either. Follow me, gentlemen. If there is a reward due, we'd best get to it.'

They had trudged through the house noisily, their heavy boots echoing on the old wooden floor below, yet even when all she could hear was silence, Letty refused to move from her position on the landing. Hearing Layton's voice just a few scant feet away had rendered her almost frozen with fear.

'Go into your bedchamber, Letty. And for God's sake don't light a candle. Sit on the bed and don't move. We don't want that man hearing a sound from upstairs. He's a canny one. And no matter how much you are tempted to look, stay away from the blasted window as well. One of us will tell you when the coast is clear.' Jamie's hushed voice floated softly up the stairs and gave her some comfort. For a brief moment, when she had heard him talk so convincingly about wanting the reward money, she had wondered if he might betray her. Now she felt ashamed at the thought.

'Thank you, Jamie,' she whispered and did exactly as he said.

The minutes ticked by slowly. Occasionally, she saw the light of one of the lanterns reflected on the walls of her bedchamber or heard muffled male voices. One thing was for certain, the search was a thorough one. Letty did not know whether that was at Jack's insistence or Layton's, but she told herself it was a good thing. If their search proved fruitless, then they would surely be less inclined to come back.

After what felt like hours, she finally heard the men stomp back into the house, where their conversation continued until she was so jumpy and panicked she could barely hear the words over the noise of her pulse beating in her ears. Snippets of conversations wafted through.

'We will keep an eye out...'

Jack's voice. *'She might well be dead...'*

Jamie. *'Nobody could survive the elements for this long without shelter...'*

'Could she have found someone on the road travelling back towards London?' That came from Dr Joe.

They were putting doubts in Layton's mind. Even when she heard the front door creak open and heard it close firmly behind them again, she could still not bring herself to move from her position perched on the edge of the mattress. Jamie said one of them would come when it was safe, and right now, being safe was her only priority.

More silence stretched out ahead of her. When Letty thought she would die from the not knowing, she finally heard footsteps on the staircase and instinctively held her breath as they moved swiftly towards her door even though she knew, in her heart, they were friendly feet.

'It's me, Letty.' She slumped at the reassuring sound of Jack's voice and felt tears wet her cheeks as the door cracked open. 'They've left. Jacob and Joe have gone to secure the gates.' Fear had closed her throat, making a verbal response impossible, so she nodded slowly and tried to stand, only to find her knees would not support her either. 'Hey—don't cry.' He crossed the room in three long strides and sat down beside her on the mattress. 'I think we did a pretty good job of convincing them you weren't here. They should leave us alone now.'

Hearing Layton's voice again had reminded Letty of how precarious her situation still was. 'Th-thank you.' Her voice caught on the final syllable and to her complete horror she was unable to stem the flow of tears which were now pouring down her cheeks. When Jack wrapped one strong arm tightly around her shoulders and pulled her closer, she burrowed against his chest and wept, conscious of the fact she was behaving like a silly dolt, yet desperate for the comfort and protection he offered.

His other arm came around her and he rested his chin on the top of her head, rocking her slightly as he soothed her with gentle words. 'It's all right, sweetheart. You're safe now. I promise.'

Letty did feel safe with him, but still she could not stop crying. After the worst of the racking sobs had subsided, Letty tried to speak.

'I w-was having such a l-lovely evening—for a while I had f-forgotten about it all.' She had as well. Despite the disastrous dinner, the easy banter and the sense of camaraderie this evening had been something special. Letty could not remember ever feeling quite as comfortable anywhere, not even her private rooms in her house in Mayfair. For a while there she had been part of the family. Except they weren't her family. She was the interloper and they had generously taken her in out of the goodness of their hearts. Her only family member had sold her to a complete villain without so much as a by-your-leave, for his own financial gain. Letty was nothing but a healthy purse to him. And Bainbridge. The thought of him sent ice through her veins. They were hot on her heels and baying for blood.

Letty's blood.

She knew too much.

Jack must have seen the panic on her face. He cupped her cheek with his palm, swiping away the fresh tears she had not realised were still falling with his thumb. 'We knew they would come here at some point. Layton's visit was inevitable. If anything, I am angrier at myself. I should have known they would turn up as soon as the weather eased. When it stopped raining earlier, I should have insisted the gates be closed before we had dinner. But they came, and they are none the wiser. I doubt we will see them any time soon. You don't need to dwell on it for every second of every day, Letty.'

'But the threat is still very real, isn't it? They haven't given up. Even after a fortnight, they are still here. L-looking for me.' Fresh tears threatened, but she ruthlessly fought against them. Self-pity was not going to keep her alive. Crumbling in Jack's capable arms would only ever bring her temporary relief as well. In a few weeks, she would have to return to London and use the power of the law to bring her uncle and Bainbridge to justice. Then she would be alone again in her big house in Mayfair, where there were no noisy males to laugh with and nobody who cared one whit about the real her. Funny, a fortnight ago, she had never wanted to leave London. Now, she could scarcely imagine wanting to go back.

Letty moved to sit upright, but Jack's arms tightened around her protectively and held her so close, she could feel the steady beat of his heart against her own ribcage so she allowed herself this brief moment of comfort. Her own heart swelled and tried to match its rhythm, as if they were meant to beat together in harmony. She felt his warm breath in her hair. 'They still have no idea what happened to you or where you are. I will keep you safe, sweetheart, in whatever way is necessary, for as long as it takes.'

Letty melted against him, needing the contact. However, it was not only the comfort of his arms she craved. Being held by Jack Warriner was a heady experience. He was so big and solid. Commanding. When he said he would keep her safe, she believed him. Time and time again he had proved himself to be trustworthy. Loyal. Kind in his own brooding way. And she liked it when he called her sweetheart. Perhaps far more than she should. Letty tilted her head back to gaze up at him. 'I can't stay here for ever, Jack. Can I?' Please tell me I never have to leave, she thought, hoping he would hear her. Because suddenly, staying here with Jack felt like exactly the right thing to do. She belonged here.

Didn't she?

She certainly felt more herself here than she did in any of the London ballrooms. There, she had to be Violet Dunston, wealthy society beauty, but somehow separate from the proceedings. Human contact was transient, meaningless. The world only saw the confident heiress, not the lonely, uncertain girl beneath. The one who had no one who really loved her, yet everyone believed they knew her because they had read so much about her. Letty had read those same accounts, bemused. She did not recognise the frivolous, but much-emulated creature they wrote about, the girl whose concept of fashion was exquisite. Who danced like an angel floating on air. Whose laugh was like the gentle tinkling of a stream. However, the more nonsense she read about her mythical self, the more Letty pathetically tried to live up to the ideals. More and more new dresses, elaborate hairstyles, honing her skills at flirtation or eyelash fluttering and practising her laughter in the mirror so that the sound of it in public did not disappoint. At best, she had become a spectator to her own life, more concerned about what others thought than being true to herself.

And all for what? A bunch of acquaintances who never thought to look past the façade? All of them far more impressed with her money than with the girl. It was laughable, how empty her privileged existence actually was. Internally, she craved a life enriched with love and genuine purpose, not money, yet she played to the gallery regardless. The Duke of Wentworth was actively courting her, yet he had no idea he was courting Violet

Dunston the *Tea Heiress*, and not her, Letty, at all. She had not even sought his opinions on her grand plans to create a foundling home. Why not? Did she really care if he disapproved? Or was she as indifferent to the perfect Duke as she was to her empty shell of a perfect life? Things she would happily walk away from as soon as she took control of her fortune and began her life properly.

Here she was Letty. Nobody cared if her hair wasn't correctly dressed or if she snorted when she laughed or failed disastrously at cooking. Being part of this family was wonderful. Bizarrely, being the butt of their jokes was also wonderful and already she dreaded leaving them. Her life in Mayfair would feel sterile in comparison. But she dreaded leaving Jack the most.

There was something about him which drew her and tugged at her heart more than any man ever had before. When she was with Jack, she could scarcely remember what the Duke of Wentworth looked like. That was hardly a surprise when Jack Warriner was quite the most spectacular specimen of a man she had ever encountered—but it was more than just his good looks that enticed her. Everything about him appealed to the woman within and his sense of duty went above and beyond. Even now, despite all of his many heavy responsibilities, he was trying to take away her pain and fear by absorbing it himself. Making her problems his and asking nothing in return.

How utterly romantic was that?

Without thinking, Letty snuggled her cheek against his chest contentedly and sighed. Except, the sigh sounded more like a groan of pleasure than an expression of relief. Probably because being held by him *was* pleasurable. In his arms, she felt dainty and womanly—while he was just so manly and strong. Letty allowed her hand to snake up to rest on his chest, splaying her fingers so that her palm could touch more of his body in one go and revelling in the solid feel of him. Wanting even more.

They stayed like that for almost a minute, just holding each other, until something shifted in the atmosphere between them. His eyes were still locked with hers, but his breathing was shallower. Next to her his heartbeat was quicker and she suspected hers was, too. She watched his Adam's apple bob as he swallowed warily and realised it was she who made him wary. Not Layton or Bainbridge. Her.

He was not immune to this intense attraction

either, yet he held himself rigid, maintaining the small distance between them because, despite his rough edges, he was a proper gentleman who would never take advantage of her. Yet Letty desperately wanted him to. Her arms brazenly wound her way around his neck and she watched his eyes darken. He stared down at her for several long seconds without releasing his tight hold on her, his mouth hovering only a few inches away from hers, giving her hope that he also felt the intense pull of desire she did, that she had not imagined the tension between them when he had lowered her from the chandelier, but then his blue eyes became stormy. His features troubled. Another minute and their perfect moment of connection would be gone. She was damned if she would let that happen again. Letty closed the distance between them and pressed her lips softly to his.

He'd almost kissed her. It took every ounce of willpower Jack possessed not to claim her mouth with his and demand she never leave him when he had thought he'd heard her ask to stay. Letty belonged here. In his house. In his bedchamber. In his arms…but common sense intervened. The girl was overwrought and understandably scared for her life. Taking advantage of her while she was this upset would make him the lowest of the low. No better than the vile Warriners of old and his father in particular. A man who had compromised a vulnerable heiress to get his hands on her fortune. Jack sincerely doubted anyone would believe he was not a chip off the old block if he actively pursued his attraction to Letty. She did not belong here—her real life was in London and it was the sort of life so far removed from his own that to fool himself she would seriously consider staying in this house, with him, was beyond even the realms of fantasy.

Jack had been about to put some distance between them, for his own heart's safety, because he feared the yearning he experienced was threatening to burst forth, leaving him exposed and vulnerable, and doomed to be in receipt of her pity. Then miraculously, it had been Letty who had kissed him and, like a starving man at a banquet, all his body could do was satisfy the physical need which had consumed him from the first moment he had seen those bare legs displayed beneath the hem of his shirt.

One gentle brushing of lips was never going to be enough to sustain him for a lifetime, so

Jack kissed her again with more urgency than he had intended, pouring all of the unexpected tenderness he felt for her into it until the emotion threatened to choke him. It made his mouth more passionate than it should have been, a kiss that should have terrified an innocent like Letty. Yet she met his lips with the same enthusiasm, winding her arms tightly around his neck as he hauled her into his lap roughly and dragged her womanly body flush against his. Because he had to, Jack buried his fingers in her hair, sliding off the ribbon which bound it back until the riotous curls sprang free.

When he felt the seam of her mouth relax, the kiss became more carnal. He explored her mouth thoroughly with his tongue and teeth and then trailed heated kisses along her throat, surprised by her needy passion and revelling in the way she arched against him in mindless desire. Through the soft, worn linen of the matching shirts they both wore, he recognised the pebbled hardness of her nipples against his body and found his hands stroking up the side of her ribcage in search of better contact. Letty did not appear to mind his presumptuousness. If anything, she welcomed it. As his hand cupped one soft swell reverently, she pressed it urgently against his palm and purred with satisfaction. Her own hands tugged his shirt from the waistband of his breeches, then burrowed underneath the fabric to stroke the skin on his back.

Blinded by another surge of desire, he eased her back on to the mattress and allowed his mouth to trail moist, searing kisses across her collarbone, then down on to the upper swells of those lush breasts. Her ribcage was rising and falling rapidly and she sighed his name with her eyelids closed, her head writhing against the sheets with each impertinent flick of his tongue. Jack's fingers pushed the fabric aside and touched her properly. Her puckered nipple hardened further when his thumb grazed it. Simultaneously, the motion caused his groin to tighten more and he kissed her deeply to hide his own needy moan. God, he wanted to be buried inside her. Deep inside her, branding her as his for ever.

'I've made some tea—shall I bring it up?' Joe's voice in the hallway below dragged him abruptly and painfully back to reality. Jack sat back, panting, only to see Letty sprawled wantonly across his bed, her hair fanned out around her head, one perfect, aroused breast bared to his hungry gaze and her desire-darkened green eyes as wide as saucers.

'No need!' he called, hoping the panic was not audible in his voice. The bedchamber door was wide open. Anybody could have seen what he had done, the full, shocking extent of how he had greedily and shamelessly taken advantage of a frightened woman in his care. He was no better than his hateful father after all. 'We are coming down now.'

As Letty had not already done so, Jack pulled the neckline of the shirt upwards to cover her modesty and tried to make sense of what had just happened. If Joe had not called out, he wouldn't have stopped. Now that he had, reason *had* to replace desire. What had just happened, should never have happened. He had put his own selfish needs above Letty's. Hadn't he?

Although she had instigated the kiss and she was smiling at him shyly. Perhaps she really did want him? If she wanted him, too, then maybe this kiss was the start of something. He glanced back at Letty, only to see her smile had gone and she was hastily tying her hair back with the ribbon. She did not meet his gaze. Did that mean she regretted it? Or was it that she was only equally as horrified as he at the prospect that they might have been caught? Jack sincerely hoped it was the latter because the glimmer of hope that she might, miraculously want him—*him!*—as much as he wanted her was overwhelming and too ridiculous to give credence to.

Except such unruly thoughts were as impractical as her reciprocating his feelings in the long term was improbable. Aside from the fact that only the biggest of cads would try to take advantage of a woman who was as distraught as Letty currently was, Jack had nothing to offer her. Nothing positive at least.

He could offer her a life of misery and of being shunned by society as his father had his mother, he supposed, or he could doom her to an eternity with a man who was as suspicious of love as the world was of a Warriner. Hadn't he seen first-hand how such a marriage could destroy a woman? Jack would not follow in his father's footsteps and simply take what he wanted, and to hell with the consequences. Letty deserved more than that. She was bright and resourceful, tenacious and charming, and so beautiful it made the air catch in his lungs every time he saw her.

Yes, she might well have been staring at him as

if he were her knight in shining armour a few moments ago, clinging to him and tempting him to
kiss her because she was desperate, so very frightened and he was the only one here. But he also
had to remember she had just been crying like a
baby in his arms beforehand. He had felt her fear
as he had held her and knew she had nobody else
to turn to except him and, under difficult circumstances, people rarely thought straight. That fact
he also knew well. After the death of her parents,
hadn't his own mother mistakenly believed herself to be in love with his father the moment she
had met him, when it had really only ever been
lust tinged with loneliness? She had ended up ruined, then embittered and resentful for ever afterwards because she had confused one powerful
emotion for another one. Such was the inevitable
way of things.

Jack watched Letty lick her plump, kiss-swollen
lips and wondered, fleetingly if she had actually
wanted him to kiss her or if, like his mother, she
had simply needed someone to be there for her.
She had unmistakeably enjoyed his kiss. He had
seen and felt her earthy response to his touch. Perhaps the very fact their kiss had turned incendi-

ary the moment it had started was a sign that she felt more for him than simple gratitude.

For a brief moment, Jack allowed hope to bloom again and then he banished the thought angrily. He was confusing Letty's obvious gratitude for an invitation, when the poor girl was terrified out of her wits. It was then that he knew if he stayed here with her for much longer, his resolve to do the right thing would disintegrate. It was sobering to realise there was more of his father in him than he had believed. The temptation to bolt the bed-chamber door and kiss her again superseded all thoughts and took every ounce of determination to ignore. But he *had* to be the responsible one. Letty was so full of life and laughter. He would not be the one to kill those lovable traits with the cold, hard truth of an eternity stuck with him, here in this demoralising place.

Of course, she would initially make the best of it because that was the way she was made, but month after month, year after year, her effervescence would diminish and the light in her lovely green eyes would dim. Letty belonged in society where she could sparkle. He had to do the right thing and nip this in the bud now for her sake, before real, irreparable damage was done.

'Tonight has been a bit of an ordeal, hasn't it? Neither one of us is thinking straight.' Jack passed her his handkerchief and watched a myriad of emotions play across her expression. One looked like confusion, another disappointment, and he could have sworn he thought he saw desire, although he could well have been mapping his own desires on to her. Wishful thinking? He just didn't know any more. In the end, she stared right at him and frowned.

'Not thinking straight? I am not a silly girl, Jack, if that is what you are implying.'

'I know you are not a silly girl. You are a frightened girl, which under the odd circumstances of this evening is perfectly understandable. And fear can unsettle us.' Jack was definitely unsettled and currently terrified that the part of him which was like his father would win. She was still frowning.

'So you are saying what we just did happened only because you think I was unsettled?' Now he heard anger, too.

'What I mean is, in view of everything that has happened, it would be inadvisable to confuse one charged emotional state with another. Kissing me is not going to make the dangerous situation we find ourselves in any better, nor is it advisable.

We both know it was nothing more than a silly mistake on your part.'

'A silly mistake.' Her tone could have curdled milk. 'On *my* part.'

He smiled as best as he could at her admission, even though he had secretly hoped she would disagree with his practical logic. At least now he had made her understand what had really made her kiss him, his conscience would be clear. Almost. 'I would prefer to pretend it never happened.' While he would cherish the memory of their kiss, the last thing he wanted was for Letty to feel awkward around him. He would feel awkward enough for both of them. And disappointed. And perhaps even a little heartbroken.

'I see.'

She wasn't looking at him again, therefore he had no idea whether she agreed with his assessment of their current situation of not. She rummaged on the bedside table for the elaborately embroidered handkerchief he had found her with that fateful night and watched her clean her face with it, then tried to smile back at him bravely. Clearly she was grateful he had extricated them out of a potentially awkward situation and was relieved to be able to pretend nothing was amiss, although the knowledge did not bring him any relief.

He had kissed her. Intimately. And not only in the physical sense. His strange, powerful feelings for her had been poured into the kiss as well. If she'd have had more experience of a man's kisses, she would now know he felt more for her than just passion. Jack had been so caught up in the moment, so caught up in the idea of him and her together, he had never wanted it to end. Even now, he felt uncharacteristically unsteady and shaken. Letty, on the other hand, was definitely *not* still reeling from the intensity of the unexpected emotional and physical bonding. She appeared to have recovered her equilibrium without much effort at all. Further confirmation he had done the right thing—if perhaps a little insulting.

'How terrible do I look?'

Not nearly terrible enough to stop his body's yearnings. 'Nobody would know you had been crying.' Jack held out his hand and tried to ignore how perfect hers felt clasped in his. She was a damsel in distress and a true knight in shining armour would put aside his own feelings for the sake of hers. Theirs could only ever be the sort of courtly love from a bygone era. Jack was her protector, nothing more. She was a princess. 'Please try not to worry about those men any more. One way or another I will get you home safely, Letty. You have my word.' He pulled her up to stand next to him and then forced himself to let go of her hand. 'Until then, you will remain here. With me.'

God help him.

Chapter Thirteen

Fifteen days and thirteen hours remaining...

With only four days to go till Christmas Eve, Letty was determined to get into the spirit of the Season despite everything that was presently wrong with her life. Even if one put aside the trials and tribulations of an uncle who had betrayed you and a gnarly old earl who intended to wed by you by force, then potentially kill you for your money, or the sad fact that not one of the London newspapers Jacob read so avidly had printed any story suggesting she was missing or so much as *missed*, there were more pressing matters which Letty found vexing. All of them involved the eldest Warriner and her stupid, pointless feelings for him.

Why Letty was so besotted with the surly brute, she could not say. He was nothing like the man she had promised herself she would fall in love with. Not that she was in love with Jack, of course. Only a fool would develop such a powerful emotion for a man who largely behaved as if she didn't exist. Ever since their kiss five days ago, he had either avoided being left alone with her, or treated her like somebody suffering from a delusional mental state. Yes, he was polite and more sociable than he had been. When he was accompanied by any one of his brothers, he laughed and chatted to her as if she were one of them. But if she tried to corner him on his own he bolted. On that fateful night, he had dismissed her one and only attempt at seduction as merely being a weakness of the mind brought about wholly because she had been distraught. As if she, Letty Dunston, thwarter of kidnappers and now master baker, was even capable of behaving like such a ninny.

To save face, she had turned into Violet once more and gone along with it, when in truth his speedy about-turn from ardent, passionate lover to patronising, overbearing protector had hurt. Letty had kissed Jack because her body had told her to, because being held in his arms had made her forget about Layton, Bainbridge and the danger she was in. Because it simply felt *right*. And not, as he had oh-so-reasonably stated, because she had been in a *charged emotional state*, brought about by fear. She had been in a charged emotional state all right, only it had been brought about by being in such close, intoxicating proximity to *him*.

And to make matters worse, and perhaps even more galling than being chastised like a child for wanting something she couldn't have, was the sorry fact that she *still* wanted him. Body and soul. Every loyal, upstanding, brave solid inch of him. He had pushed her away and then, to her utter mortification, informed her he would rather pretend it hadn't happened. Letty was so angry at him, and so utterly demoralised and humiliated by his rejection, that five days had done nothing to close the wound. Yet barely an hour of the day went by when she didn't remember how marvellous it had felt to have his mouth and hands on her. Or to have her hands on him. She had never behaved in such a scandalously wanton manner—but acknowledged honestly to herself that she happily would again.

With him.

Any time that he saw fit!

Angry and frustrated in equal measure, Letty stared down at the bread dough on the table in front of her. After her disastrous Fowl à la Braise, and after failing so spectacularly as a seductress, conquering *The Art of Cookery Made Plain and Simple* had become something of a mission. Everything in her life might well be miserable in the here and now, but she could at least learn to make bread. Punching the air out of the soft dough gave her some satisfaction and she continued to pummel it, imagining it was Jack Warriner's handsome, patronising, kissable face.

If he were a normal gentleman, he would be flattered by her interest. In Mayfair, suitors had been queuing up to catch her eye. Some handsome, almost all titled and eligible. It was rare a day went by without a bouquet arriving from one of her admirers, complimenting her on her beauty, charm and wit. Any one of them would have been thrilled if she had kissed them—not that she had ever wanted to kiss any of them. But when the patronising, supercilious, condescending Jack looked at her, all he saw was an emotionally feeble girl with an addled mind, so of course, the *responsible* thing to do was to pretend it hadn't happened or avoid her like the plague. Nobody had ever avoided her before—and certainly not someone she had a soft spot for. Yet despite his annoyingly patriarchal manner and apparent immunity to her charms, Letty still had a particularly soft spot for the vexing man. When she didn't feel the overwhelming urge to kiss him, she simply wanted to hold him and talk to him. Be there for him as he was for her. Ease his many burdens.

From the sounds beyond the back door, and the way her traitorous skin tingled, the vexing man himself was back from the village. Irritated at the realisation her body now apparently sensed his presence before her eyes did, Letty continued to ferociously knead her bread dough and did not do him the courtesy of looking up as he burst through the door.

'You're back then,' she said with her eyes fixed on her dough.

She heard him and Jamie take off their greatcoats and shake the rain out of their hair like a pair of wet dogs.

'They've gone—Layton and his men.' This came from Jamie, never one to mince his words or over-embellish a sentence with more words than were absolutely necessary. Letty did look up then.

'Gone where?'

Jack shrugged. 'Bound for London, we believe.

Three weeks of fruitless searching, constant rain and the rapid approach of Christmas have forced them to give up. The innkeeper said they paid their bill in full and passed on a forwarding address in Mayfair in case anyone heard anything interesting.' He thrust a piece of paper at her and she stared down at the address dispassionately. She had been expecting to see her uncle's address— *her* address—and she was not disappointed. She hardly needed further proof of his treachery.

'Do you think they will come back?'

His blue eyes flicked briefly towards hers. Obviously, even looking at her for short periods of time was something he found distasteful. 'Hard to say. The reward is now a thousand pounds, so even with them gone, finding you is a massive temptation for the locals. Except now the reward is for any information that leads to your whereabouts or the discovery of a body…so perhaps they have given up hope that you're even still alive.'

'Well, my uncle will be in for a surprise when I turn up on my birthday then, won't he? You must be relieved, Jack. You only have to suffer through another two weeks of my burdensome company.' Letty was not sure what sort of reaction she had been expecting from that harshly delivered statement, but with hindsight, she supposed she should have anticipated stony indifference. Jack did stony indifference so well.

'I'm going to chop some wood.' He stalked to the door and retrieved his sodden coat from the peg. The door slammed behind him and Letty punched the dough again, feeling decidedly shaky and thoroughly upset. Jamie limped around the table to sit opposite her and stared.

'Have you two had an argument?'

'Of course not, to have an argument, one would actually have to converse in private. In case it has escaped your notice, your brother prefers to avoid me.'

'He has been absent quite a bit lately. And now that I think upon it, he's been rather quiet. For him. Clearly you bring out the worst in him.' His mouth quirked in an approximation of a smile.

'I am well aware he doesn't like me, Jamie.'

'Oh, I wouldn't say that…'

Letty snorted her disbelief. 'I would! Of course he doesn't like me. Aside from that one night… when Layton turned up here…we have scarcely exchanged any words which were not completely necessary or spoken across the dinner table.'

'The night Layton turned up, you say? Wasn't that the night the pair of you kissed?'

Letty's head shot up and she felt the beginnings of a blush stain her cheeks. 'He told you about that!'

Jamie tried to act innocent and then grinned. '*He* never said a word—*he* didn't have to. I have eyes. Even a short-sighted fool with no sense could have worked out what the pair of you had been up to that night. You both arrived downstairs looking rumpled, couldn't meet each other's eyes and had those swollen mouths that only come from some serious—'

'Stop!' Her cheeks were now positively steaming so she covered them with her hands. Not much got past Jack's intuitive brother. 'Does everybody know?'

He shrugged. 'Hard to say. We haven't spoken about it—but they have eyes, too.'

This was awful. 'Oh! I feel like such an idiot.'

'Don't. Jack is a big boy. If you didn't want to be kissed, you had a right to put a stop to it.'

'What?'

'Well, I assumed from his odd mood, longing glances and solitary tendencies you refused his advances.' His blue eyes, so like his older brother's, but not as addictive to her, narrowed as he scrutinised her. 'Am I wrong?'

Letty stared down at the floor, willing it to open up and swallow her whole. When it didn't, she covered her face with her hands again so that Jamie would not see her shame. 'I kissed him. *He* was the one who put a stop to it.' As she had always suspected, when you put aside her fortune, there was nothing particularly special about her.

This statement was met with silence. After several moments, Letty peeked out between her fingers to gauge his reaction. Instead of looking amused at her confession, Jamie appeared exasperated. 'My brother has a very distinct sense of right and wrong. And it usually works to the detriment of himself.'

'What is that supposed to mean?' she asked curiously.

'Jack will always blame himself or put himself last. He always *has* to be responsible.'

'You are talking in riddles, Jamie. Whatever it is you clearly feel the urge to say, I wish you would just say it and be done with it. I am already completely mortified. With any luck, any further shame will result in my immediate death from it.'

'For goodness sake, Letty! For a beautiful woman you can be daft sometimes. Did *he* put a stop to it immediately?' Of course he hadn't. If he had, then she would not have had to deal with the shame of knowing he'd seen her bare breast. Touched it. At the time, she had hoped he would very much want to kiss it, too. 'I shall judge from your colourful reaction, that things developed into a bit more than a chaste kiss.'

In the absence of anyone else to confide in, Jamie, it seemed, would have to do. 'Jack said I was in a *charged emotional state*, brought about by fear due to Layton.'

'And were you?'

'Not at that precise moment, no.'

Jamie stood awkwardly and began to limp out of the kitchen, their uncomfortable conversation now obviously at an end. What was it with the Warriner men that they were happy to leave so many important things unsaid? She pouted. 'So that is it, is it? I bare my soul and you walk away.'

'I assumed you were off to the barn.'

'And why would I go there?'

Jamie sighed and raised his eyes heavenwards. 'I'd have thought it was obvious.' She watched his retreating back as he disappeared down the hall, but still heard his parting words as they drifted back to her. 'My principled brother is clearly as daft as you are.'

The log split with a satisfying sound. Only two more weeks to go. Two weeks and she would be back where she belonged, being courted by her rich Duke and robed in her missing finery. Then Jack would be spared the torture of seeing her every day. Perhaps then he would finally locate the peace of mind which was currently evading him.

He would take her back to London, they would say a stilted, awkward goodbye, and then he would head back here where he belonged. And as long as he never read one of Jacob's blasted newspapers, he would never again be confronted with the temptation she presented. For the sake of certainty, Jack would even speak to Jacob and warn him never to tell him any news about her. All talk of Letty would be forbidden from that day forth, so Jack could properly banish her from his mind. The very last thing he ever wanted to hear was a story about Letty marrying her wealthy, powerful Duke. He didn't want to have to picture her in another man's arms, in the full throes of passion, making those arousing, sensual noises she made and pushing her perfect, bare breasts greedily into another man's filthy hands.

The axe came down on the next log with such force it embedded itself in the ground and, for a moment, he experienced a raw surge of hatred for the faceless Duke he had never met. A man who, in all probability, never had filthy hands. Whoever he was, however much money the man had, and however clean his hands were, he did not deserve Letty. But then again, neither did Jack. Therefore, all of this effort he was putting into yearning, and being consumed with irrational jealousy, would be better directed elsewhere—and perhaps, in view of the wall of chopped logs stacked neatly along one whole side of the barn, he would do better to vent his frustration elsewhere as well. At this rate, they wouldn't need wood for several months. Another week and there would be no more trees left on his land.

He heard the barn door creak open behind him and turned. Then wished he hadn't.

'Can we talk?'

Typically, like the uncivilised savage he was, he had discarded his coat and waistcoat again. He was sure the sight of him sweating from exertion in only his shirt was offensive. And he probably should have shaved this morning as well. Her Duke would have shaved. 'If you want.' Which Jack certainly didn't. He placed another round log upright on the floor and swung the axe again. If he kept busy, remained aloof, she would leave quicker.

'Why don't you like me?'

The next stroke was off, splintering through the bark and sending the log rolling towards her legs. If he went to retrieve it, he would have to offend her nostrils with the scent of honest labour. If he began chopping a new piece of wood, he would look like he was scared to go near her. Neither option appealed, so he leaned his forearms on the axe handle and tried to appear bored.

'Letty—I have work to do. I don't have the time to flatter your ego. When you go back to London, I'm sure there are plenty of gentlemen there who will fall over themselves to tell you how wonderful you are.'

'I don't care about their opinions. I want yours. And I don't want you to spare my feelings. What is it about me that you find so distasteful?'

'I think you are imagining things.'

'And I think you are patronising me and doing

your level best to avoid answering my question. Why don't you like me, Jack? Do you find me irritating? Am I huge burden? Or do you think me silly and empty headed? Or perhaps you find me unappealing. And if that is the case, why did you kiss me back?'

Chapter Fourteen

Fifteen days and twelve hours to go...

Letty had gradually edged closer towards him and reached out to touch his arm. 'Does the sight of me disgust you?' Because she had to know. No matter how difficult it was to hear, she had to know why Jack had recoiled from her that night the very moment he had come to his senses.

'Of course not!' He looked and sounded outraged. 'I thought we agreed to pretend it never happened.'

'But it did happen and now you cannot even look at me without wincing.' He stubbornly stared back at her, but she saw the slight flinch anyway. 'There it is! You're doing it again. Just admit you can't stand me.'

'Oh, for goodness sake!' He raked one hand impatiently through his overlong dark hair and huffed out a sigh of complete exasperation. 'The thing is…I like you well enough. It's just after what we did, it makes things awkward.' He was resolutely staring at his folded hands on the axe handle. 'It shouldn't have happened, Letty. Everything about it was wrong.'

It. He couldn't even say the word kiss. That did not instil her with confidence in her abilities as a temptress. Automatically, her fingers went to her lips as she tried to recall exactly where she had gone wrong. 'Did I do it incorrectly? Was I too brazen?' Those intense blue eyes almost popped out of their sockets as he glared at her, then quickly looked away to hide his reaction, giving her all the answer she needed. 'Oh, my goodness! I *was* too brazen. I'm sorry, Jack—I don't have much experience of kissing and…well…kissing you was more than a little bit overwhelming.' Letty had the urge to cover her breasts with her hands because he'd seen them, or at least one of them. Her hands flapped ineffectually in the vicinity of them, causing his eyes to widen even more, so, swamped with shame and self-loathing, she covered her face with them instead. 'I behaved like a hussy, didn't I?'

There was a long, loaded pause. The only sounds

filling the silence were the laboured sounds of Jack's breathing as he tried to think of a polite way to tell her she had disgusted him with her shamelessness. Letty heard him move towards the hay bales and lower himself heavily on to one of them. It sounded as if he was trying to calm his breathing by inhaling deeply.

'No, you didn't. Please don't think you did anything wrong. I just… God, this is awkward.' Jack sounded as miserable as she felt. She risked a glance at him and saw his expression appear completely wretched as well, sat there with his hands tucked underneath his thighs, his posture rigid. 'You are under my care, Letty. I cannot protect you properly if my mind is elsewhere. Does that make sense?'

'And kissing me sends your mind elsewhere?'

'Kissing you sends me out of my mind, woman! I'm only human.'

Although it was a pretty compliment, he did not appear to be particularly happy about it. Carefully, she moved towards the bale and sat down next to him. 'Kissing you sent me out of my mind, too, Jack. If we both feel the same way about it, surely that is a good thing?'

He shot her an odd look through half-hooded

eyes and shook his head decisively. 'It's lust, Letty. Pure, raw, human lust. Nothing more. Don't try to rationalise it as anything else.'

'It could be…' He stayed her with his hand.

'No, Letty. It couldn't.' He shook his head again and sighed. When he next spoke, he did so kindly, as if to a child. Or a woman with an addled mind who struggled to see the nose on her own face. 'I won't lie to you and pretend it could lead any-where, even though doing so would be in my best financial interest and would completely benefit me in the long run. Once the lust is spent, Letty, there would be nothing left between us and I re-spect you too much to ruin your life like that. If things had gone any further the other night, we would have had to marry, and once you realised the truth, you would quickly have come to regret it. We Warriners are not good with wives.'

Well, that killed her blossoming hope stone dead, swiftly and clinically.

An emphatic no.

No maybe. No perhaps. No hesitation. Just no. He desired her body, albeit temporarily, but not her. Whilst the rejection cut like a knife in her gut, at least he was honest. There were no games with Jack Warriner. 'I suppose I should thank you for your principles. Most men of my acquaintance would have happily ruined me in order to marry me.'

'I dare say they would happily marry you before ruining you, too. You are a beautiful woman.'

'I doubt they truly notice my face. My looks, nor my character, hardly matter when I come with such an enormous mountain of money.' Letty stood despondently and walked towards the door. At least being desired for only her body was marginally more palatable than just her purse. There was something about her that Jack found attractive, even if the idea of spending a lifetime with her was wholly unappealing. His passion and desire had been genuine. He simply knew he could never love her enough to spend a lifetime with her.

'You are being too hard on yourself. I am informed you are courted by all manner of worthy men. Even a wealthy duke. Once I return you safely home, you will see things with clarity again. You belong in Mayfair with a man like him, with your fancy clothes and an army of servants. I don't mean to hurt your feelings, Letty. I am simply being a pragmatist. You have a particular life to live and so do I. Your life is in London, at parties and soirées, surrounded by your admirers, and mine is here, and that is how it should be. You were not born to be a Nottinghamshire farmer's wife any more than I could pretend to enjoy the superficial conversation of the privileged.'

He smiled, as if it could soften the blow he had just dealt her. 'The trouble with our current situation is that everything is exaggerated. We have been thrust together, when under normal circumstances our paths would never have crossed. But they did, under an extreme set of conditions where our emotions are heightened and everything feels intense. But it's not real, Letty. We are like oil and water, you and I. No matter how hard we tried, we could never mix.'

More painful honesty that threw salt on her already gaping wound. She should have ignored Jamie and continued pummelling her bread dough. At least then she had been only angry and confused. Now she felt truly bereft, spoiled and insignificant. *Superficial*. The first time she had made tentative advances towards a man she actually trusted, a good man who would not take her money, and humbled herself by suggesting that there could be more between them because she had *wanted* there to be more between them, and her worst fears were confirmed. When the lure of her fortune was stripped away, Letty really had nothing except a pretty face going for her. It was a hard, cruel way to learn that lesson.

Letty lingered in the doorway, tempted to tell him that there was more to her. That she had plans to help people with her money. Make the lives of lonely orphans, like her, easier. Make a difference because she hated the parties, soirées and disingenuous admirers—but she knew he wouldn't listen. Like her uncle, he did not think her capable of such depth so she painted on one of Violet's sunniest, emotionally vapid smiles. The one which told the world she was perfectly comfortable with a situation and had already forgotten why she had been bothered by it in the first place. 'You are probably right. The circumstances we find ourselves in are somewhat unique. Thank goodness you are so sensible.' She only had to survive for two, interminable weeks in his company, then she could go home and lick her wounds in private. Immerse all of her frustration and passion in the poor foundlings and prove everyone wrong about her. Including him. It was cold comfort. For the first time since she had arrived at Markham Manor, Letty wanted to leave.

'I suppose we should begin to plan how I am to

safely return to London now that the Earl of Bainbridge has seemingly given up his search here. I don't want to walk straight into a waiting trap—and I suspect that will be their next plan of action in this whole ghastly mess.'

Jack, understandably, appeared greatly relieved by her change of subject. 'Yes...definitely. Why don't we all discuss it over dinner tonight?' He retrieved the fallen log from the floor and placed it end up on the ground, effectively dismissing her from his presence with the gesture. He was already swinging his axe before she closed the door behind her.

The loud explosion made the windows rattle while the accompanying burst of lightning lit up the bedchamber with the mouldy walls. Jack forced his exhausted, sleep-numbed mind to focus as he sat bolt upright in the bed he'd slept in ever since Letty had recovered enough not to need him to sleep on her floor. The leadlight glass sounded as if it was being pelted with handful after handful of gravel. He came to rapidly, blinking hard to squeeze blurriness from his eyes, then padded to the window and yanked open the heavy curtains to squint outside and groaned.

The storm that raged was one of the most ferocious Jack had ever witnessed. He could just make out the shapes of trees in the darkness, their branches bent over from the power of the wind. Rain fell in sheets rather than drops, pouring down the window pane like a waterfall. Another clap of thunder rumbled ominously, closely followed by the blinding light of a mighty fork of lightning. It split the sky and briefly, terrifyingly, illuminated the swollen banks of the river. So swollen now, the trees on the top of the steeply inclined bank were standing in a foot or more of boiling, furious water.

Another handful of gravel hit the window and he realised it was hail. Only small hail, but enough to panic the sheep, who were probably already panicked quite enough by the wind, rain, thunder and lightning. If they ran for the cover of the trees near the river bank, the stupid animals would likely be swept away on the current. And there he had been, less than an hour or so ago, praying for something, anything, which would take his mind off Letty and allow him to finally get some undisturbed sleep. There was nothing like the threat of impending doom and the prospect of several hours outside battling against the elements to distract him from his unwanted, but incessant, thoughts about her.

Jack was in the process of buttoning the falls on his hastily dragged-on breeches when Jamie stepped through his door. 'Good. You're up.'

As his brother was already wearing his greatcoat, it was fair to assume that Jamie, as usual, had not bothered going to bed. 'Have you woken Joe and Jacob yet?' Jack tugged on one boot as he hopped on the spot before collapsing to sit back on the bed to pull on the other.

'They're dressing, too. I'll meet you downstairs.'

Less than a minute later, Jack strode on to the landing, only to be confronted by the sight of Letty looking deliciously sleep rumpled at her door. She had only opened the door enough to poke her head around, but Jack saw the tantalising glimpse of a female leg where it poked beneath the hem of yet another one of his shirts and the sight irritated him. The blasted woman was handy with a needle. She had started embroidering little patterns on everything from napkins to pillowcases. Weeks ago, she had begun making a dress—which was still not finished—so why could she not fashion herself a proper nightdress? One that came to the floor and covered all of her soft, silken skin. And while she was about it, she should probably plait the wild, golden riot of curls that hung past her shoulders and tempted him to touch. An ugly nightcap would not go amiss either.

'What's happening?' she asked.

'There's a storm. We need to round up the animals. Go back to bed Letty. You're in no danger.'

'I can help.'

Jack was in no mood to be tactful. 'No, you can't. Go back to bed.'

The storm would take his mind off her; he didn't need the additional burden of an heiress faffing about and getting in his way when he had a serious job to do. He saw her fine eyes narrow just before she slammed the door shut and he turned away, striding briskly to the stairs. It was just as well. If she had argued with him, he would have bitten back twice as hard. Lack of sleep always brought his temper close to the surface and, as Letty was responsible for the deficiency, he doubted any confrontation would end well tonight. Not after their splendid chat in the barn earlier, when she had thanked him for being so sensible, then blithely gone about her day as if the words he had wrenched out of his gut and choked hollowly out of his mouth had not sounded the death knell on all his secret hopes of a miracle.

She might have argued then, as she was prone to when she heartily disagreed with something, and perhaps given some credence to the idea that their two worlds could merge if they both wanted them to. But of course she hadn't. Only a tiny part of him had expected her to—a part which he hadn't even realised existed until he had categorically listed for her all the reasons why there was nothing except lust between them. Even as he said the words he knew them to be false. What he felt for Letty was more than just desire. He genuinely admired her tenacity and her sunny disposition. Her indomitable spirit. The woman never let anything beat her, whether that be kidnappers or roasted chickens. And since the very first moment he had found her frozen and terrified in the road, a part of his jaded, wary, Warriner heart would always be hers. Yearned to be hers. Maybe those rash feelings were due to his customary and ever-present sense of responsibility—but if that was entirely the case, why, when he had held her chilled body in his arms that night, had her presence in them felt so very…right?

If only she had been a random, ordinary girl of

no consequence instead of The Tea Heiress. Then maybe he would have stood a chance and taken a gamble. It didn't help knowing, thanks to hours of rifling through Jacob's collection of newspapers when nobody was looking, that when the newsmen wrote the words *Tea Heiress* they were always put in italics, as if she were so special, so above everyone else, that only a select few in society were on a par with her. Now he knew her, he realised they were right. Letty was an incomparable...and so very far out of his reach as to be laughable.

Unfortunately, that same tiny part of him which had held out for the miracle earlier was now disproportionately grieving the inevitable loss of her in his life, even though he never really stood a chance of her remaining in it. He had also read about *her* life in those same newspapers and it was a life he could never hope to give her. The finest clothes, balls, jewels and a prominent and revered place in society. The moment Jack had reminded her of her wealthy Duke, she'd nodded and smiled and immediately switched her thoughts to getting home to Mayfair. Which had been his intention. Because any hope of a future between them was ridiculous. Wasn't it? So he should be happy he had been the sensible one.

But he wasn't.

'We need all the ropes we can carry.' His three brothers were assembled in the kitchen, the lanterns already lit. 'The river has burst its banks. If one of us has to venture into it, then we'll be tethered to something first. If we drive the sheep to the west pasture, they will be safe. Jamie—check on the horses, then the cows. See that none of them have injured themselves.'

His brother's face clouded with barely suppressed fury. 'I am not a blasted invalid, Jack. I'll help you three with the sheep first. The horses and damned cows can wait!'

'I'll see to the horses and cows.' Jack spun around to see Letty marching towards him in a greatcoat that swamped her and wearing an expression of complete and total defiance. Jamie nodded and handed her a lantern, clearly delighted not to be relegated to lighter duties because of his injuries.

'Go back to bed, Letty! It's dangerous out there.' And Jack could already feel the beginnings of a knot of worry at the thought of her out in that storm. The last time she had been exposed to bad weather she had almost died. 'This is no place for a woman like you.'

She marched fearlessly in front of him and stuck out her chin, not the slightest bit intimidated by the angry way he loomed over her. 'I am not some silly, spoiled, empty-headed fool.' Her finger prodded him firmly in the chest. 'And whilst your brothers might well listen to your orders, you are not my master Jack Warriner. Or my husband. And you never will be. So don't expect me to obey you. I am helping. Deal with it.' She spun on her heel and stomped stubbornly towards the back door. Without a backward glance, she flung it open and flounced into the raging tempest.

Chapter Fifteen

Fourteen days and approximately twenty-two hours of misery left...

The tiny hailstones burned her face as they blew about in the wind, but Letty ignored them. Jack's idea that she should stay in bed when there were potentially distressed animals on the estate was ludicrous. It was not as if she had actually been sleeping. Try as she might, sleep had proved to be elusive after he had knocked her down a peg or two earlier. More than a peg or two, if she were being honest with herself. In actual fact, Letty felt as if her legs had been brutally cut out from under her. Now the hurt she had felt at his words had curdled and marinated into anger. How dare he suggest she was not up to the task of being a Nottinghamshire farmer's wife! Since she had been ripped from Mayfair, she had attacked task after task and emerged victorious.

Jack's pithy assessment of her lifestyle grated. Superficial conversation for the privileged. Balls, soirées, jewels, fancy clothes. All external trimmings which had absolutely nothing to do with who she really was inside. Just like everyone else of her acquaintance, the thick-skulled eldest Warriner could not see further than skin deep. Letty was more than all that and, if Jack couldn't see it, then, quite frankly he didn't deserve her either. And she was not some feeble, delicate ornament incapable of knowing her own mind!

She slammed into the cow barn first. Aside from the noisy mooing one would expect from cattle in the midst of a thunderstorm, everything appeared all right. To be sure, Letty held her lantern aloft and checked each beast as best she could for signs of injury or undue distress. Finding nothing, she distributed some fresh hay and water before securing the barn door carefully closed and battling her way across the yard to the other barn where the horses were kept.

The closer she got, the clearer Letty could hear the door to the barn swinging noisily against the hinges. The wind must have dislodged it and the bashing sound would only serve to spook the horses. She dashed inside and was not even slightly surprised to hear the sounds of agitated animals in the pitch-black enclosure. Again, as she had in the cow shed, she raised the lantern to check on each one and began soothing the mounts by stroking their muzzles and whispering words of reassurance. It took a few moments to realise the end stall, Satan's stall, was open.

Letty went to it, peered inside and, finding it empty, used the glow of the lantern to search the rest of the cavernous building for signs of Jamie's temperamental horse. But it was nowhere. Outside, in the storm, with thunder, hail and explosive lightning, she seriously feared for the animal's safety. This was really not the night for the horse to go wandering around loose.

Making sure the rest of the animals were secured, Letty grabbed a set of leather reins hanging on the far wall. If she could locate Satan, she would need to put him in a halter in order to bring him back safely. She bent to pick up the lantern again, then plunged into the dark field beyond the barn, hoping against hope it would be miraculously easy to find a jet-black horse in the oppressive darkness.

* * *

After twenty minutes of searching, she caught sight of the men in the field beyond. With their similar heights and appearances, it was difficult to discern who was who from a distance. However, the closer she got, it became obvious which one was Jack. It stood to reason that he would be the one who put himself in the most peril. Currently, he was thigh deep in the raging water, holding a wriggling sheep in his arms and wading back. Behind him, the river gushed violently, tossing the occasional broken tree branch effortlessly up into the air before sucking it mercilessly under the water. Surely, he didn't put the life of his sheep above the safety of his own?

Without thinking, she broke into a run to drag him away from the danger. When she got nearer, Letty noticed he had thick rope knotted around his waist and shoulders. The other end of the rope was tied to Jamie and wound around the trunk of a sturdy tree. Jamie spotted her first and waved. She could just about hear his voice over the gale as he pointed.

'Help Joe and Jacob move the sheep!'

For a second, she hesitated, as the need to reassure herself of Jack's safety warred with her desire to help, but when she saw him deposit the sheep carefully on solid ground and glare back at her menacingly, the decision was easy to make. She knew exactly what he would say. *Go inside, Letty.* As if she were wholly useless. This field, in the midst of this storm, was no place for a silly, decorative society princess. Letty turned to search for the two youngest Warriners and saw them just to the west. She headed directly towards them until something else, something big, frightened and horse-shaped appeared in her peripheral vision.

It took Jack far longer than necessary to reach his brother. The ground was like a bog, sucking on the soles of his boots and hampering every stride. When he reached him, Jack didn't mince his words.

'Go after Letty and send her indoors!' He had no idea what Jamie had thought he was doing to send her to help the others, but a raging storm was the very last place on earth he wanted her to be. Not after the last time.

'Don't be daft, Jack. Letty is perfectly capable of rounding up some sheep.'

Jack folded his arms belligerently in the stance he knew his younger brothers called his Do-As-

I-Command posture. 'I don't *want* her rounding up sheep. I *want* her out of harm's way. She's not built for this sort of work. Any fool can see how delicate she is!'

'Letty? Delicate? That girl is as strong as an ox. She can move furniture on her own, remember? And clean several years' worth of grime in minutes.'

Jack winced. He hated the fact that Letty still cleaned for them. When he had initially told her to earn her keep, he had never actually intended for her to do anything, it was merely a tactic to put her in her place that one time. Very well, she had done a splendid job that first time and one which had made him feel bad for underestimating her, but he had certainly not wanted her to continue to do it. Yet every day, his house improved as a result of her labours and every day he felt guiltier and guiltier she had to demean herself like that. His mother had never lifted a finger. Would never have dreamed of lifting a finger. And now Letty was demeaning herself here, too, being pelted with rain and hail, getting soaked to her lovely skin and covered in muck. 'I want her inside!' he roared.

Jamie nudged him and pointed back towards the river bank. 'There's another one.'

The stupid sheep stared back at him in a blind panic, its hooves slipping as it struggled to maintain its footing on the steep bank already under several inches of water. With a groan, Jack ensured the rope about his middle was tight and trudged back towards the water.

Being a sheep, and therefore in possession of absolutely no sense, the animal fought against being rescued. Jack was breathless by the time he had wrestled it free and his leg muscles were screaming from the exertion. His passage back towards firmer land was painfully slow and, as he traipsed towards his brother, he automatically scanned the horizon to check on Letty. He soon spied Joe and close by him Jacob, but there was no sign of the petite, stubborn vixen who didn't do as she was told. Perhaps she had found the going hard and given up already? He certainly hoped she had.

Relieved, he turned back towards Jamie, only to see his brother's eyes widen ominously. Jack followed his gaze off into the distance and made out the small square of light from a lantern on the ground. Thunder began to rumble, then an enormous fork of lightning crackled overhead, illuminating the field and silhouetting Letty. She was walking, hands outstretched, towards a rearing, kicking Satan. Jack experienced a moment of sheer, gut-wrenching terror.

'Letty, stop!'

The gale took his warning and blew it back in his face and the pasture was plunged into darkness again. Both Jack and Jamie hastily tugged at the rope that bound them together, clawing at the sopping knots with chilled fingers until they gave.

'That horse will kill her if she goes near it.'

His brother's stark words echoed Jack's own fears. Letty might well have a soft spot for horses, but Satan had earned his evil name fair and square. Once he was untied, he stumbled towards her, calling for her to put a stop to her madness. Either she did not hear or she did not listen, leaving him powerless to do anything but watch the awful drama unfolding before his eyes.

She lunged and caught the horse around the neck, hugging him and, from his position too far away, it looked as if she was talking the beast. It fought against her hold at first, then miraculously stilled. He watched her retrieve a halter from her shoulder and slip it over the animal's enormous head, all the while soothing him with her palms and voice. Within moments, the horse was obediently following her as she tugged gently on the reins, but not back towards the barn, towards the low stone wall which separated this pasture from the next. It was only when she clambered to stand atop the wall that Jack realised what she intended to do and fresh panic surged through him, forcing his tired legs to pump the ground to reach her before she effectively committed suicide.

But without a saddle, and while another rumble of thunder sounded ominously overhead, she climbed on to Satan's back, her golden head bent low over his so that he could hear her. The huge horse reared then, causing Jack's heart to skip a beat, yet she held her seat magnificently, holding the reins with one hand while the other smoothed down the stallion's mane. Satan's jerky motions calmed slowly, and as if nothing at all was the matter, he finally came to stand obediently beneath her.

They stood like that for several moments while Jack stood frozen to the spot, too scared to move in case he spooked the horse and signed her death warrant. But to his horror, Letty gathered the reins tighter, and before Jack knew what was happening, she set off swiftly. Fearlessly. Heading towards the scattered sheep, leaving Jack powerless to stop her.

He stood breathless and gaped at the spectacle. Despite the howling wind and violent storm, Letty had full control of the enormous beast. As another tremendous crack of lightning set the sky ablaze, she galloped to the rear of the furthest sheep and began to herd them towards the open gate of the west pasture, using Satan like a mighty, disciplined sheepdog, which she rode instead of whistled at. By the time Jamie caught up with him, all the pair of them could do was stand and watch as she made short work of finishing what the men had started and failed to achieve.

'I see exactly what you mean,' Jamie drawled as the last sheep disappeared into the adjoining field, 'Your Letty is a delicate one.'

'For the last time, she's not *my* Letty,' he said through gritted teeth.

'Yes, she is. The girl is mad for you. It's beyond me why you are so hell-bent on resisting her.'

Jack felt his throat constrict at the memories. 'You know why, Jamie. This place is not suitable for a gently bred woman.'

Jamie turned slowly and stared. 'Because of what happened to our mother?'

Jack did not want his brother to see how much the painful recollections hurt and how much his feeble attempts at easing her burdens had failed, so he stared out towards the raging river rather than meet his eye. 'She came from London, too. You saw what living here did to her.'

'Our mother was delicate—that I do agree with. But in spirit, Jack, not body. Every memory I have of the woman is of her complaining about her lot in life, blaming our father, or us, for her situation rather than doing something about it all.'

'She was miserable because of our father's self-ishness. I won't do that to Letty.'

'No, Jack. Our mother was just miserable! Did it ever occur to you that she had a hand in what happened to her, too? Our father had a terrible repu-tation long before he met her, yet she allowed him to seduce her. People don't change. Did she think he would? She was one of the most selfish people I have ever known. All she ever cared about was herself. How unhappy with her lot she was. How difficult her life was. She wasn't a mother, Jack. As a parent, she was no better than our useless father. Thank God we all had you, else I don't doubt we'd have turned out little better than feral.'

In the distance, they heard the whoops of joy as

Joe finally closed the gate on the last of the sheep. Letty held Satan on the spot, effortlessly using only the lightest touch on the reins while Jacob appeared to be congratulating her. She threw her head back and laughed, enjoying her moment of triumph, then her gaze locked on to his across the field and neither the distance nor the darkness could not diminish the defiant pride which radiated off her as she sat astride Jamie's unmanageable horse.

He could just imagine her thoughts. *You underestimated me, farm boy, and I proved you wrong.* She kept proving him wrong. So much so, he was starting to doubt his own firmly held beliefs.

'Letty wasn't born for this sort of life.' Just because she could round up frightened, scattered sheep in the rain didn't mean that she should. In her world, such degradation would be unheard of.

'You're probably right, Big Brother.' Jamie spun on his heel and began to limp towards the celebration. 'The girl managed to thwart a gang of kidnappers and escape from a moving carriage unaided. She should have frozen to death or died of fever afterwards, but within a few days she was up and about. And, of course, she is so delicate that she doesn't balk at the challenge of single-handedly cleaning a mansion *and* she can tame a crazed, temperamental horse by riding it bareback in a thunderstorm. The more I think upon it, Jack, the more she resembles our mother in her weak character. Being leg-shackled to an imbecile like you might be the one thing that breaks her.'

Chapter Sixteen

Eleven interminable days to get through...

It had been an uncomfortable few days. In a reversal of roles, it was Letty who now avoided Jack. The bitter sting of his rejection still hurt and she was counting down the hours until she could leave so that she would be spared the trauma of seeing him again. Each time she looked at him, his well-meant words flooded back and alternately upset her or spiked her temper. To make matters worse, Letty was certain she kept catching him staring at her, a slightly perplexed expression on his handsome face, almost as if she were some peculiar specimen she was studying through a microscope and one which he could never hope to understand. It was most unnerving.

Even mealtimes were awkward. Not with everyone else, of course, just with Jack. Both of them actively joined in the boisterous conversations, but they were careful to avoid directly answering or directing comments at each other. At times, it became almost impossible to keep track of it all and Letty's near-constant state of self-consciousness, growing lack of confidence and her determination to hide it all behind the cheerful façade of Violet was becoming exhausting.

The only light at the end of the tunnel was that Letty would be leaving in a week. Four days before her twenty-first birthday Jack had decided they would journey to London. He planned to do the journey in segments, travelling overnight so as not to arouse suspicion and resting during the daylight hours well away from prying eyes. With a reward for one thousand pounds hanging over her head, reporting a sighting of Letty was potentially the most lucrative Christmas present anyone would ever receive. She made no arguments on his insistence they err on the side of caution. Once in London, she would be handed over to the authorities where she could finally bring her uncle and Bainbridge to justice.

Whether or not Jack would be staying to witness the ugly aftermath, she had no idea and her pride would not allow her to ask. She was putting all of that nonsense out of her head for the time being. It was what it was. All she could say with any certainty was that she would soon be all alone in the world again, devoid of any real human attachments and with only her money to keep her company. It was cold comfort for a woman whose dearest wish was to belong somewhere and be understood. No, that was a lie. She wanted to belong *here*. With Jack. Never mind—she had had real plans before she had met the man, plans that did not include a patronising male who thought he knew best, and she would start on them the second the ink was dry on the official papers giving her control over her own fortune. Jack might not need her. but those foundlings did. She would belong with them and he would be forgotten.

Or so she hoped.

With a sigh, she reached for the greatcoat by the back door. Today was Christmas Eve, and Letty was damned if she would allow her melancholy to spoil her plans for the festivities. Right now, because she could finally risk going outside in daylight, she was going to fetch holly to decorate the great hall in readiness. Tomorrow afternoon, after the essential farm chores were done, they were going to celebrate properly. Jamie had killed a fat goose which was hanging ready to be roasted in the oven and Joe had gone to the village to buy some wine to accompany their feast. With Jacob, Letty had organised games for afterwards and she had made each of the brothers a small gift. It was nothing special, only handkerchiefs she had embroidered using their mother's old silk threads, but each one had the man's name and a pattern which suited his character. Jamie's had colourful paint palettes and brushes, Jacob's had books and newspapers and for Joe she had recreated the snake-and-staff motif used by healers since ancient times.

Jack's handkerchief was a cause for concern, but it was far too late to change it now. She had been umming and ahhing for days about whether or not it was appropriate, being uncharacteristically indecisive, to the extent that it was now far too late to change it even if she wanted to. Which she definitely did. Unsurprisingly, she had made his first and put far too much care into the design. If compared alongside his brothers', it would be plain to see it had been made by a woman completely besotted. But Letty had made it before she had humiliated herself before him in the barn and then could not bring herself to change it because to do so involved thinking about him, when she would prefer to avoid doing that at all costs. It was a decision which would probably come back to haunt her. Everyone knew what a lion symbolised.

The whole of England was peppered with them. The monarch's crest had three, for pity's sake, and every other door knocker in Mayfair had one. Lions stood for power, strength, courage and fortitude. Four attributes which Jack Warriner possessed in spades. However, for Letty it stood for Jack's other attributes, too. Loyalty. Self-sacrifice. Leadership. He was the unchallenged leader of this pride. The king of all beasts had seemed strangely fitting for a man who allowed himself no time for hobbies. Their protector. Her protector.

Her rejecter now as well, which was as devastating as it was humiliating.

Why hadn't she chosen something more innocuous and perhaps a little insulting, like a sheep? Jack owned sheep and they vexed him a great deal. He thought them stupid creatures. Last night, she had considered unpicking her work and replacing the majestic lion's head with a fat, woolly sheep just to spite him, except, she was concerned he might see this as a reminder of her shameless reaction to him when she had first witnessed him pulling one of the stupid creatures from the mud. He must have noticed she had become a flushed, stuttering fool at the sight of his bare chest. Jamie certainly had. However, the awful truth was that Letty would blush scarlet when she gave it to him, no matter which design she had chosen. At least she could fib her way out of the lion.

It could, she reasoned, also represent his superior, dictatorial manner, aloofness and coldness. From what she had read, your average lion would not think twice about ruthlessly killing its prey and eating it, just as Jack had not so much as blinked when he had denounced her existence as superficial and privileged. If questioned, she had already prepared a little speech to make the others laugh and put their eldest brother in his place. Letty hoped she didn't have to use it because none of it was true. She adored the fact he was noble and steadfast. In a world where Letty found it difficult to truly trust anyone, she trusted Jack implicitly. Heart and soul. He always did what was right and proper. He was reliably, solidly responsible.

However, she hated that he insisted on maintaining those iron-clad morals all of the time. Just once, she wished he would forget about them, kiss her and lose his mind completely. The noble Jack was so frustrating, or perhaps it was simply because *she* was frustrated.

Using shears, she snipped boughs of holly from a bush which was a bit sparse. The leaves were curled and browning without a single berry in sight. Disappointed, she scanned the grounds for a better specimen. Off into the distance, close to the river's edge, she thought she spied something red and walked towards it. On closer inspection, it proved to be the perfect example of a Christmas decoration. Shiny, waxy green leaves resplendent with ripe, crimson berries. She was so excited with the find and engrossed in cutting armfuls of the stuff, she failed to notice the two children peeking at her from behind a matching holly bush on the opposite bank. Nor did Letty see them scurry off before she bent down to gingerly pick up her thorny decorations and drag them carefully back to the house.

Jack had got up especially early today in order to be finished, and bathed, in time for the planned dinner. He couldn't remember when he had looked forward to a Christmas Day as much as he did this one. Christmas had always been a day much like any other in Markham Manor. When his mother had been alive, he had vague recollections of fraught Christmas dinners in the formal dining room, which inevitably deteriorated into another violent argument between their parents. After his mother had died, his father preferred to spend the entirety of Christmas in a state of constant inebriation, but then again, as he was so regularly in that state, it had not exactly been a surprise. He couldn't remember presents or games, and the Warriner brothers had barely acknowledged the significance of the day in the years since. It was just another day of sweat and toil.

This time, there was an unmistakable atmosphere of excitement in the house which dragged him along with it, whether he wanted it to or not, and that came directly from Letty. The woman was determined to have a proper Christmas and had roped his brothers into her plans. Entertainments were planned, every nook, cranny and surface in the great hall was bursting with sprigs of holly and the festive aroma of cinnamon and baking had tickled his nostrils whenever he set foot in the kitchen. Joe and Jacob had been talking about it for days and even Jamie appeared a little cheered by the prospect.

All three of his brothers had quietly explained to him that there would be presents, all homemade and inexpensive, and that he should probably acquire something nice for Letty. After racking his brains for ideas and having no talent for making anything at all, he was quietly confident he had found her something nice although it was not homemade. It also, in all probability, would earn him a sound ribbing from his brothers. But she deserved it regardless. A small token of his gratitude for all of the work she had done in his home and for bringing the old place alive these last few weeks. He already knew Markham Manor would feel cold and empty when she left. He felt cold and empty himself knowing that day was rapidly drawing near.

Since their last conversation, she had resolutely, but politely, avoided him. Not that Jack could blame her. With the benefit of hindsight, he could see he had been dismissive and harsh, and a huge part of him bitterly regretted it. At the time, he had hoped to nip their inappropriate attraction for one another in the bud. He had been convinced Letty was unsuited to the life he could offer her. After witnessing her conquer Satan during the storm, he was prepared to concede he had unfairly underestimated her, which then led to him wondering if he had made a terrible mistake. Perhaps, at the time, he should have welcomed her tentative suggestion that there could be more between them? Jack still couldn't get over her admission that his kisses had driven her out of her mind. Only a fool would turn down such a wonderful woman, which meant, as he had long suspected, he was the biggest fool to ever walk the earth.

However, in view of her new reluctance to have anything to do with him, and her constant excited chatter about her impending return to Mayfair, it was probably for the best. Even if he had succumbed to temptation, she would have come to her senses eventually and regretted him—regretted them—and he was not certain he could bear that. It was better to extinguish all hope than to have to witness her inevitable disgust of him.

He hoped this little memento might make her eventually come to remember her time with him fondly, but he suspected once he was out of sight, and she was surrounded by her sort of people, Jack would be out of her mind. Ironic, really, when he was slowly going out of his. Good grief, she had made him utterly pathetic!

Jack dragged on a clean shirt and popped his

gift safely in his pocket before heading downstairs. His brothers were already seated at the formal dining table, each with their hair combed and wearing their Sunday best. Dishes filled with potatoes and a steaming array of vegetables covered the linen-draped table. Where had she found a tablecloth? Jack never knew they possessed one. It all looked, and smelled, quite splendid. He scanned the room quickly for Letty, which typically, Jamie noticed straight away.

'Letty has gone to get the goose,' he explained, starting to rise. 'I should probably help her. That bird is heavy.'

Jack quickly stepped in. 'I will go.' It might be his only opportunity today to see her on her own and give her his inappropriate gift away from prying eyes. He walked briskly towards the kitchen and stopped dead.

Letty was wearing a dress.

Jack had never seen her in dress before, aside from the one ruined, soaked one she had arrived in which didn't count, and the unexpected sight of it was quite overwhelming. She turned towards him and he watched her green eyes widen with surprise.

'Oh! Hello, Jack.'

Her golden curls were arranged on top of her head, exposing the swanlike curve of her neck. The bodice of her dress was cut in a scoop. The merest hint of cleavage rose above it; acres of creamy, alabaster skin were on display for his greedy gaze to feast upon. Even the sight of her bare arms, beneath the feminine capped sleeves, reminded him that he was a man and she was a woman. A very beautiful woman. A beautiful and very passionate woman. Instinctively, and completely beyond his control, his groin tightened and Jack was grateful that, for once, he had put on a coat.

'I've come to carry the goose.'

His voice came out gruff, angry. Hardly festive. And he had no idea what to do with his hands. Why now, after all of this time, had she decided to finally finish making the blasted dress? Letty in breeches was a temptation. Letty in a gown was pure torture.

'Here it is.' She smiled tightly and gestured to a huge platter on the table. 'If you carry that in, I shall bring the gravy.'

She picked up the gravy boat and briskly manoeuvred around him to lead the way, clearly keen not to be left alone with him. With a sinking feeling, Jack heaved the platter into his arms and trailed after her. The view was almost as breathtaking from the rear. The neckline of the gown dipped low, showing the delicate shape of her shoulder blades and the velvety skin on her back. The fabric draped along the contours of her body, highlighting the womanly flair of her hips and the juicy peach of her bottom as it swayed before him. Jack gripped the platter for grim death, fearing his stupid knees might buckle from sheer lust, sending her lovely Christmas dinner crashing to the ground.

They sat at the table. As far as Jack could see, the impact of Letty in a gown had no effect on the others. Either they had already seen her and recovered from the shock or the only man she had the power to bewitch was him. To his consternation, his brothers insisted he carve the bird as the head of the household, effectively putting him on display when he was in no fit state to be so. Having a throbbing bulge in his breeches, obviously he made a hash of it. Stupid, *stupid*, uncultured, clumsy fool! It would have been more fitting if he had simply torn the goose limb from limb with his bare hands like the most uncivilised of savages.

Conversation flowed around him and Jack did

his best to join in, only his eyes kept drifting towards Letty as he picked at his food and chewed without tasting it.

'What is the first thing you are going to do when you get back to town, Letty?' Jacob kept asking for titbits of society gossip because that world intrigued him. Each one served to remind Jack he was unworthy of her.

She shrugged her slim shoulders and beamed at his brother. 'I don't know. Something *frivolous*, I suppose, like shopping on Bond Street.' Jack could have sworn he saw her eyes flick to his defiantly on the word frivolous, but it was so fleeting he might have imagined it. 'Actually, the truth is I am going to build a home for foundlings. It breaks my heart when I see those lonely children huddled on the street begging for scraps because they have no one to care for them.' The passion in her tone humbled him. 'I have visited some of the orphanages in town and they horrify me. The children are treated like prisoners, as if they have committed some heinous crime rather than suffered the death of their parents. I want to create something different. Not a cold institution, but a home with a heart. My children will be taught to read and trained to earn a decent living when they are finally old enough to go out into the world. I don't want them having to resort to crime or the worst sort of menial work in order to eke out a living.'

It was all so worthy and he realised, with shame, something too close to her heart. Most people would see only her money and not the fact that she was an orphan.

'Well, I think that is admirable,' Joe said, obviously impressed. 'I should like to see it when it is built, Letty.'

'You must come and visit me, and I shall take you to see it myself.'

She was only being polite, but Jacob jumped at the invitation. 'We would love to. Can I come and visit you during the Season, too?'

Letty patted his arm affectionately. 'Of course. I shall have you escort me to all the *superficial* balls, parties and *soirées* I attend.' This time Jack was certain that her eyes flicked towards him with undisguised hostility before she grinned back at his brother. 'You can charm all of the young ladies.'

'As if an eligible young lady of the *ton* would look twice at him!' Joe scoffed just before he popped the last fluffy roast potato into his mouth.

'I believe I would cut quite a dash there,' said Jacob in his usual good-natured, slightly arrogant way.

'With your roguish charm, I fear for the hearts of the ladies, but then again I believe you would all cut a dash there. Three handsome brothers.' Another pointed look of disgust in Jack's direction as she deliberately cut him out. 'What young lady could resist you? One twirl around the dance floor and they would all be smitten.'

'Then I'm done for,' said Jamie wryly. 'My twirling days are over.'

'Ah, but, Jamie, you don't need to twirl. Once I casually drop into the conversation that you are a returned war hero, the women will swarm around you like flies around honey. The same goes for you, Joe. There is something about a learned doctor which ladies adore.'

'Will you introduce us to your dashing Duke as well?' Jacob said this without so much as a flicker of an eyebrow, but Jack was no fool. It had been a jibe designed to get a rise out of him. Ever since the night of the storm, all three of his brothers regularly pumped Letty for information about her Duke. Probably in a thinly veiled attempt to get him to show them he was jealous. He let the barb slide, as he had all the others. They could not understand why he resisted Letty—but then Joe and Jacob had been so young when their mother had died, so he doubted they remembered how living here, isolated in this desolate, crumbling prison, had ultimately destroyed her.

'I should be honoured to introduce you to the Duke of Wentworth. I am certain he would insist on meeting my brave rescuers without my having to prompt him.'

Jack forced himself to swallow the mouthful of food which had suddenly turned to chalk dust in his mouth. To hear Letty speak, the man was a paragon of virtue and the most perfect example of a proper society gentleman. Yesterday, he had endured the lengthy tale of how the illustrious Duke of Wentworth filled his splendid mansion with the most exquisite *objets d'art*. Soon, he would add Letty to his collection and Jack would hate him more than he did already.

'Then it's settled,' said Jacob decisively. 'We shall all visit you in Mayfair for the Season.'

The very last place Jack ever wanted to see Letty was in her natural habitat, with blasted Wentworth, surrounded by her own swarms of worthy flies he would enjoy personally swatting. With his fists.

'And who would run the farm, Jacob?'

Why had he sounded so churlish? His three brothers stared back at him with varying degrees of pity and despair as the atmosphere became strained. It was Letty who fixed things.

'Why, Jack, you would, of course. I doubt he has any interest in the *superficial* conversations of the privileged. I dare say, you three will have to visit me without him.' Hoisted by his own petard, he could do nothing but smile tightly and wish he was outside vigorously chopping wood. 'Shall we retire to the other room and swap presents?'

Letty sailed past him regally, apparently completely unperturbed by his curmudgeonly outburst, barely gracing him with a glance. Keen to regain the celebratory mood, his brothers tumbled out of the dining room behind her. Jamie punched him hard in the arm as he limped towards the door.

'Cretin.'

Jack supposed he deserved that, too. Letty was doing her best to behave as if nothing had happened, as Jack himself had implored, so why couldn't he? It had just been a harmless, meaningless conversation, with no firm plans set in stone. Why had he needed to throw his oar into the water and sour the mood?

Because he wanted her to believe he didn't care about her fancy Duke and was pretending nothing had happened, when *everything* had happened. Everything about the situation confused him, leaving Jack for once all at sea with no rudder to guide him. He set his shoulders and trudged into the great hall like a man on the way to his own execution.

Chapter Seventeen

Nine days and approximately six hours until it's over...

Letty took her seat around the roaring fire and tried not to focus on Jack's blatant refusal to even consider maintaining their acquaintance once she was gone. At the very least, he could have pretended to care, although she already knew pretending was not something the man was capable of. If something was amiss or not to his liking, he was one for telling it like it was. Unfortunately, every time he told her what was what, Letty was always left feeling hurt by his brutal honesty. It was probably for the best. Her stupid, misguided heart would heal all the quicker knowing his was blissfully indifferent.

Joe walked towards her smiling, holding out a small gift wrapped in one of Jacob's newspapers.

She decided there and then not to let Jack spoil her only family Christmas in almost four years. She grabbed it eagerly and undid the string which bound it. Two perfectly square cakes of perfumed soap sat within the wrinkled paper.

'I made them myself. I found a recipe for medicinal soap in one of my books and substituted the lye for lavender oil.'

Letty grabbed his lapels and kissed him on the cheek. 'I love them! Thank you. Before I go to bed I shall lounge in the bath for at least an hour.'

'You can have my present next.' Jamie reached behind his chair.

His present was bigger and also wrapped in newspaper. She unwrapped it and gasped at the beautiful watercolour in her hands. The detail was exquisite. 'Markham Manor...' Without thinking, Letty ran her fingertip lovingly along the painted edges of the quaint Tudor manor house and felt a surge of emotion. She was going to miss this place. It had become home in such a short period of time. But not as much as she would miss her temporary family. Jack's brothers had become her brothers. Losing them would be like a death and she would mourn the loss of them. 'I thought you might like something to remember us by.'

Tears formed in the corners of her eyes and Jamie stared back at her, alarmed. 'No waterworks, if you please, madam! I don't do emotional outbursts.' That was an understatement. Yet Letty knew his disinterested demeanour hid a deep well of emotions.

'You are a lovely man, James Warriner.'

He pretended to find her hug of gratitude distasteful. 'That's quite enough, thank you.'

'You're already wearing my present.' The youngest Warriner grinned. 'I already know you love it.'

'Yes, indeed. You certainly know what a lady likes.' All of the other brothers, including Jack, regarded them quizzically. Jack, she noted, also looked quite peeved. 'Jacob got me some hairpins.' Letty patted her coiffure for emphasis. 'Hence, I no longer look like a poodle.'

'Hairpins!' Jamie turned to his brother, outraged. 'Please tell me you didn't put Letty's safety at risk by buying them in the village.'

'Of course I didn't. What do you take me for? They came by way of that farmer's daughter I have been courting. Once I took them all out, I pretended to have lost the majority of them in the haystack we happened to be lying in. I would like it noted, I sacrificed *myself* for Letty's hairstyle.'

'And it was a very noble sacrifice, I'm sure. How you must have suffered...' Letty practically skipped over to the sideboard where she had hidden her gifts. 'I have made some things for you all, too.'

'Wait,' said Jamie pointedly, 'We haven't seen what Jack has got you yet.'

Much as she did not want to look directly at him, with so many eager onlookers, to do otherwise was rude. Jack met her gaze and appeared mortified. He stared down to his lap awkwardly. It was obvious he had not got her anything.

'You didn't forget, did you?' Joe asked slowly.

'Of course I didn't forget!' Jack unfolded his big body from the chair and edged towards Letty, looking likely to break into a run at any minute if given half the chance. Once he was in front of her, he frowned, appearing all stiff and, to her complete consternation, totally adorable. 'I wanted to give you something special. Seeing as you have worked so hard on behalf of myself and my brothers.' He still didn't look her in the eye. 'And... well...'

'Oh, spit it out, man!' Jamie rolled his eyes. 'I've never seen you so inarticulate.'

He shot his brother an evil glare, but he rummaged in his pocket and then unexpectedly took hold of her right hand. Letty watched transfixed as he slid a ring on to her finger. The band was gold; the square stone was a beautiful flat emerald.

'It's very old. Tudor, I believe. From Sir Hugo's day... Well anyway, I thought the emerald would complement your eyes...'

Her heartbeat suddenly speeded up as she stared at the lovely piece of jewellery, trying not to think about her body's immediate reaction to his touch or the fact she desperately wanted to tell him he had put the ring on the wrong hand.

'It's lovely. Thank you.'

He had noticed her eyes? What did that mean? And was he blushing? She was sure he was.

Letty had kissed the cheek of every man in the room except the one she most wanted to. All eyes, she realised, were now watching the pair of them closely. Too closely. Her breath became ragged and her lips tingled. To not kiss him would be poor form. But kissing him, after what had happened the last time, terrified her. Even a chaste kiss would serve as an uncomfortable reminder that he knew her passions were fired by him. Just thinking about doing it again made her limbs feel heavy and her head feel light.

She had also dithered a beat too long and Jack had taken a stilted step backwards. For some reason, even though she knew his true feelings, he appeared wounded by her hesitation. If ever there was a time for Violet's charming bravado, it was now.

'I shall treasure this, Jack.'

In one swift, decisive motion, Letty took a large stride forward and stood on her tiptoes, intending to bestow a light peck on his cheek, but his head turned towards hers and their lips brushed instead. The kiss was quick—but no less incendiary for it. Letty felt the power of it throughout her body as her nerve-endings positively exploded as if a fuse had been lit within her. Those first breaths afterwards were erratic. Jack stared back at her, stunned, and for one, brief moment, she considered kissing him again before she remembered she was currently supposed to be Violet. Charming. Detached. Superficial. As unaffected by him as he was by her. Except she might have begun the kiss as Violet, but it had been Letty's lips his had touched. Letty's heart which had soared. In a panic, she put some well-needed distance between them and her words tumbled out in a rush.

'I want you all to open my gifts at the same time, because, rather unoriginally, you all have the same thing.' Quickly, she distributed her packages and clapped her hands to signal the unwrapping could begin, all the while trying to ignore the shaky feeling in her legs and the steady, sure sound of her heart knocking against her ribs. Jack was too focused on untying the ribbons she had secured the tiny gifts with, so Letty assumed he was not similarly affected by the brief, intimate contact. He had probably done it on purpose to put her in her place for all of those petty jibes she had thrown at him over dinner. A reminder that he knew she was bluffing when she pretended he didn't matter. A way to regain the upper hand.

His fingers refused to work properly as Jack did his level best to undo the endearingly feminine bow and conceded he was having a bit of a moment. The emerald ring might as well have been a declaration of love! Good grief—what had he been thinking? And then he had had to touch her velvety skin and slip the ring on to her finger, and that felt like a declaration, too. A man only gave a woman one sort of ring… Oh, why had he done it in front of his brothers? The three of them now kept glancing at him knowingly and he would probably never live it down. There had been a ruby pendant in the box of old jewellery he'd unearthed. He should have given her that.

Not a ring.

But the ring, with its emerald the exact shade of her beguiling eyes, had called to him and, like a fool, Jack had listened. Then, because politeness, and only politeness, had dictated it, she had kissed him and instinctively he had turned to kiss her back, almost as if there was some sort of magnet pulling his mouth to hers. To all intents and purposes it should have felt like the platonic kiss she had meant it to be, except, the instant those soft lips had touched his, his skin had caught fire and his heart had literally swelled in his chest. Unfortunately, it was not the only swelling he was dealing with.

By accident, rather than design, the ribbon came apart at almost the same moment his brothers' did.

'Would you look at that?' Jamie actually grinned as he held up his gift. 'You're a fellow artist, Letty! The detail in this is astounding and the pattern is so personal to me.'

'Mine, too!' Joe displayed the medical motif. 'When I finally qualify I shall carry this with me on all of my house calls.'

Jacob began to laugh at his. 'Letty, you are priceless.' He passed the square of fabric to Joe, who scrutinised the intricate stitching and began to laugh as well. 'Newspapers filled with gossip around every edge and a farmer's daughter in one corner! What did she make for you, Jack?'

In truth, he wasn't entirely sure what to make of it. The handkerchief was more elaborately embroidered than those of his brothers, but the golden lions around the edges in various poses all looked towards the magnificent male in the centre of the linen, who sat proudly staring out at him. He turned and searched Letty's face for clues and became more baffled when she refused to look at him. Was she blushing?

'I thought a lion would symbolise…um…the fact you are the undisputed leader of—'

Joe intervened. 'Our pride?'

'More like he's got too much stupid pride,' Jamie hissed in a poor attempt at a stage whisper.

'Lions are proud, noble and brave and so is Jack.' Letty's voice sounded a little squeaky, although she was smiling at everyone serenely. Jack didn't know whether to read anything more into her gift, or not.

Jacob leaned over to examine the handkerchief. 'Do lions usually have turquoise eyes?' Then he made a point of examining Jack's face and smiling slowly. The smile was apparently contagious, because it crept on to Joe's face next, then Jamie's, until the three of them were grinning like fools. 'Why, yours must have taken so many more hours to complete than ours!' It did beggar the question. If she had taken more care over his gift, did that mean she cared more for him? 'But I suppose Jack gave you an emerald when I only gave you soap, so I suppose his superior gift is fitting.'

Poor Letty appeared about to combust with embarrassment, she was so crimson, and, like Jack, she was clearly mortified by their reactions. They were reading meanings into Letty's gift which probably were not meant to be there, even though he now desperately hoped they were. In such situations, attack was always the best form of defence, although he could not think of anything to say which would not make the sudden disquiet worse. Instead, Jack glared at his brothers menacingly, letting them know purely by the ferocity of his glare that he would flay the skin from any man who dared to say what they were blatantly thinking. The boisterous male grins slipped off their faces smartly and the three of them stared at their boots like naughty children. The ensuing silence was so brittle it made Jack cringe. So he filled it, for her sake.

'Thank you for your lovely gifts, Letty. They were very thoughtful.'

She grinned again, making everyone, except him, feel better about what had just happened. She did it with such aplomb, she had almost convinced Jack she was oblivious to his brothers' blatant innuendo. Almost. But not quite. He was coming to believe Letty often hid her real thoughts behind an innocent, smiling façade which never quite touched her eyes. 'I thought we were going to play some games?'

In his head, he had just invented a new one, and it was called *How Quickly Can I Strangle My Brothers*. But he smiled and played along for her sake, and his. As the hours flew past pleasantly, Jack's fingers kept touching the square of linen in his pocket and hoping that proud lion was exactly how she saw him rather than the fortune-hunting cad everyone else would assume he was if he ever dared lay another hand on her.

* * *

When, inevitably, the time came to go to bed, his three brothers disappeared with alarming haste, although Jack was glad that they did. He was so confused he simply had to talk to her. Letty was almost through the door in their wake when he called her back.

'Letty—can we talk?'

She stopped and slowly turned around, but not before he witnessed her posture become rigid. Something about it did not bode well.

'Of course.' She clasped her hands tightly in front of her, almost defensively.

Like an idiot, he had started the conversation without a clear idea of what it was he was going to say. He wanted to ask about the turquoise lion eyes and if she liked her present. He wanted to know if her feelings for him were the same as his were for her. He wanted—*desperately* wanted—to know if there could still be more between them than the physical attraction he had stupidly dismissed it all as, even though he knew nothing good could ever come of it. 'I wanted to...' Her expression was unreadable, but her green eyes were stormy. 'The thing is...'

'Yes?'

Did she look hopeful? Eager? Letty stared back down at her hands, playing with the silly ring he had given her in a moment of mad weakness. In desperation Jack took her hand and she stared at it wide-eyed. She was definitely embarrassed by this unwanted conversation, too. Her cheeks were pink and he saw her swallow awkwardly at his clumsy attempt at…whatever it was he was clumsily attempting. It was probably better to let sleeping dogs lie. She was leaving in less than a week. Which was for the best. For her at least. Any declaration now was as ludicrous as it was futile.

What exactly did he expect her to do? Stay here when she had every luxury in Mayfair? Be content to live with a farmer? Kiss goodbye to her high position in society and be shunned by everyone she knew? Marry him when she had a duke waiting for her at home? There was wishful thinking and then there was fantasy.

'The thing is, I wanted to thank you for all of the effort you have put into today.' And inevitably, common sense returned.

'I see.' She stared at him levelly. 'Was there anything else you wanted to say?'

I think you are wonderful and I'm a fool. A stupid, penniless, unworthy fool. I wish I could turn back time and do it all again differently. This isn't just lust...I truly care about you.

Who was he kidding? He loved her.

'No. Nothing else...just thank you.'

Hell's teeth! He loved her. The room began to spin.

'Then I shall say goodnight.'

Please don't go. Not just now, but ever. Stay here with me.

'Goodnight, Letty.'

Chapter Eighteen

Five days left...

Tomorrow she would leave Markham Manor, yet even thinking about it hurt. Letty supposed she should be frightened about the potential for danger on the long journey or apprehensive about all the nastiness which would inevitably follow her return home, yet strangely both of those things paled into insignificance when compared to saying goodbye to this house and the men within it. She tried not to specifically link these feelings to Jack because she had already accepted the end of whatever it was they had. As each day passed and the time of her departure drew nearer, they conversed less and less. Yesterday, they had barely exchanged more than three sentences and two of those had consisted of 'Good morning' and 'Goodnight'. This, apparently, was something they were both responsible for. Today, Jack had left to begin his work long before Letty had come downstairs. If his most recent behaviour was anything to go by, she doubted she would see him until dinner. Their last dinner together.

Without thinking, she touched the gold band he had placed on her finger. Soon that would be the only thing she had left of him. It would always be her most treasured possession. His token of thanks which she had desperately hoped would be more. But, of course, the anticipated declaration of his affection had turned out to be nothing but a forlorn hope. Jack had not changed his mind about her unsuitability and Letty's heart had shattered.

Despite her mood, she wanted to mark the occasion, and to do it she was making chicken à la Braise again. The only twist, she hoped, was this time it would be edible. She had learned a great deal about the art of cooking in the last few weeks and was determined to do it properly. It was almost a badge of honour. A statement about how far she had come. The two sacrificial chickens were already roasting away nicely in the oven, completely devoid of feathers, and nesting in a rich, aromatic sauce made from reduced wine and herbs. Now she actually knew what *reduce* meant in a recipe, the final dish was definitely showing some promise. She plopped the last peeled carrot into the waiting pan of water to cook later, as vegetables, it turned out, did not need to be boiled to death for two hours. Then, with all the preparation done, she headed out into the hallway to freshen up and put on her homemade dress for the last time, too. Inside, Letty might be broken, but only Violet would be visible on the outside. She did not want their last memories of her to be of the real girl who didn't quite pass muster.

When the tears came, and they would, only Letty would ever see them. If this whole experience had taught her anything, it was that she was not prepared to settle for someone who did not adore her with the same depth and ferocity as she adored him. She was worth more than that. If Jack couldn't see it, when she had bravely let her guard down for the very first time, then perhaps, some day, someone else would. And perhaps, if her heart ever healed, if the big gaping hole shaped like Jack Warriner ever closed, Letty would move on with her life as well. Because she, Letty Dunston, thwarter of kidnappers, housekeeper, maid, cook, sheep rescuer and soon to be benefactor of London's most sympathetic foundling home, was worth it. So she would do her hair and dress prettily, and allow the *Tea Heiress* to sit at dinner in her stead one last time. When she got to Mayfair, she was determined not to bring her alter ego with her ever again. This was definitely Violet's last performance and Letty was glad to be rid of her, so something positive had come from this whole heartbreaking experience. She knew she had outgrown the confines of her old life and was more than capable of tackling the challenges of the new one. More than capable and now completely independent for the first time.

Rather bizarrely, she felt the vibrations of the approaching hoofbeats first. They resonated through the old wooden floorboards, sending tingles of alarm through her feet and legs as she realised those foreboding hooves came from more than the one horse. An entire team of horses was pounding up the driveway at speed, almost in synchronisation, which suggested a carriage.

Instinctively, she bolted up the staircase and camouflaged herself in a dark corner on the landing and listened as the carriage rattled to a stop outside the front door. Several pairs of boots jumped and crunched on the gravel before the threatening pummelling of a fist against the oak front door sent tentacles of fear whipping throughout her body.

'Open up! We know she's in there!' The tentacles wrapped themselves around her organs and squeezed like a vice. The Earl of Bainbridge's sinister tone did not brook any argument. He was coming in. Nothing was going to stop him. 'Go around the back. Check there are no other escape routes!'

Letty heard boots crunch away at speed from the front of the house. In moments they would reach the open kitchen door and swarm into her safe haven, defiling it. If they found her, she wouldn't stand a chance.

Panic glued her feet to the floor and caused her breath to saw in and out of her lungs painfully. Where was Jack and the others? Were they on their way to rescue her? Were they oblivious to the violation? Or worse, had they already been silenced?

The pummelling on the door began again in earnest. 'We know you are in there, Violet! Did you think you could escape me?'

The menacing words galvanised her. Bainbridge couldn't succeed now, not after everything she'd been through. She had to escape. She had to think. She had to focus on the practicalities.

Going back downstairs was suicide—however, staying up here, where there was no escape route, was almost worse. For a second she contemplated barricading herself into her bedchamber. The heavy wooden wardrobe would offer her some protection, if she could move it. But if she, a lone woman with a woman's physical strength could move it, so too could a group of angry men. Then what?

Blindly, she ran along the landing as the first voices appeared inside the kitchen, unsure of which way to turn. Then she saw the eyes. The bright blue eyes, identical to Jack's, staring out at her from the portrait. Sir Hugo's priest hole! Weeks ago, Jack had told her to hide there if the worst happened.

Her clumsy fingers struggled to release the hidden panel, yet the men were now noisily marching their way down the hallway, kicking open doors as they passed them. Searching for her.

Letty almost whimpered as the secret door finally swung open, but bit down hard on her tongue to stop herself. Stealth and silence were imperative. She slipped inside the tiny room beyond and forced herself to close the door slowly, even though she could already hear a pair of heavy boots on the stairs. With the door closed, she was plunged into blackness. Not so much as a crease of light bled through the ancient panelling, so she had to locate the sturdy bolt blind, with trembling fingers, and carefully, quietly, slide it until it locked.

The footsteps reached the landing.

'Pull apart every room. She could be hiding anywhere. Cupboards, under the beds, behind the curtains. You two check the attic! Leave no stone unturned.' Layton's cold, calculating voice issued orders rapidly. Letty could barely hear him. Her pulse was so noisy the sound of its drumming dominated the inside of her head, yet she knew her rapid breathing might betray her. Any sound she made might betray her. Carefully, she stepped cautiously backwards until she felt the hard press of brick against her ribs.

'Someone was here when we arrived. There's food cooking in the kitchen.'

Letty did not recognise that voice, but it was coming from only a scant few feet away from where she was. On the landing. She held her breath and stared into the darkness, praying she would hear the man's footsteps as he walked away. In the distance, the unmistakable sounds of the downstairs being ransacked, with no thought or care for the family's possessions, piled misery on to her terror. All the Warriners had done was help her, and now, everything they owned would likely be ruined by these monsters. If she survived this, she vowed to replace every stick of furniture damaged.

If she survived.

'Violet is definitely here.' The unmistakable sound of her uncle's voice. So he was here, too. She supposed he would be. Too much was at stake to risk not finishing the job properly. And this time, they would finish the job. She knew that with absolute certainty. They would kill her for sure now. 'Look.'

'It's just a handkerchief,' Bainbridge said dismissively.

'It's an embroidered handkerchief. My niece's work. I'd recognise it anywhere.'

The voices became more muffled as they walked away from her, the noise of the destruction of upstairs replacing it as wardrobes were ruthlessly, mindlessly emptied. Powerless to do anything other than listen and hope, Letty carefully lowered herself to the floor of the little priest hole, wrapped her arms tightly about her knees and silently pleaded for a miracle.

'Let's call it a day. It's almost dark.' Joe stood stiffly below him, stretching out his back.

It had taken all four of them to replace the roof on the dilapidated cottage, but after two days of intensive work, largely because Jack had needed a proper challenge to stop his mind constantly wandering to Letty, it was almost done. One more tenant cottage finished would mean another tenant and another meagre rent. 'All right. You three head back. I will finish these last slates.'

'No. It's Letty's last night with us and whatever nonsense is going on in that stubborn head of yours, you owe it to her to be there for dinner.' Jamie glared up at him, his arms folded. 'We are all going back together. Now.'

'Fine.'

Jack feigned disinterest, although his gut was already clenching. Pathetically, he wanted to hide away from the grim reality of her going in the hope it would actually stop hurting. Fat chance of that. There was a pain in his heart so acute it kept making him physically flinch. But it was for the best because he had to think of her welfare before his overwhelming feelings. Reluctantly, he climbed down from the roof and helped the others pack away the tools. Their pace back was leisurely, in deference to Jamie's sedate speed, and he was grateful for that at least. In a few hours, he would watch her climb his stairs for the last time. This time tomorrow, they would set off to London. Less than two days after that, they would say goodbye.

The silhouette of Markham Manor loomed darkly in the twilight. It was odd that he should be thinking negative words like loomed again already, when for the last few weeks, the sight of his home had warmed him. It had warmed him, Jack recognised, because Letty had made it into a home rather than a responsibility. With her inside waiting for him, it no longer felt like a millstone around his neck, but more a place of light and hope. His feelings for the house would soon become as dark as the windows once more…

Something was not right.

Since Letty had taken charge of the house, those windows always glowed a golden welcome and tonight they were black. He began to run.

'What's wrong?'

'There are no candles burning. We left the gates unguarded.' Jack had left Letty unguarded.

The closer he got to the house, the more the cold despair of dread settled in the pit of his stomach. They had been gone for hours. Letty could have been gone for hours.

Jack smashed through the back door and saw the carnage. The kitchen table was lying on its side, chairs scattered this way and that. All his worst fears were confirmed. They had come for her and he had not been here to stop them.

Behind him, he heard someone strike a match and the dim light highlighted that the wanton destruction went way beyond this room. Jacob thrust a lantern into his hand.

'Letty's a smart girl, Jack.'

She was. No matter what life threw at her, she always proved herself to be resourceful. She could have escaped. Or she could have hidden. 'Search everywhere.' Jack plunged into the chaos of the hallway and took the stairs two at time, heading to the one place he had told her to go.

'Letty!'

The he stopped in front of the secret panel. 'Letty, sweetheart, it's me. Jack.' The deafening silence caused his throat to constrict, strangling his words. His fingers fumbled at the concealed latch and his heart only began to beat again when he realised it was locked. From the inside. Thank God!

'Letty, sweetheart.' He lowered his voice, trying to sound calm even though he had never felt so far from it. 'Unlock the door, darling. They've gone.' At least he hoped they had. In his haste to find her he hadn't checked.

Joe poked his head round the banister. 'There's no sign of them—not in the house at any rate. I've come to get Jamie's guns. We're going to check outside.'

He nodded, too petrified for Letty's safety to do any more. 'Did you hear that, sweetheart? There's no sign of them. Please. Talk to me.' *Please be in there. Unharmed.*

'J-Jack?' Her voice was so small, barely a whisper, but his heart soared at the sound.

'Yes, sweetheart. It's me. Unlock the door.' He needed to see for himself all was well. Touch her. Hold her.

'Are they really gone?'

'There is nobody here except me and you.'

He pressed his ear to the wood and heard movement. After an age, and a great deal of fumbling, she slid the bolt open. Jack yanked open the panel and watched her wince and cover her eyes against the weak light from the lantern as she knelt on the floor in front of him. She had been in the dark in there. All alone. Terrified. He could tell by the tiny quiver of her shoulders she was on the cusp of tears.

Automatically he dropped to the floor, crawling into the tiny space and gathering her against his chest tightly, tucking her head under his chin, needing to comfort both of them with the embrace. She burrowed against him, wrapping her arms around his neck, and he noticed her fingers were chilled, too. Jack pulled the edges of his greatcoat around her, rocking her as he tried to warm her skin, grateful at the reassuring, rapid beat of her heart against his.

'I thought they had taken you!' He ignored the crack of emotion in his voice; for once his manly pride could go to hell. She was safe. That was all that mattered. 'Are you injured? Did they touch you?' Because if they had, then they would have to die. It was as simple as that.

She shook her head against his shoulder. 'Th-they never f-found me. I came here as soon as I heard them. Oh, J-Jack, I could hear them pulling apart all the rooms. I thought they would never stop. Your poor house.'

'It's just a house, Letty. Things. None of them are important.' He kissed the top of her blonde curls reverently. The only thing of any importance was safe in his arms.

'I was so frightened. I thought they had hurt you.' An anguished sob escaped her lips. 'Are all your brothers safe, too?'

'Shh, sweetheart…everyone is all right.'

'I've put you all in such danger—I never should have stayed here. I'm so s-sorry, Jack.'

'This is my fault, Letty. If anybody should be sorry it is me. I left the gates open. I became complacent, so sure they were gone, I left you unguarded. If something had happened to you…' Emotion clogged his throat, preventing him from finishing the sentence, but Jack would have not been able to live with himself.

'You're here now. That's all I care about. You're here and safe.' Her slim body shook as the tears she had been bravely holding back came unabated. Jack didn't try to make her stop. After the ordeal she had just been through, she deserved the release and he needed the closeness. All he could do was hold her tight, smooth his hands over her hair and thank God she had had the wherewithal to seek the shelter of this ancient refuge, grateful it had finally hidden someone worthy.

How long they sat there like that, curled together on the floor, he had no idea, but it was long enough for his brothers search the estate and return to find them still there. Jamie wore a grim expression.

'We can't find them in the grounds. That doesn't mean they are not in them. It's just too damn dark to search properly. But the gates are secured and so is the house. Joe's guarding the front door and Jacob the back. If anyone tries to come in, both boys know to shoot first, ask questions later.'

'They know I've been here. My uncle found my embroidery and recognised it. They'll come back.'

A sobering thought. Jack exchanged a meaningful glance with his brother to silently gauge his opinion; the gloomy certainty he saw in Jamie's eyes terrified him. 'They won't be far away. Someone will be watching the house. More men will be guarding the lane. They will have seen us searching for them—but they are waiting now. To see what happens next.'

Jack felt Letty stiffen in his arms and pulled her closer. 'We won't let them near you, Letty.'

This place was a fortress, perhaps they could hold Bainbridge and his men at bay. But even if they could, it was only a short-term solution. 'We need to get her out of here.'

'Agreed.' Jamie nodded, his jaw firm and his shoulders set for battle. 'I have a plan.'

Chapter Nineteen

Four tense days and twenty-three hours to go...

Just after midnight, Joe and Jacob set off to check the grounds. The light of their lanterns and the movement near the gates were designed to draw attention away from the three cloaked figures heading towards the barn. Jamie pushed bales of hay in front of the doors in case thin slivers of light from their single candle bled out into the darkness. Silently, Jack saddled two horses while Letty pushed their hastily procured provisions into saddle bags. Just before they extinguished the candle, Jamie pressed a pistol into her hand. The feel of something so deadly in her palm should have been frightening, but its cold weight was reassuring.

'Remember what I told you. Pull back the hammer, aim it at the head and squeeze the trigger.'

She nodded her affirmation and put it into the belt tied around her waist. Jamie turned gravely back to his brother. 'Wait here till you see the light of my lantern. Once we are sure they've gone, we'll follow. Take care, Big Brother.'

With that he blew out the weak candle, pushed away the hay bales and limped back towards the courtyard. She and Jack waited in tense silence, holding their respective horses by the reins. Not more than two minutes later they saw the glow of Jamie's lantern at the back door of the house. It moved slowly away from both his other brothers and from where they stood. Another decoy to fool whoever happened to be watching that the Warriners were either searching for Letty or for potential intruders.

'Let's go,' Jack whispered and led the way behind the barn, towards the dark, forbidding woods. Letty had to trust he would be able to find his way out of them and take them safely, directly to the Great North Road almost four miles away.

They walked the horses until the blanket of trees surrounded them. She let him boost her on to her mount, then waited while he hoisted himself into the saddle. 'Once we get to the river, we have to veer south, keeping the water to our right.

That way we will bypass Retford altogether. The stretch of the London-bound road we should meet is fairly isolated. It should be easy to spot from the cover of trees if anyone is there waiting for us. If they are, we will simply remain hidden.'

He sounded so supremely confident, it went some way to allay the worst of her fears, bringing down her level of fear from completely petrified to merely terrified. If—no, *when* she got through this, it would probably take Letty weeks to feel anywhere near normal again.

But Jack's solid, calm presence did help. Ever since he had found her in the priest hole, she had drawn comfort from his strength. His house had been ransacked, the family's belongings ruthlessly strewn on the floor and trampled over. Yet Jack had simply cast his eye over the damage and shrugged. He tasked Joe and Jacob with clearing up the worst of the mess in the great hall so that they could all sit down and took Letty into the kitchen where he set the kettle to boil, keeping her busy by distracting her with mindless chatter while he made them all some tea. By the time it was ready and they carried it back into the hall, his brothers had almost put the room to rights and had hidden any evidence of the wanton destruction created by her would-be captors.

Then, the five of them had planned and prepared for the dangerous journey back to London. Too shaken to really participate, Letty had been grateful Jack had taken the time to seek her approval of every decision that was made, making sure she understood exactly what to expect. If they reached the Great North Road safely, they would travel to London under the veil of darkness, resting during the daylight hours so that there was less chance of anyone seeing her. It would take longer, and there were the added dangers of footpads to consider, but as those scoundrels would only want her possessions, of which she currently had none, they were a lesser evil than Bainbridge and her treacherous uncle. For safety's sake, any rest stops would likely not be in comfortable inns for the first day or two. Once they were closer to the capital, and as long as they had encountered nothing hostile on their route, they might be able to risk one of them. But it had to be a busy one, Jamie had cautioned, because people saw far less in crowds. London, Jamie claimed, would be the very best place to hide and Letty believed him. The circles she moved in were small and close knit. Those well-heeled, well-spoken paragons of society rarely ventured out of Mayfair or the usual fashionable haunts. If they took a room somewhere like Cheapside, while the ugly legal necessities were dealt with, she sincerely doubted her peers, or more importantly her uncle, would be any the wiser.

Their horses picked slowly through the black forest. Letty made sure she was close on Jack's tail; it was too dangerous to risk even the dimmest of lights. After what seemed like an eternity, they heard the unmistakable sounds of rushing water. Jack stayed his horse so Letty could move up alongside him. He reached out one hand and gently cupped her cheek for a second. 'Are you all right, Letty?'

He had been doing that a lot since he had found her, she realised, taking every opportunity to touch her. Almost as if he needed to reassure himself she was safe and whole. Letty liked it. The gestures suggested he cared about her, and right now he was her whole world.

'I will feel a whole lot better when there is a good hour or more between me and the Earl of Bainbridge.'

His hand sought hers, held it, his thumb massaging her palm. 'I will not let him near you, sweetheart. I promise.'

And every time he called her sweetheart, her silly heart soared, even though he only ever used the endearment when she was upset or distressed. It didn't really mean anything. Any more than the emerald had meant anything more than what it was. A gesture of thanks. A small token. Yet Letty had been supremely conscious of the gold band encircling her finger from the second Jack had put it there. He let go of her hand and she automatically brought it to touch the ring, her index finger tracing the smooth stone. It had become a habit. A ritual. Soon, the small, old heirloom would be all she had of him.

Jack directed his horse south and she followed. Their progress was painfully slow as the forest closed in on them. Proud, tangled roots prevented the horses from building up any speed or momentum while low-hanging branches caught against her sleeves. With them came the dreadful memories of the last time she had been here, terrified and alone, yet determined to escape. In such a short time, she had now come full circle. The irony of the similarity was not lost on her, although this time Letty was not alone. She had

Jack. And for the first time, he was bathed in moonlight. Ahead of him, she could see why. The trees had thinned and there appeared a valley cut through them. They had reached the road.

Jack slid off his horse and handed Letty the reins. She tried to remain calm when he retrieved the pistol from his belt and she heard the hammer cock with an ominous click.

'I am going to check we are alone. Stay here.'

He crouched down and manoeuvred his way deftly through the trees to step on to the lane, then for several heart-stopping minutes, he disappeared from sight. A twig on the ground snapped and she almost jumped out of her skin, until she saw him, smiling sheepishly, emerging from the undergrowth.

'Sorry. I should have said something. I didn't mean to scare you.'

'As I haven't stopped being scared for hours, a puff of wind would likely scare me. It was sensible you didn't warn me. Anything above a whisper has the potential to get us both killed. Is the coast clear?'

'I checked both ways. I never saw a thing. I think it is fairly safe to assume they will be watching the road closer to the house rather than here.

We are at least four miles away from the village and there is not another one for ten miles.' She watched him haul himself effortlessly back into his saddle and nudge his mount down the small incline to the road. He waited patiently at the bottom while Letty did the same. 'It's pitch black and thankfully not raining. If ever there was a good opportunity to make some headway, it is now. If you're up for it, I say we push these horses for the next hour or so.'

They both set off simultaneously, varying between a trot and a canter until they approached the outer edge of the next village when Jack slowed and signalled her to do the same. 'Two fast horses clattering through the centre of a village in the small hours might arouse suspicion. Let's keep to the grass and avoid the cobbles.'

This formed the pattern of the next couple of hours. As they tore up the miles, Letty began to relax, although as the night time began to dissolve, she also realised she was exhausted. Jack found a road marker which warned they were only a few miles from Grantham. Even Letty knew it was too popular a stopping point on this road and would soon be filling up with early morning travellers keen to be on their way. Wearily, they turned their horses and plunged across fields instead, hoping they would find a suitably deserted place to rest in until the evening.

The big barn had an air of dereliction about it, perched as it was on a hilly pasture and well away from the rest of the farm buildings. As Jack had suspected, it was a spare hay store which was mostly empty, therefore they were unlikely to be bothered as the farmer's cows would all be closer to home in the dead of winter. Letty helped him to settle the horses at one end and fed them while Jack found water for the animals to drink. Once that chore was finished, they hungrily ate some of the food they had packed, swilling it down with milk.

Neither of them spoke, they were both dead on their feet. The hours of stress had taken their toll. Letty was so pale it worried Jack. The strain of her most recent ordeal was written all over her lovely face, yet she had not complained once on their long and arduous journey through the cold, damp night air. She needed several uninterrupted hours of sleep in a comfortable feather bed. Unfortunately, this ramshackle barn was going to have to do. It was about as far away from the luxury she was used to in Mayfair, but it was remote and almost watertight.

Letty packed away the uneaten rations in a saddle bag and fetched the blanket they had brought while Jack built her a nest to sleep in at the top of the haystack, away from view. If anybody did happen across them while they were sleeping, it would take a goodly while to find her and hopefully by then she would be prepared with her pistol. She smiled at him gratefully as he helped her to climb up and sank into the straw with a sigh. 'I can't remember ever looking forward to sleep more.'

Jack unravelled the bedroll and draped it solicitously over her. 'Where is your pistol?'

She retrieved it from her waistband and waved it at him. 'I know. I shall sleep with it close by.' He made to clamber back down from the stack and she frowned. 'Where are you going?'

'I shall sleep down here—near the door.' He wasn't particularly looking forward to lying on the draughty wooden floor, but with a bit of straw he supposed he could manage well enough.

'No. That will not do. You need your rest, too, Jack. I thought you were going to sleep up here. With me.'

The sudden surge of desire cut through his exhaustion very effectively, until he realised it was not a romantic invitation at all. 'That would hardly be proper, Letty.'

She giggled, the sound so unexpected after everything she had been through, clearly amused at his feeble attempt at behaving like a gentleman. 'Nothing about our association has been proper, Jack, so I hardly think we need to bow to propriety now. Come up here.' She patted the straw next to her and, to his consternation, his body took it as a signal. His groin tightened involuntarily.

'I shall be quite all right, Letty. If I am near the door, I can keep watch.'

'If you are near the door, you will freeze to death. Besides, I should feel much safer with you next to me than all the way down there.' If it made her feel safer, then perhaps he should sleep up there. With her. How exactly was he supposed to sleep, while his body was rampant with need and the woman he wanted more than anything else on earth was lying next to him? She saw his hesitation and inadvertently used it against him. Her eyes were wide and troubled and there was a definite, fearful catch in her voice. 'Please, Jack. I do not want to wake up in this strange place and wonder where you are. Don't leave me up here on my own.'

It was the tiny tremor in her voice which sealed his fate. Underneath her façade of bravery, Letty was terrified, as anybody would who had spent several hours alone, locked in the darkness, listening to the men who wanted to kill you pull apart a house as they searched it. Compared to that experience, his unfortunate physical discomfort paled into insignificance.

With leaden feet, he grabbed his own blanket roll and climbed reluctantly to the top of the hay stack. There was hardly room for two, so he did his best to put some distance between them and stretched out next to her. Letty rolled on to her side and smiled sleepily at him, conjuring up thoughts of what waking up in the morning with her every day would be like. This close, even in the dampened early morning light in the barn, Jack could see the darker flecks of green which ringed her pupils. He supposed they gave her mossy eyes the depth which made them sparkle like emeralds. Her golden hair was almost the same shade as the hay she lay on, except the hay was coarse and lacked lustre; Letty's curls shimmered like the finest silk embroidery thread.

'I think we made good time last night. I hope your brothers are safe, too.'

'Jamie will see them off. And if they won't leave, he has a veritable arsenal in his bedchamber. I don't fancy Bainbridge and your uncle's chances against him.'

'The last thing I want is any one of them hurt on my behalf. I have developed quite an attachment to the three of them.'

But what about him? Had she developed an attachment to him? Jack wanted to ask so very much. Was there more to the precious lion embroidery, as there had been to his ring, or was he pathetically reading something into their relationship which was no longer there? Jamie was convinced she was—how had he put it?—mad for him. Mad being the operative word. Jack was certainly mad for Letty. Today he had been ready to commit murder on her behalf. The acute, visceral fear he had experienced when he realised she had been in danger had unmanned him. Seeing her so frightened, curled up in the priest hole, yet utterly relieved she was alive and unharmed, he had very nearly succumbed himself and wept with joy. Afterwards, when she had clung to him, he had almost told her exactly how he felt. Only common sense and his own deeply held beliefs that people under duress do not think entirely straight had stopped the ardent confession spilling from his lips. Despite the fraught circumstances, Jack suddenly decided he had to know if the hope in his heart, which refused to die, stood any chance whatsoever.

'Letty…I was wondering…' Jack turned his body to properly face her and noticed her shivering beneath the thin blanket and completely forgot what he wanted to say. 'Oh, sweetheart, you're frozen. Come here.'

It had been an unconscious, natural decision to pull her into his arms. Sharing body heat and blankets made perfect sense, the pragmatist in him knew that, yet he had not fully thought the ramifications through. Letty eagerly cuddled up, wrapping her arm around his waist and hooking one leg snugly over his in order absorb the maximum amount of heat from his body.

'Oh, that's lovely. You're so warm, Jack.' And getting warmer by the second, but there was nothing to be done about it except grin and bear it. One arm curled possessively around her back, while the other fumbled for both blankets. He dragged one on top of the other, then bundled them around the pair of them so that only Letty's golden head poked out. She sighed contentedly and burrowed into the crook of his arm. 'I think we have discovered the perfect way to sleep outdoors. Perhaps sleeping in a barn isn't quite so bad after all?'

And perhaps he should just shoot himself now and put himself out of his own misery. Hours of potential torture stretched before him. By the deep rhythmic sounds of her breathing, Letty was not similarly overwhelmed with lust and longing. Her dark blonde eyelashes formed perfect crescents on her soft cheeks and her arm across his middle, scant inches away from the particular area which was causing him the most angst, was weighted with sleep. Stifling a groan, Jack pressed his lips to the top of her head.

'Goodnight, sweetheart. Sleep tight.' At least one of them would.

Chapter Twenty

Only two days to go...

Letty woke slowly, enjoying the weight of Jack's arm looped around her waist and the feel of his strong, broad chest pressed flush against her back. In the two nights they had been travelling, she had learned a few things about Jack Warriner's sleeping habits which utterly charmed her. Firstly, he talked in his sleep. The occasional word made sense, but most of the slurred mutterings which came out of his mouth were complete nonsense. Secondly, if she inadvertently moved away from him, he would instinctively roll towards her, curl his big body around hers and anchor her to him with a possessive arm across her middle. And thirdly, and perhaps not at all charmingly but quite thrillingly, just before he awoke the hard evidence of his desire nestled snugly against her bottom as it did now. All three things, he was blissfully unaware of she knew.

Yesterday, to spare his blushes, Letty had pretended to be asleep when he stirred and had remained like that until he had hastily released her and clambered down the haystack. This morning, she was severely tempted to see how he reacted when she didn't pretend, because his need to touch her constantly and call her sweetheart was not diminishing, no matter how many miles they put between themselves and her treacherous uncle. Something in their relationship had shifted and she was keen to explore what it was. Letty was beginning to hope Jack felt far more for her than simply lust—but the lust was a very good start.

Like the shameless harlot only he brought out in her, Letty wiggled her bottom against him until she heard him stir. Jack shifted slightly and pressed that intriguing part of him closer, so she wiggled some more. He sighed blissfully and nuzzled his nose into her hair affectionately, then, to her complete delight, the hand which had been thrown over her waist snaked up and firmly cupped her breast. It all felt very nice and very naughty. Too nice and too naughty to suspend the experiment any time soon.

She twisted slightly, to give him greater access to her neck and chest, and allowed her fingertips to stroke the exposed skin on his forearm while her wayward bottom continued to brush against him. When his thumb began to rub lazy circles around her nipple and his lips found her ear, Letty felt a momentary pang of guilt. The man was clearly still half-asleep and she was taking blatant advantage of him. How would she feel if he had tried to take advantage of her while she slept?

It was then that she smiled. Because if Jack had not been such a gentleman, Letty realised she would have been thrilled to bits. Boldly, she splayed her own palm flat on the hand which was currently lightly touching her bosom and shamelessly pressed it more firmly against her body, holding it in place as she shimmied her body around to lie flat on her back. Only then did she slide her palm under the hem of his shirt and caress the warm, smooth skin just below his ribcage. Jack mumbled some nonsense, but at the end of the incomprehensible sentence was one word which made her heart sing.

'Letty.'

It was half-sighed, half-groaned, yet it left her

in no doubt he was thinking about her alone and not just any random woman, either remembered or imagined.

'Yes, Jack. It's Letty.' Her hand smoothed its way to his shoulders and her mouth was barely an inch away from his. She would not be the first one to succumb to a kiss this time. If it was going to happen, it had to come at his instigation.

'Mornin', sweetheart.' It was late afternoon, but she didn't bother to correct him, because his hand had found the undone top of her shirt and was burrowing underneath it decisively. She moaned when long fingers touched the sensitive bare skin of her needy breast, but that moan was stifled by his lips on hers.

As sleepy kisses went, this one was earth-shattering. It was soft, shockingly intrusive and delightfully intimate. His tongue tangled with hers as he rolled his weight on top of her and, in case he suddenly came to his senses and stopped his sweet torture, Letty wrapped one leg around his hip. Aside from holding him in place, this also served to cushion all that glorious hardness in the cradle of her thighs. Only two pairs of soft breeches separated their bodies. If Letty had had a wand or supernatural abilities, she would have used magic to instantly dissolve the unwanted barrier.

Jack had to be awake now, because surely no man was capable of causing so much carnal pleasure in his sleep. His lips strayed away from hers and trailed hot, open-mouthed kisses down her neck, over her collarbone and deliciously over the covered swells of her breast. His mouth tortured her nipple through the linen, then with a growl, he grabbed the hem of the shirt at her waist and hoisted it up, exposing both of her breasts. His tongue swirled hotly around one aching tip before sucking it into his mouth. As Letty writhed in unashamed appreciation, he swapped sides and hungrily worshipped the other one before seeking her mouth again.

Letty desperately needed to feel him properly. Skin to skin. Heartbeat to heartbeat, so she clawed his shirt up to his shoulders and yanked it over his head. She arched against him wantonly, grazing her pebbled nipples against the solid wall of his chest and plunging her fingers into his thick hair, moaning her encouragement into his mouth. Everything blurred except the glorious sensations he was eliciting from her body.

She felt his hand rummage between their

squirming bodies for the buttons on the falls of his breeches. Letty's fingers hungrily joined his to assist. It was then that he pulled back, although not far enough to detract from the intimacy of the situation. His hardness still pressed against her core, one hand still cupped her breast, but his lips stilled and he lifted his head to stare down at her, somewhat alarmed.

'We shouldn't be doing this.'

His breathing was laboured, his sleepy eyes darkened and stormy with desire.

'Why?'

'You have been through a terrible ordeal. You are still overwhelmed with stress.'

To tempt him, Letty threw her arms back over her head. It brought her bare breasts into his eye line, one of them still covered by his big hand. 'Do I look stressed to you?' For good measure, she ground her hips against his and let him see the pleasure it brought her.

His thumb grazed her nipple once. Twice. He was not as immune to her as he had claimed. In that one moment, she could see how much he wanted her in the intensity of his deep blue stare. He closed his eyes and swallowed, clearly having an internal battle with himself.

'I want this, Jack. I want you.'

'I want you, too, Letty. More than anything...' He closed his eyes again and sighed. She watched a myriad of emotions chase across his expression before he severed all contact by rolling on to his back. 'But I won't ruin you like this. Not now. Not when so much is still unsettled and fraught and you have no idea how being with me will seriously impact on your life. But...' He sat up and stared down at her. She watched his eyes feast on the sight of her shamelessly sprawled on the hay, lingering on her breasts hungrily before he wrenched them away. 'When this is over, when you are home and safe, then perhaps we can discuss this again. I shall lay out all the pitfalls and all the reasons why I am not a good choice of husband, and then you can rationally decide what you want to do.' He located his shirt and hastily pulled it on. 'Things will be different then, I can assure you.'

Letty forced herself to stay exactly where she was, displayed for only his eyes to see her as nature had intended. 'Do you think my feelings will be different?'

'Yes. Until the dust has settled, your feelings are bound to be confused.' His words might have upset her, except his hand had come down to rest on her belly. They both watched its progress as it edged up her body, gently kneaded her breast and then came to rest lovingly on her cheek. 'Passion isn't love.' Before she could argue, he jumped decisively down to the floor. 'I'll ready the horses. We leave in fifteen minutes.'

The weather matched Jack's mood. The rain had begun again shortly after midnight. Fine, misty rain at first, but then it came down with a vengeance. About an hour ago, it had turned to sleet. Another partially frozen droplet hit his neck and dribbled under his shirt, compounding his misery further. The only part of his body that had been spared a thorough soaking was his backside. However, the same saddle which had kept his posterior dry was now almost torture to sit on.

This leg of their nocturnal journey had been interminable. Partly because there was once again an atmosphere between him and Letty and partly because he could not seem to get the image of her sprawled in the hay out of his head. Jack might well be frozen to the bone, miserable and saddle sore, however none of these ailments apparently affected his rampant male parts one little bit.

Why had his sense of responsibility chosen to rear its ugly head when it had? A few minutes later and his lust would have been thoroughly sated and the dilemma he suffered would be moot. They would have had to have got married and that was that. Except, his heart wanted more than a wife by default. He would absolutely not be his father and trap her. He wanted Letty to choose him. Not because she was frightened, or lonely or unsettled or grateful, but because she had properly considered her decision and decided he was worth all the trouble. This last month had not been normal for either of them. Letty needed some normality to rediscover herself.

And once she did, then she would realise the concept of them as a couple was sheer folly. When the danger was over and she was back on familiar turf, he had to be prepared for Letty to see the potential misery of marrying a Warriner and making the considered decision that it was not worth it in the long run. In Jack's experience, hope in any form had always been the kiss of death. He needed to stop hoping, stop thinking they might stand a chance, and focus on getting her home safely.

He risked a glance sideways and saw she looked

as miserable as him. The few strands of hair visible under the hat she wore pulled low were stuck to her face. Her long eyelashes were spiky from the rain and, more worrying now that the first light of dawn pushed forth, there was a distinct bluish tinge to her lips. She needed a warm bath, plenty of bedcovers and a roaring fire. The last time she had suffered exposure to the elements like this, she had been sick for days and he had feared she would die.

The last road marker had warned that they were only a few miles from Baldock, a busy little town where several roads merged with the Great North Road. Trusting Jamie's advice, this might be the perfect place to risk stopping at an inn. People apparently saw less in crowds and they could both do with a proper bed, hot food and dry clothes before they set off on the final leg of their journey. Tomorrow morning, with any luck, they would finally arrive in the capital, and once they got there, the next instalment of Letty's ordeal would begin. She would need all of her strength for that, so the risk of the inn was worth it. They would also benefit from having a brick wall between them when they slept. Two separate rooms would give them both some space. Letty would be able to think about their situation dispassionately and Jack would be able to avoid all temptation.

'We will find an inn in the next town.'

Letty nodded, her expression wretched, clearly too cold and too tired to comment, so they trudged on until they saw a suitably busy inn. The morning carriages were already loading in readiness of leaving and the tantalising scent of cooking bacon wafted in the air. Jack handed her some coins and sent her to the dining room to order them both some breakfast.

'While I sort out the horses and the accommodations, Letty, you should probably try and appear as inconspicuous as possible.' She nodded listlessly and walked off, and Jack went first to the stables.

A lad relieved him of the horses and led them inside to be rubbed down and fed. Jack went in search of the innkeeper, only to find his frazzled wife instead. 'I should like two rooms, please.'

'And I should like an ermine cloak and a husband who wasn't workshy and still abed—but we don't always get what we want. You can have one room or none at all.'

'But I need two.'

'We're full. The world and his wife are travelling back to London now that Christmas is over. I have one room spare, it's a fine one and plenty big enough for two. Take it or leave it, sir. If you don't want it, someone else will snap it up within the hour, I'm sure.'

Jack wavered for a moment. All manner of mischief could occur in one room as it had this morning when he was still half-asleep. Sharing a room with Letty, one in possession of a proper bed, was a temptation he did not need if he was to keep his vow of not ruining her…but on the other hand, Letty was frozen and exhausted. And the innkeeper's wife did say it was plenty big enough for two. There might be a place for him to make up a bed on the floor. If it came to it, he could probably bed down in the stables. Letty's health and wellbeing had to come first.

'I'll take it.'

He found Letty sitting hunched at a small table in the far corner of the crowded dining room. 'They only had one room.'

She shrugged and Jack couldn't tell if she was peeved at him, the lack of a second room or merely bone tired. 'It will have to do.'

'I've ordered a hot bath to be drawn. It should be ready in half an hour.'

'I wasn't sure what you wanted to eat, so I have ordered you pretty much everything.' She smiled then and the odd atmosphere began to float away. 'Personally, I could eat a horse.'

The meal turned out to be both enormous and delicious. The hot tea was even better and it revived them both. Thankfully, Letty was her usual cheerful self and made no mention of their earlier indiscretion. It suited Jack fine. Talking about what had happened would make him think about it and it was already proving to be near impossible to forget the glorious feel of her perfect bare breast squashed into his palm, or the way her body had fitted so splendidly against his and how she had writhed in pleasure... All at once, his breeches tightened again and remained ruthlessly so during Letty's third, painfully slow cup of tea.

By the time they had finished and located their room, the steaming bathtub was already waiting and, thoughtfully, the maid had also arranged a screen for privacy.

Jack had intended a swift exit as soon as he was sure Letty was properly settled, followed by a brisk and necessarily bracing wash from the pump out in the courtyard to cool his ardour, but the room was warm and the lure of proper armchairs to rest on was too strong, so he stepped inside. When he gave in to the urge to sit briefly in one of the chairs, his bones gratefully sank into the soft upholstery and his good intentions did not shout loud enough to drown out the sound of sheer contentment. The freezing pump could wait a few minutes more.

'Do you want to bathe first or second?'

More temptation Jack did not need—but, oh, how his aching body would enjoy the soothing relief of a nice hot bath. Now the chance to soak in a hot tub had presented itself, he was reluctant to turn down the opportunity. Besides, he was also reluctant to leave the wonders of the chair just yet.

'You go first.'

She disappeared behind the screen and Jack began to pull off his sodden boots. Letty's wet clothing came off piece by piece and she slapped them noisily across the top of the screen.

He really hadn't thought this through.

Now he knew she was completely naked behind the screen—and that was far too unnerving to contemplate for long. He needed to do something practical to distract himself. After he heard her sink down into the water with a throaty sigh, he retrieved the sopping clothes and arranged them near the roaring fire to dry. His own clothes stuck wetly to his body and he realised they were probably the reason his spine was aching with cold. He dithered as to whether or not he should take his off in readiness for his turn in the bathtub, then realised she had already seen him stripped to the waist, so the sight of his hairy chest was hardly going to come as a huge surprise. And he was cold, after all. He peeled off his shirt and breeches, wrapped a towel tightly around his waist and placed them next to hers to dry, trying to ignore the sound of splashing water as she soaped her naked skin only a few feet away.

The next ten minutes were the longest of his life. His imagination was out of control, his body was primed for action and the sounds of her bathing behind that blasted screen were possibly the most erotic noises he had ever heard. Who knew the sound of soap being rubbed on to a flannel would be so potent?

When she emerged swaddled in another towel, the skin he could see was all pink and it took all of his strength not to go to her, snatch away the towel and drag her into his unworthy arms. Her hair hung damply around her shoulders and down her back. She stared at him for a second or two, blinking rapidly, then smiled shyly as she padded past him. The back of the towel draped low, displaying the graceful lines of her back and the hint of the curve of her bottom. His big, calloused hands longed to be filled with it.

Feeling awkward, self-conscious and beyond aroused, Jack gratefully hid behind the screen to take his turn in the water. He undid the towel and stared down at his arousal mournfully. Was it ever going to subside or was he doomed to spend all eternity as stiff as a board? He should have washed at the pump. The cold water would have done the trick instantly. If he took a long bath, he reasoned, she would be tucked safely in bed by the time he finished. And if he stayed in it long enough, the water would chill and his rampant body might finally calm down. With any luck, it would take such a long time, she would already be soundly asleep by the time he felt settled enough to emerge.

Chapter Twenty-One

One final day remaining...

His skin was covered in goose bumps by the time he finally emerged from the bathtub. The dark, downy hair on his chest and abdomen clung wetly to the muscles beneath and his male nipples were puckered with cold. To say he made her mouth water was an understatement. A wet, half-naked Jack was even more appealing than any version of him she had seen previously. It took all of her resolve not to lick her lips at the sight.

He appeared surprised to see Letty sitting at the hearth drying her hair. Or perhaps he was simply stunned to see her shamelessly wearing nothing but a towel. Although it was tucked securely under her armpits, it was not long enough to cover her legs. His blue eyes flicked to them before he dragged them back to her face. When he spoke, his normally deep, commanding voice was a touch higher than usual.

'I thought you would be in bed.'

His eyes dropped to her legs again and she watched his Adam's apple bob in the thick column of his neck. Had he not been naked under the towel, he probably would have bolted for the door. She bothered him. And judging by the interesting bulge under the waistband of the towel, he liked what he saw. As reactions went, it did a great deal to boost her confidence. However, that was not the sole reason she had waited for him to finish bathing. There were things they needed to talk about and Letty was not inclined to wait, as Jack had wanted, for the *dust to settle.*

'My hair is almost dry. Why don't you come and sit with me and keep me company?' There were things that needed to be said. Letty had several pertinent questions for him which positively demanded answers. She had had hours to mull over his words when he had put a stop to their intimacies this morning and his choice of phrasing had been telling. At no point had he mentioned *his* doubts about the pair of them, only *hers.* Why did he think she would suddenly change her mind about her feelings for him when she got back to London?

Jack walked stiffly to the chair, clutching the towel for grim death and doing his best to hide what was going on underneath it. When he sat down, he made sure the towel was suitably bunched to disguise his obvious arousal and stared back at her awkwardly.

'Tell me about your family.'

This appeared to flummox him, because his dark eyebrows came together and he suddenly appeared even more uncomfortable in the chair.

'What exactly do you want to know?'

'I want to know all of the terrible reasons why the world apparently distrusts the Warriners.' Because somehow, that was at the heart of his dilemma and the reason he held himself back from her. Letty had seen the effect she had on him. He wasn't immune to her charms, nor was he indifferent to her character. In the last two days, he had proved he would move heaven and earth to see her safe. Jack cared about her. She felt it.

'There are so many reasons, it would take days to tell you everything. All of them were a bad lot.'

'But you and your brothers aren't.'

'Mud sticks, I'm afraid. We have been ruthlessly

tarred with the same brush. I have tried to allay people's fears over the last few years. So far, all my efforts have been in vain. As a family, we are universally disliked by all.'

Letty had heard versions of this comment frequently from all four of the brothers, yet they had been reticent about elaborating. 'Then start with your parents. What did they do to upset the world?'

She watched him take a deep breath and stare down at his hands. He didn't want to talk about it, she realised. He would use it as a barrier to stop him being happy—but it was not something he was keen on sharing. His fingers began to play with an edge of towel, alerting her to the fact he was uneasy about her potential reaction, but he met her gaze squarely. Almost defiantly. 'My father was a complete scoundrel. He drank too much and had a tendency not to pay his debts. He was untrustworthy and lacked morals.'

An interesting assessment, but severely lacking in tangible evidence. Letty already had the impression getting the whole truth out of this proud man would be tantamount to drawing blood out of a stone, but there was too much at stake not to ruthlessly squeeze the stone for every drop. 'What morals did he lack?'

Those disarming blue eyes narrowed. 'When my father saw something he coveted, he did whatever he wanted to get it. Often, that meant he used foul means over fair.'

'Are you saying he cheated people?'

He nodded curtly. 'He was famous for it. Nobody would do business with him.'

'And now you suffer by default as nobody will do business with you either.'

'Nobody local will. I have found a butcher in Lincoln who will suffer my lamb and another merchant who will take the corn.'

'Suffer? Take? I've seen how hard you work and the quality of your stock, Jack. They are hardly doing you a favour.'

'Oh, they are. I assure you it's taken years to get anyone to do even that much.'

Years of listening to her father had given Letty a sound understanding of business. 'Do they pay you market price?'

'Almost.' The proud gleam was shining out of his eyes and those spectacular shoulders had risen defiantly. He knew he was being fleeced. Knew and accepted it because he had no choice. Further discussion on the topic would likely result in Jack's lips sealing up tighter than a drum, when for once he was talking, albeit with great reluctance.

'What other morals did your father lack?'

'He could be violent. He had a habit of punching people when he had a drink inside him. That also made him unpopular with the locals.'

It probably also made him wildly unpopular with his family. Letty feared she knew the answer to her next question already, but wanted to gauge his reaction to it none the less. 'Did he use his fists on you, too?'

He shrugged. 'Better on me than the younger boys or my mother.'

Poor, loyal, steadfast Jack.

'Is that why she took her own life?'

'Partly—but she was never happy at Markham Manor.' He raked an agitated hand through his damp hair. 'I am under-exaggerating. She *loathed* Markham Manor. She loathed my father. And because we all had the misfortune to be born the spitting image of him, she loathed us, too.'

Jamie had claimed Jack always had to be responsible. He absorbed other people's problems unconsciously, seeing it as his place to shoulder them as the head of the family. Hardly a surprise when his parents had let him down so dreadfully.

'Do you blame yourself for her death?'

He paused, as if giving it some thought for the very first time, then shook his head. 'No. I blame my father. Plunging herself into the river was far more appealing to her than living the life she had foisted upon her.'

'In what way was her life foisted upon her?'

Those proud shoulders deflated and his eyes became troubled. Darker. Bluer.

'My mother came from London. Like you. My father charmed her, ruined her and then took her away from the life she loved. They were ostracised from society. My mother never got over it.'

Another interesting insight into this complicated, stubborn man. 'You think the same would happen to me?'

He looked at her grimly. 'Don't you see, Letty? Everything about our situation has been fraught with danger from the outset. You have been through a great deal and do not know who to trust. But you trust me and perhaps you've fooled yourself into thinking those feelings mean more than gratitude. I cannot, in all good conscience, pursue whatever may, or may not, be between us until your life is normal again and you can see things clearly. It's not easy being a Warriner.'

His flippant dismissal of her emotions as being fickle and interchangeable galled. 'Oh, for goodness sake! I am neither that shallow nor that addled! I know my own mind perfectly well. And as for your claim about it not easy being a Warriner, perhaps you should try being the Tea Heiress for a few weeks. That is not easy either! We all have our crosses to bear, Jack.'

'I should imagine having a great fortune and society practically falling at your feet is a great chore!' he shot back sarcastically.

'Urrgh! How typical. Now *you* are tarring *me* with the same brush I have always been tarred with!' Gripping the edge of her towel, Letty stood up abruptly and stalked towards the window. She had hoped he would understand or think differently seeing that he actually *knew* her. But then again, why would he? Jack had always struggled to make ends meet. He had no concept of what being an orphaned heiress was like. If she wanted him to open up to her, then it stood to reason she should entrust him with the same honour.

'Do you know what it is like to be all alone in the world, Jack? I doubt you can even begin to imagine it, because you have your family. Three noisy brothers who are always there for you. You might fight, disagree, rub each other the wrong way, but there is always somebody for you to come home to. To talk to. Since my parents died, I don't have that.'

She turned and walked slowly back to her seat, all the while watching him digest the information. 'But the newspapers always talk of all the parties and balls you attend.'

It stood to reason he would compare what he thought to be true with her version of the truth. How best to explain it?

'I have a big house in Mayfair. It is filled with servants and fine furniture, I eat the best food, wear the nicest clothes—but it is a house without a heart, Jack. It intimidates people, so they rarely visit. And if they do, it is out of either curiosity or to gain gossip to pass on to their friends about the mythical Violet Dunston who resides within. Sometimes the house feels like a prison, except I am the only inmate.'

Letty sat down slowly and reached for his hand.

'You already know my uncle is not exactly the model guardian. At best, he has always been indifferent to me. He moved in and fulfilled his legal obligations, but we rarely spoke. Yes, I do go out to balls and parties. I rarely turn down an invitation, but that is not because I particularly enjoy them, it is because if I don't go to them, I never get to have a conversation with anyone. Except, they are never *really* the sorts of conversations I would wish to have. You were right when you called them superficial. Everybody believes I live this charmed existence. It never occurs to them that I am lonely or that Violet Dunston is a character I play in public. Nobody wants to see the reality of who I actually am.'

'You're lonely.'

This, apparently, was a grand epiphany because he appeared both shocked and horrified in equal measure. Seeing his expression of pity, for her, made her want to weep.

'One never quite knows who to trust. Are they really my friends or is it the fortune which attracts them? Being one of my acquaintances has its benefits. I am famously generous.'

'I thought you had men lining up outside your door to marry you?'

Letty laughed without humour, because it really would be laughable if she was not on the receiving end of it. 'They do line up. It's terrifying. But it's not me, Letty, that they want. I sincerely doubt any of them truly see me at all. I sometimes wonder if the real me is completely invisible to everyone. It's the enormous pile of banknotes they see when they look at me which attracts them. You might think I have everything, yet I envy you your riches, Jack. You have three brothers who love you unconditionally, a noisy, cheerful house and a purpose every morning when you get up. I get up alone in the morning, make myself busy with trivialities which bore me senseless and go to bed alone again every single night. It is humbling to learn that I am of such little consequence to people that none of my so-called friends and acquaintances have even noticed I am missing. My uncle picked the perfect time. Christmas is a time for families. And I don't have one.'

'I never realised your life was like that.' His fingers had laced with hers somewhere during her monologue and it made her sadder, yet she did not want his pity.

'What do you see when you look at me?'

He was silent for ages, his thumb gently tracing lazy circles in her palm.

'I don't see a pile of banknotes or a superficial spoiled girl.' His intense gaze finally locked meaningfully with hers. 'I see the most beautiful woman in the world. I see a woman who never ceases to amaze me. One who rises to every challenge. One who is tenacious and kind, who can laugh at herself and stand up for herself. One who never gives up and who cooks chicken with the feathers on.' He smiled then, except it was not any normal, everyday smile. It was an intimate, knowing smile. 'I never see Violet. I only ever see Letty.'

Something finally fell into place inside her, some misplaced part which had been missing all of her life. With it came her own epiphany. He loved her. She could see it in those fathomless blue depths without him needing to say the words. The words were superfluous anyway. His feelings came out in every solicitous action, every noble deed. Not only that, but she loved him in return. She recognised that now. It was more than attraction and lust, or the need for him to like her. Her heart belonged to him and always would. Every sinew and fibre of her being wanted only to be with him. The knowledge gave her inner strength. New purpose to crack through the noble fortress he hid behind because it was *he* who felt unworthy.

She stood and let the towel slither to the floor, watched his eyes widen, then darken with desire as they raked her naked body, even though he remained rooted to his spot in the armchair. Feeling the weight of his stare, she turned and slowly walked towards the bed, feeling every inch the temptress she wanted him to see. When she reached the bed, Letty slid between the crisp, clean sheets and propped herself up seductively on one elbow, making sure the covers only covered her up to the waist.

'Come to bed, Jack.'

He sat as still as a statue, his eyes locked on her and his breathing erratic. 'No. I won't ruin you, Letty.'

Oh, bless him! she thought as she giggled at his ridiculously noble gesture. 'Don't you see, Jack? You *can't* ruin me. I could take a hundred lovers and it would make no difference. The majority of my suitors would overlook my lack of virginity in much the same way they ultimately overlook the real me. I'm Violet Dunston, remember. It's my fortune they want to take to bed. The lack of my maidenhead would hardly deter them—yet it would be such a shame to waste it on one of them when they wouldn't appreciate it. You would appreciate it, wouldn't you, Jack?'

She let him war with himself for a few moments, watched the interesting battle being fought in his expression. The responsible gentleman fought the human man with basic human urges. When he stood up, it was hard to discern which one of them had won. He strode towards her, suddenly appearing quite furious.

'I won't offer you marriage yet, Letty. I am not a fortune hunter.'

'I don't recall asking you to marry me, Jack. I'm asking you to come to bed. To make love to me. If anything, you silly, stubborn man, it is me who is intent on ruining you. In fact, if I do it properly, I will ruin you for all other women except me.'

Then he grinned. It was the same roguish smile which had dazzled her weeks before. 'You want to ruin me?'

'Indeed I do. I promise not to view it as a declaration of marriage or even a promise of one. I am perfectly happy to wait and see if my feelings for you are real.' Which of course they were, except the idiot was too proud to see it. He couldn't accept that anyone would truly want him for the man he was. However, there was no point in arguing with him about it now. Not when his obstinate, responsible mind was made up. If she was going to get her way, then she had to give him another reason to willingly come to her bed. Fortunately, she did not have to make anything up. 'The truth is, I want you. I want that big, brutish Warriner body on mine. I want your hands all over me. I want to know what it feels like to be bedded by a man who doesn't care about my money. I want to give myself to the only man who sees the real Letty. And if you don't take me soon, all of this burning desire that consumes me will send me mad from the wanting.'

From the heated determined expression on his handsome face, her words might well have hit their mark. His mouth began to curve up slowly. It was all male and deliciously predatory.

'Brace yourself, Letty. You are about to be thoroughly ravished.'

'I am?'

She rolled languidly on to her back and stretched her arms out on the pillow like a cat enjoying the sunshine, but she could not hide her smug smile of victory. It slid off her face when he dropped his own towel on the floor and she caught her first glimpse of him completely naked. Every inch of him was firm, solid male.

Every single inch.

And, good grief, there was a lot of inches to accommodate.

He saw her reaction and gave her a very self-satisfied, confident smile. 'Try not to panic, sweetheart. If I do it right, we shall likely both lose our heads and you will have a splendid time in the process.'

'I—I will?'

His big body slipped under the covers next to her. One strong arm snaked possessively around her hip and tugged her until her body was flush up against his.

'You will. I promise. *This* Warriner always keeps his word.'

Chapter Twenty-Two

Twelve glorious hours to go...

Jack did not disappoint. From the outset he assaulted her senses with all manner of new sensations, each one a revelation. Just being so intimately aligned, bare skin to bare skin from head to toe, was an experience. His body was solid and unyielding. He was hard where she was soft. Flat where she had curves. Her hands enjoyed shamelessly exploring those masculine planes and her eyes hungrily watched as certain muscles tensed or jumped under her touch. Because she had to, Letty placed her mouth on his chest, inhaling the intoxicating scent of him as she ran her lips over his body.

Jack was doing some exploring of his own, except his lips followed his fingers everywhere they went. He started with her mouth, kissing her until her body ached for more, then he tortured her by licking and nibbling his way slowly down her neck and shoulders. He stayed longer on her breasts, his clever tongue working her nipples into such a state of arousal that she had to grab his head and hold it in place. But even that did not ease her body's urgent cravings and Letty found her hips straining to meet his, her legs falling open wantonly in invitation, desperately wishing he would put an end to the delicious torture and fill her body with his.

He knew what she wanted and denied it. Letty felt him smile as he twisted his hips out of her reach and placed soft kisses over her belly—which did nothing to satisfy her overpowering desires. There were other, better places she wanted his mouth. Her breasts, for example, still ached for his touch.

She tried to drag his mouth back to hers, but he would have none of it, preferring to trace the outline of her navel with his tongue, and she growled in frustration.

'You're a wretch, Jack Warriner.'

His returning laughter was muffled. 'Why am I a wretch?'

'Because...'

'If you cannot tell me, then how can I know what it is you want?' His teeth scraped her hip and began to nibble their way down the top of her thigh.

'You know perfectly well what I want...'

Those lips were torturing the sensitive skin on her inner thigh now. It was a vast improvement on having them on her stomach, but as pleasant as it was, it did absolutely nothing to lessen the ache between her legs. An ache which was causing her to writhe desperately on the mattress. His splayed hands rested on the very top of both thighs, so very close yet still so far away from where she craved them. Her hips bucked instinctively and he stared up at her with the most wicked smile she had seen yet. It was no wonder. From his position he could see all the secret parts of her which remained a mystery to even her own eyes and, heaven help her, she didn't care one whit.

'Jack...please.'

He smiled knowingly and dipped his head, and to her complete surprise, and utter mortification, placed a hot kiss *there*. Instinctively, Letty went to close her legs, only to find his hold on them made it quite impossible. She tried to sit up, but then his tongue touched something which sent ripples of pure pleasure through her entire body.

'Oooooh…'

The noise she made came out part-sigh, part-groan, and she quite forgot that she was outraged by the improper intrusion. When his tongue stroked her again intimately, Letty sank back on to the pillows and decided she did not want to fight him. Clearly the man knew exactly what he was doing, so who was she to argue? Within moments, nothing else existed other than his clever mouth on her most secret place and the mounting pleasure that tiny intimate movement was creating. Words would not form, only noises. Soft sighs, urgent moans. One hand plunged into his hair, the other gripped the sheets tight and her heels dug into the bed so she did not move a muscle, fearing if she did he would leave that one, delectable sweet spot she had not known had existed just a few minutes ago.

Jack could feel the tension build in her body and like the novice she was she fought against it. Her head thrashed from side to side, her hips strained against his mouth, while she hovered on the cusp. Gently, he eased his finger inside her to massage the inner walls of her body. Nobody else had touched her like this.

Just him.

If nothing else came of their relationship, he would always be her first and he was going to make sure she never forgot him. He was determined to spoil all other men for her, just as she had ruined him for any other woman. Letty was so warm and wet and tight it made him groan as he stroked her. His own body was screaming for release, but he wanted her to know what pleasure felt like before he stole away her innocence. Yet, it didn't feel like he was really stealing it from her. She was giving it to him, freely and with such trust it humbled him. When her hips began to buck, he sucked the sweet bud into his mouth and heard and felt her release joyfully. He shifted so that he could see her face. Her eyes were closed, her corkscrew curls were fanned over the pillow and her lips were parted in ecstasy.

She sensed his gaze and her eyes fluttered open and stared down at him. Jack had never witnessed anything so utterly perfect as Letty was right then. His heart stuttered and his breath caught, and his body throbbed with need. He should stop now. That was the gentlemanly thing to do. Slowly he sat back on his heels and sucked in calming breaths.

He watched, slightly unnerved, as Letty's small hands reached out to touch him. She traced his hardness reverently, her fingertips so gentle that Jack had to clench his teeth to stop crying out. Now would be the perfect time to rise from the bed and leave her, because if he stayed a moment longer his resolve would evaporate. He should leave her a virgin. That was the right thing to do. But against his wishes, his hand closed around hers, showing her how to hold him, and from then on he was lost. When he could stand the exquisite torture no more, he lay down beside her again and, like the trusting angel she was, she opened her arms in invitation.

Her lovely body was still trembling when he positioned himself between her legs and the happy, pleasure-filled smile she gave him, and the way her arms looped languidly around his neck let him know she welcomed this part of the act, too. Emotion clogged his throat. This beautiful, perfect, angel wanted him.

Jack Warriner.

What had he ever done to deserve such a gift?

'I love you, Letty.' The words tumbled out before he could claw them back. Her kiss-swollen lips parted and he just knew she was going to say the same words back. But he wanted them to be real, not uttered in the heat of the moment when her passions were inflamed. Jack placed his fingers gently on her mouth. 'Not now, Letty. Tell me in a month or two, when all the danger is over. If you still mean it.'

She sighed and kissed him deeply instead, pushing her hips against his in encouragement. He kissed her back, the tip of his arousal nudging her entrance, and then, with painful, tender slowness, pushed inside.

Her tight heat encased him. Jack's body urgently wanted to move, but he held back. He stopped when he met the barrier of her maidenhead. Only then did he break the kiss to stare down into her face. He did not need to tell her he did not wish to hurt her. She understood. Her hand came up to cup his cheek and she shrugged her shoulders.

'Just do it. I trust you to make it right.'

So he did. He pushed past the barrier swiftly, burying himself deep inside her and then stopped dead, feeling like a savage brute for causing her pain. It was Letty's hips which moved first, undulating against his, enticing him to continue and driving him mad with need.

When he moved, he intended to do so slowly, but it was Letty who spurred him on. She met his tentative thrusts eagerly, staring deep into his eyes, a beautiful, contented smile on her face. When she wrapped her legs around him and he saw her eyes flutter closed in pleasure, he quite forgot his oath to go slowly. The faster he moved, the deeper he plunged, the more Letty moaned her enjoyment. When her hands came down to grab his buttocks and he felt her pull them roughly, urgently towards her body, he gave up trying to fight it and let the desire take him. To his relief, she cried out first and her body pulsed around the entire length of him, and Jack finally lost his head and joined her, crying out her name in exultation as he pulled out and spilled himself beside her, protecting her even in the heat of the moment.

Knowing she had made good on her promise.

She had ruined him for all other women. He would never be able to look at another one again because no one else was Letty and he belonged to her.

They slept for a few hours before Jack could not resist the urge to make love to her again. Slower this time, because he knew it might well be for the very last time. When they next awoke it was already dark and way past the time they should have started on the road. He was tempted to ask her to stay until the morning, but knew what they had come to do could not be put off. If they made good time tonight, they would still see London in the morning and, as much as he feared what returning her home might do to them, it was long past time they banished the threat from her uncle and the Earl of Bainbridge from her life. Once that was dealt with, fate, no doubt, would have its rightful say and all Jack could do was hope and pray that, for once, it might take pity on him.

Jack lifted her on to the saddle carefully, his expression rueful. 'Are you sore, sweetheart?'

She was, a little bit, but it was a pleasant sort of soreness which reminded her of what they had done. The very last thing she wanted was to make him feel guilty for it. 'Not really. I quite like how it feels.'

'I shouldn't have woken you and—'

'Don't you dare apologise for our second time together. I thoroughly enjoyed myself.'

A smile played at the corners of his mouth as he

hoisted himself on his own horse. 'It was rather spectacular.'

An understatement.

Intimacies with Jack Warriner were yet another revelation and not something Letty had any intention of giving up while he *waited for the dust to settle* and he decided they were meant to be together. Why was he so determined to be stubborn? What did she have to do to prove her feelings for him were as real as his were for her?

'It's insulting, you know.' Letty hadn't meant to think out loud, but decided not to be sorry for the sudden outburst.

'What is?'

'Your ridiculous insistence that I do not know my own mind.'

'You have been through such a terrible ordeal…'

Letty rolled her eyes in irritation. 'Oh, please! Not that speech again. It's becoming very tiresome. To be frank, Jack, I really haven't been through a terrible ordeal at all. Yes, I have had a few terrifying moments in the last month, I am not denying that, but overall, it has been a very positive experience.'

'The devil it has!' It was his turn to appear agitated now. 'Being kidnapped has been a positive experience?'

They turned their horses into a narrower section of the road, riding side by side while they bickered. 'Yes, it has. I have really enjoyed living at Markham Manor. I liked being part of the family and learning new things.'

'Like how to clean nooks and crannies and do laundry?' He was staring at her as if she had gone quite mad.

'Yes, I did, as a matter of fact. It made me appreciate my life more. I got a great sense of achievement from doing those chores and it made me happy to know I was helping you and your brothers.'

'So you do admit you are *grateful* to me, then?'

She was going to kill him. He was determined to twist her words to justify his own fears about them. 'Of course I am grateful. You saved me, sheltered me and took care of me. Who wouldn't be grateful? But *that* is not the reason why I gave myself to you. I was not *that* grateful, I can assure you. I was merely trying to explain why the past month has not been the dreadful ordeal you seem to think it was and you are determined to find reasons why I couldn't possibly love you, when I know quite well that *I do* love you. And a few weeks of contemplation in London is *not* going to change that.'

He pulled up his horse smartly and appeared to be quite annoyed with this statement.

'I've told you not to say anything like that until you are certain.'

But she could see the hope shining in his troubled blue eyes despite his words. If he hadn't been so much taller and broader than she was, and if they had not both been sat astride horses on the Great North Road, Letty would have grabbed him by those splendid shoulders and tried to shake some sense into him. Denied that satisfaction, words would have to do.

'I am certain, you stubborn fool! I have never been more certain of anything in my entire life.

'I.

'Love.

'You.

'There! I said it again. And I'm not addled, or suffering from misguided gratefulness or blinded by lust to the detriment of all else. It is *you* who is uncertain, Jack. And rather insultingly, you are uncertain of me!'

He went to interrupt, but she didn't give him the chance.

'You're convinced that after a few weeks, I will grow to resent you, like your selfish mother did your father and grow melancholy and perhaps fade away. What evidence do you have to support such a preposterous notion? I am not like her, Jack. I am not some silly, spoiled, weak-willed woman who cannot cope without the finer things in life. I can bake bread, for goodness sake, and round up sheep and thwart kidnappers all on my own. I am not now, nor will I ever be, the sort of woman who feels sorry for herself or throws herself into a river.'

When he opened his mouth once more to refute her, she gave him her parting salvo. Something, apparently, he had thus far not considered.

'You think my life with you will be hard. You believe I will be shunned and ostracised by society. If I am, it will be a blessing. I loathe society. I am sick and tired of pretending to be Violet and feeling lonely. But that aside, I think you are missing one very pertinent detail. I am *the Tea Heiress*. I have far too much money for anyone to shun me, and, in case it has not crossed your stubborn, proud, obstinate mind, *when* you marry me—and you will marry me, Jack Warriner, because *we* love each other to bits—you are going to be obscenely wealthy, too!'

Neither of them saw the four armed men at the side of the road waiting for them until it was too late.

Chapter Twenty-Three

Two precarious hours left...

'Hello, Violet. Did you miss me?'

The Earl of Bainbridge's face was suddenly illuminated when he struck a match. Jack glimpsed the yellowed whites of his eyes and the pistol in his gnarled hand before the match spluttered and died. Jack did his best to shield Letty with his body while he scanned the dark road for a way to escape. Dense tangled bushes flanked both sides of the road, too high for their horses to jump without momentum and too thick to be able to charge through. As he considered galloping back towards Baldock, a dark carriage rolled out behind them, blocking the *road* completely. Another man climbed out, the same sort of age as Bainbridge and clutching another pistol which he aimed directly at them.

'Uncle William. Have you come to do your own dirty work this time?' Letty glared at him defiantly, her delicate chin lifted and her fine eyes colder than Jack had ever seen them.

'You should have married Bainbridge, Violet. If you had, then we could have avoided all of this nastiness.'

'My father entrusted you with my safekeeping. He would be turning in his grave to know how you have betrayed me!'

'Perhaps if your father had distributed some of his wealth to me, then I would not have had to resort to this. But I did.'

Layton stepped out of the shadows, his white, jagged scar more apparent in the moonlight. Jack heard the click as he cocked the hammer of his pistol and pointed it menacingly at Letty. 'Get down from those horses.'

The cold calm delivery sent a chill down Jack's spine. Resisting the urge to pull his own pistol from his belt, he put his hands in the air.

'Do as he says, Letty.'

On foot, if he could distract Layton, there might be a way of slipping Letty behind the bushes so she could escape.

Unfortunately, as soon as her feet touched the

ground, Letty decided to go on the attack. She made to lunge towards her uncle, but Jack caught her and shielded as much of her straining body as he could with his own. Being restrained did nothing to stop her resolve.

'Do you seriously think I will allow you to drag me to Gretna Green again and force me to marry *that* man?'

Her uncle frowned, his own temper dangerously close to the surface. 'I'm afraid that option is now closed, Violet, thanks to your intrepid escape. It will be easier all around if Bainbridge just kills you.'

'Are you too cowardly to do it yourself?' Good grief, now she was baiting the man. Jack shot her a warning look, hoping she would back down. Could she not see that while he was holding her back, he was unable to facilitate her escape?

Being Letty, of course she ignored him.

'Here I am, Uncle. Look me in the eyes and then put a bullet between them.'

'I have no taste for murder, Violet.'

'Yet you sold me off to a murderer quite happily! Does that alleviate your warped conscience in some way?' She gave a scornful laugh.

'I did what I had to. Now that I think about it,

we should have done that from the outset. There was never any need for you to actually marry Bainbridge in the first place because, with you dead, all of your fortune automatically comes to me. But I wanted the deed done far away from London. There are too many curious onlookers there, all so keen to know the next thrilling instalment in the life of the charmed Violet Dunston.'

Jack saw Letty's eyes widen in terror a split second before he felt the cold press of a steel barrel against his temple.

'Step away from the lady, Mr Warriner.' Layton's voice was laced with malice. 'Or should that be *your lordship...* The people of Retford were very *eager* to tell us all about your family. A bad lot, by all accounts, cheats, thieves, debauchers—*earls* who would do anything to line their empty pockets with gold. It works in our favour.'

The bottom of Jack's gut sunk to his knees as he experienced a strange premonition of what they had planned. Whatever crime would be committed here tonight, the Warriners would be blamed for. 'Aren't you forgetting one thing? There are four of us. Or I am to commit your atrocities alone?'

Jack saw the moment realisation dawned in Letty's wide green eyes. So did the Earl of Bainbridge. His dry cackle of amusement was the only sound in the still, dark night. 'You picked a fine family to align yourself with, Violet. They have such a bad reputation I doubt anyone will question their guilt or their hand in your murder. Once the true horror of how they kidnapped you, demanded a huge ransom from your dear uncle, then tried to renege on the deal at the exchange by demanding even more money is known, no one will question it... Fortunately, your uncle had the wherewithal to come with armed men. Shots were fired. Your degenerate Earl was killed—and you, dear Violet, were accidentally caught in the crossfire. It will all be very tragic. Very fitting. One last, splendid story for the newspapers. We will arrange your funeral for the day his wastrel brothers are rounded up and hanged.'

Her eyes darted between Jack, the pistol at his head and the other men, the panic in her eyes clear to see. Eventually, they settled on Bainbridge, pleading.

'None of this is Jack's fault. I will do whatever you want—just let him go.'

She was trying to save him? Jack's temper surged forth. Of all the stupid, misguided, dangerous, selfless things to offer. If they got out of this alive, he might just kill her himself. But Letty wasn't anywhere near finished making sacrifices. Like a lioness protecting her cub, she placed her body in front of his. Jack heard the hammer of another pistol cock.

'Take that gun away from his head.'

When, miraculously, Layton complied and Jack stepped away, he saw Letty had her gun pressed hard into the man's belly. She turned her head slightly, never taking her eyes off Layton and whispered, 'Run, Jack!'

Oh, for goodness sake! This was getting ridiculous. As if he would leave her? As if he could? He loved her, for pity's sake. When you loved someone you didn't abandon them. You tried to save them—

Just as she was trying her level best to save his sorry skin by sacrificing hers, he realised. A lioness to match his lion. There were certainly better ways to be confronted with the full extent of his utter, blind stupidity. Perhaps he wouldn't kill her after all. He would marry her instead—but first he had to find a way to get them out of here.

Before Jack could react, both Bainbridge and

her traitorous uncle raised their own weapons and aimed them directly at him.

'What do you hope to achieve, Violet? You are outnumbered. Once your shot is spent, you will still have to watch him die.' The Earl walked towards him purposefully, his gun arm outstretched and his jaw set firm.

Despite Letty's brave façade, the impending threat made her waver. She tossed her pistol on the ground. 'Please! Don't hurt him. I'll marry you. I'll marry you willingly and then you will have all my money, just don't harm Jack.'

For the second time, a pistol was pressed against Jack's head, except this time he experienced the utter devastation which comes from defeat. She loved him and he loved her, yet now they were both doomed to die. Fate always had the last laugh at the Warriners in the end. Well, if he was about to die, he would do so bravely. Jack stood proudly, squared his shoulders and stared at Letty. Better her face was the last he saw...

But the blasted woman suddenly darted out of Layton's grasp and ran like a banshee towards the carriage.

'Take me to Gretna Green! Marry me to Bainbridge…I won't tell a soul.' Frantic sobs made her voice catch. 'Just leave Jack alone!'

It was her uncle who stalked towards her and grabbed her arm roughly. He tried to drag her back towards Jack, but she fought him, wrestling out of the confines of his arms and pushing him back against the door of the carriage. A sharp cutlass suddenly appeared out of the darkened window of the carriage and pressed against her uncle's neck.

Then came Jamie's calm but incredibly menacing voice.

'As I see it, Bainbridge, this whole sordid plot relies on this snake inheriting all of Letty's fortune. Once I kill him, even if you do kill her, all of that lovely money goes directly to the Crown, which leaves you with precisely nothing. Unless, of course, you can breathe some life into what will be left of his sorry carcase when I am finished with him.'

Jack saw the fear in Bainbridge's eyes and did not waste his chance. He reached under his greatcoat and retrieved his own pistol, taking great pleasure in aiming it at the old, wrinkled Earl and slowly dragging the hammer back.

'You are still outnumbered, Warriner!' he spat

back defiantly as Layton and the remaining lackey aimed their own weapons straight back.

In the brittle silence another pistol clicked. Joe emerged from the bushes and poked his weapon into the lackey's back. 'And now there are three of us.' For a man who was more likely to heal a fly than hurt it, even Jack was convinced his brother meant business.

Jack's relief at his brothers' arrival was palpable, but the battle was still far from won. At best, it was a stand-off. Layton was only inches away from Letty—one false move and she might be hurt. He glanced at her and he saw nothing but determination and strength in her lovely eyes. For his benefit, she flicked her eyes to her abandoned pistol on the ground. It lay between them like a beacon, too far for either of them to snatch it up. Their only hope now was Jacob—but he had yet to make an appearance...unless he had stayed behind to look after the farm...

With a sinking feeling, Jack realised he might well have done. If he had been in charge, he might well have insisted someone stay behind to shoulder those important responsibilities. As if any of that was as important as Letty's life?

Jamie yanked back her uncle's head by the hair

and pressed his blade against the whimpering man's neck. 'Drop your weapons now, or I will sever his treacherous head from his quaking, cowardly body.'

'Do as he says!'

It gave Letty some satisfaction to hear her uncle was terrified. However, it did not deter from the fact that all four of them were in a very precarious position. There were still two pistols pointed at Jack: Bainbridge's and Layton's. Only one would be required to kill him. Fortunately, all eyes were on her squealing uncle—not her. With one decisive lunge, she threw herself at the abandoned pistol, landing on the cold ground with a thud.

Layton instantly turned his gun towards her as she scrambled to grip the weapon in her hands. Letty rolled on to her back and aimed right back at Layton. 'Now you are outnumbered.'

But only just. Jamie had a sword to her uncle's neck, Jack had Bainbridge in his sights, she had Layton and Joe had the remaining man.

'Then we have nothing to lose.'

Letty watched in horror as the Earl's index finger began to squeeze the trigger. She twisted to aim her gun at him, and pulled the trigger. The bullet tore through Bainbridge's leg, sending a spray of blood and flesh into the air, and at the same moment Jack knocked the pistol from his flailing hand.

Layton made a grab for her and Letty scrambled to her knees to try to crawl away. He fisted his hand in her hair and yanked her roughly back.

'Get your filthy hands off her!'

Jack went to attack, but stopped when he saw the man's pistol pressing into her neck. Behind her, Letty could feel Layton's laboured, frightened breathing and tried to remain calm.

She had to focus on the practicalities.

They were winning and Layton sensed it. A cornered animal was always the most dangerous.

'Go ahead, Mr Layton. Shoot me. It will be the last thing you ever do and we both know it.'

Beneath her, Letty could feel vibrations through the ground. Someone was coming. Layton realised it, too. His hold on her hair tightened and he gazed around him in panic. 'Murder is a capital offence, Mr Layton. If I die, you will be hanged. That is if my fiancé doesn't shoot you first.'

The hoofbeats came closer. Lots of them. In the distance there was the sound of voices, too. All she had to do was keep him from pulling the trigger until they arrived. 'You can't escape, Mr

Layton. You are surrounded. Your accomplices have already lost.'

Her eyes locked with Jack's, warning him to stay back. The last thing they needed now was for Layton to shoot him in panic. His stormy eyes were furious, but he nodded curtly, he had delegated the responsibility for saving them to her and she loved him for that. Jack never relinquished control. Ever.

'If you surrender now, the worst you can be charged with is kidnap. If you are lucky, you will be transported.' She felt his fingers uncurl against her scalp and pressed her advantage. 'Throw down your weapon, Mr Layton. Don't let them see you holding a gun to my throat.'

The 'them' she was referring to trundled noisily towards them and Layton finally complied. He let go of her hair and threw his pistol down angrily just as Jacob arrived at the head of a large mob of men. His eyes took in the scene and he grinned down at her.

'I see I timed my arrival perfectly.'

He grasped her hand and hauled her up. A middle-aged man next to him stepped forward.

'Are you the Tea Heiress?'

When she nodded he appeared relieved.

'Miss Dunston, we heard you were in distress. Kindly point out the scoundrels who tried to kidnap you.'

Letty happily pointed at the guilty four, taking great pleasure in seeing them manhandled by the rescue party. Jamie kept his sword pressed against her uncle's throat while his hands were bound. Only then did he lower his weapon and climb out of the carriage. Two men took Layton by the arms, and he stood in quiet fury as he, too, was bound. Jack roughly hoisted Bainbridge by the shoulders and, in spite of his shattered leg, dragged him unceremoniously towards Letty and dropped him at her feet.

'I want to kill him.'

She threaded her arm through his and rested her head gratefully on his powerful arm. 'He will get his come-uppance. It's best to let the law deal with him. You can say your piece at his trial.'

Jamie limped beside them. 'With any luck, they'll hang. Did the fools not realise? When you mess with one Warriner, you mess with us all.'

Chapter Twenty-Four

Finally, midnight, 4th January 1814...

Letty and the four Warriners watched the locals make short work of securing the prisoners. Then they all returned to Baldock. The middle-aged man, it turned out, was the local constable and a great reader of the gossip columns. He gave orders for her abductors to be locked up in the local gaol and accompanied Letty and the brothers to the inn to hear their testimony. They all crowded around one big table, sipping steaming cups of tea, while he began with the formalities.

'I shall need your full names for the record.'

'Well, you already know my name is Violet Elizabeth Dunston. And this is my fiancé Jack Warriner, the Earl of...?' She turned to Jack in question as it occurred to her she didn't know.

'Markham.'

'Oh, that's nice. Your title is named after the house.'

'Actually, the house is named after the title. But that is neither here nor there.' He smiled at her indulgently before turning towards the constable. 'These are my brothers. Captain James Lionel Warriner, Joseph Lucas Warriner and Jacob Lawrence Warriner.'

More information Letty had not known. 'You all have exactly the same initials?'

'My parents were creatures of habit.'

'Does your middle name begin with the letter "L" also?'

Letty watched matching slow grins creeping up his brothers' faces and wondered why. She turned to Jack to see him smiling in amusement.

'Clearly it's a stinker if you are all grinning like idiots. Well? What is it, then?'

Joe answered for him. 'It's Leo. Like the constellation.'

'Leo?' Letty started to giggle, not caring that she snorted twice in the process. 'Leo the lion! Of course it is.' And never had a middle name suited its owner more.

The constable was extremely thorough. By the time they had all finished answering his questions, and writing down their personal version of events, it was almost two o'clock in the morning.

'What I don't understand,' Letty asked the brothers after he finally bid them goodnight, 'is how you came be in the exact right place at the exact right time?'

'You can thank Jamie for that,' Joe replied. 'We hid in the woods after you left Markham Manor and fooled them into thinking we had fled, too. When they headed to London in pursuit, we followed them. Jamie, apparently, can track anything. It was all very exciting and they never suspected a thing. We were less than a mile away when you decided to stop off at that inn.' He began to blush and Letty realised they had guessed what she and Jack had been up to in there.

Jacob, who clearly did not feel even slightly embarrassed, grinned. 'While the pair of you were *indisposed*, Jamie managed to get close enough to Bainbridge to hear what they were planning. Seeing as they were stupid enough to consider doing it so close to a town, we decided to let them ambush you in order to trap them. Catch the scoundrels in the act so that we had irrefutable proof of their guilt. I was sent to gather reinforcements.'

Jack appeared perturbed by this. 'How did you

convince so many men to accompany you? Did you neglect to tell them your surname?'

'Oh, for goodness sake, Jack! Nobody in Baldock has ever heard the name Warriner. But they had all heard about Letty. Once they realised it was Violet Dunston who was the heiress in distress, they were surprisingly keen to offer their assistance.' Jacob screwed up his face, suddenly a little sheepish. 'I might have mentioned there would be a reward. Sorry, Letty—but I promised them five pounds apiece.'

Letty rose from her chair, grabbed his face and kissed him soundly on the forehead. 'I can afford it. It was good thinking on your part and I will be eternally grateful.'

She then marched to Joe and enveloped him a hug. 'Thank you, Dr Joe. For everything. You were very brave. And frightening. The ladies are going to love you.' The most studious Warriner blushed profusely and earned a ribbing from his younger sibling.

Letty finally stood in front of Jamie and felt a knot of emotion. For all of his inscrutability and curt comments, he hid a heart of pure gold. 'Thank you for saving me.'

'That's what families do, Letty—and I assume you are about to become family and that my pig-headed oldest brother has finally come to his senses.' Jamie offered her one of his almost smiles. 'Consider it our birthday gift and wedding gift combined. And you can stop those tears right now before they fall, madam. I don't do waterworks.'

Letty felt Jack come up behind her before he curled his arm possessively around her waist. 'Now that we are not in such a hurry to get to London in the morning, shall we see if there is room for us all at this inn?'

'Inn? Haystack? I don't care so long as I am with you.' And she didn't. 'But I don't want to go to London. I want to go back home to celebrate my birthday—to Markham Manor.' Because there was nobody important in London apart from her solicitor and he could jolly well come to her. She would build her foundling home in Nottingham instead. It was equally as rotten and just as desperate.

Jack winced and heaved out a deep breath. 'With all of the worry and excitement, I completely forgot that today is your birthday. Now I feel bad. I haven't given you a gift.'

Letty grabbed his lapels and kissed him noisily. 'Yes, you did. You're my birthday gift. And don't let it go to your head, but for a girl who has everything, you, Jack Warriner, are the best present I have ever had.'

Joe and Jacob grinned. Jamie groaned.

'Seeing as you two are getting all soppy, I'm off to bed.' He tossed Jack a room key. 'Come on, boys. Let's leave the Earl of Markham and his beloved to it.'

Even though she knew they were creating a shocking spectacle, Letty could not bring herself to let go of Jack just yet. She needed to keep touching him to reassure herself that he was safe. And she didn't want to cry, even though the tears were so close to the surface. Her new life had already started and she was not going to spoil it with tears. They would fall, she knew, but not tonight. Tonight, she just wanted to enjoy being unashamedly with Jack. Her Jack. A farmer and, apparently, an earl.

'Why did I not know you had a title?'

'I've never had cause to use it.'

'I used to want a title. It was on my list of attributes for any potential future husband.'

'What other attributes did you want your future

husband to have? I should be interested to know how I measure up,' he teased.

'Let me see…' Letty tapped her chin and pretended to consider it. 'He had to be handsome, which of course, you are. So that is good news. He also had to be witty, and whilst you are nowhere near as funny as I am, you can hold up your end—when you are not being stubborn and dictatorial, that is. I wanted him to be an excellent horseman. I like to ride and I needed my husband to have a fine seat on a horse. You ride well enough, but your seat is most excellent.'

She wiggled her eyebrows shamelessly and he grinned wickedly at the compliment. 'Aside from my superior posterior, is there any other criteria I will be judged against?'

'Of course! I am very particular. My future husband would have to be a connoisseur of the theatre—and I know you read plays when you can tear yourself away from those awful ledgers—and I suppose I could loosely class your portrait of Sir Hugo as evidence of your being a patron of the arts. I also wanted my husband to be the absolute envy of all of my society friends, but seeing as I am not altogether sure I have any *real* friends there, that hardly counts any more.' Letty wrapped her arms around his waist and stared up into his hypnotic blue eyes adoringly. 'Most importantly, my future husband *had* to be *hopelessly* in love with me. Which, it goes without saying, you are. And who could blame you. Just as I am hopelessly in love with you.'

His hands came to rest gently on her shoulders. 'You do realise absolutely everyone will assume that I have only married you for your money.'

'Not everyone. I know the truth. Your brothers know the truth. I don't care what anyone else thinks. Just as long as I get to marry my handsome, responsible, proud, stubborn Earl.' She walked her fingers up his broad chest suggestively before placing her palm flat against his steadily beating heart, secure in the knowledge it belonged to her, not the pile of banknotes which came with her. If it took her for ever, Letty was determined to banish all of his insecurities about his unworthiness away. 'Have I already mentioned how determined I was that my future husband would have a title? It was the one frippery I never had.'

With great deliberation, Jack took her right hand in his and slid the emerald ring off her finger. Then he took her left hand. He slipped the gold band slowly on to her ring finger, arranged the stone just so, then brought her hand up to his lips.

'Well, I am glad I can offer you that, at least. Once we're married you can call yourself Countess. No more Violet Dunston, the Tea Heiress. You'll be Letty Warriner, the Countess of Markham.'

Letty held out her hand to examine the ring's new position and grinned. 'I quite like the sound of Letty Warriner—but I find myself surprisingly ambivalent to being a countess. It sounds so… superficial and privileged, don't you think? I believe, going forward, you should simply call me sweetheart.'

Jack kissed her long and hard until the walls of the inn swayed and her knees almost buckled. When he finally prised his mouth from hers, he stared down at her and smiled. It was his roguish smile. The one which always did funny things to her insides.

'Happy Birthday, sweetheart.' His deep blue eyes swirled with mischief and promise. 'If you follow me upstairs, I might be persuaded to let you unwrap your present.'

* * * * *

*If you enjoyed this story, you won't want to miss
these other great reads from
Virginia Heath*

*MISS BRADSHAW'S BOUGHT BETROTHAL
THE DISCERNING GENTLEMAN'S GUIDE
HER ENEMY AT THE ALTAR
THAT DESPICABLE ROGUE*